P9-CIV-936

Received On

JAN 2 3 2021

Magnolia Library

THE
TOWN
CRAZY

NO LONGER PROPERTY OF
SEATTLE PUBLIC LIBRARY

GIBSON HOUSE PRESS
Flossmoor, Illinois
GibsonHousePress.com

© 2020 Suzzy Roche
All rights reserved. Published 2020.

ISBNs: 978-1-948721-12-7 (paper); 978-1-948721-23-3 (ebook)

LCCN: 2019953837

Cover and book design by Karen Sheets de Gracia.
Text is composed in the Odile and Antraste typefaces.

PRINTED IN THE UNITED STATES OF AMERICA
24 23 22 21 20   1 2 3 4 5

⊗ This paper meets the requirements of ANSI/NISO Z39.48-1992
(Permanence of Paper)

THE TOWN CRAZY

SUZZY ROCHE

GIBSON
HOUSE
PRESS

CHICAGO

*"My imagination makes me human and makes me a fool;
it gives me all the world, and exiles me from it."*

URSULA K. LE GUIN

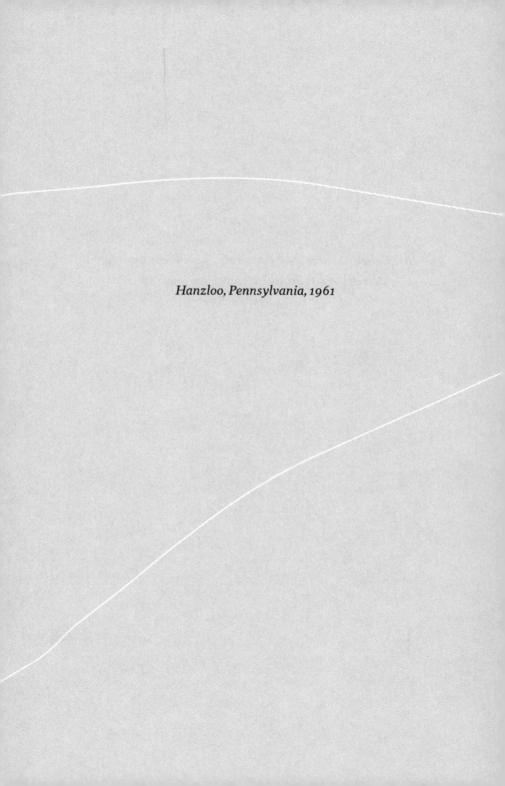

Hanzloo, Pennsylvania, 1961

You are now entering Hanzloo
Where dreams come true

ONE

On a muggy Sunday morning in late August, parishioners knelt in the pews of Immaculate Conception, fidgeting and fanning themselves with church leaflets, while Father Bruno lifted the host toward heaven and droned on in quiet prayer, "Domine, non sum dignus": *Lord, I am not worthy.*

Jim O'Brien, who for the past few months had skipped church, was taking his seven-year-old daughter, Alice, out for a drive. They didn't get far.

He turned his green Impala onto the Post Road, pulled into the empty A&P parking lot, and shut off the engine. It was only ten thirty, and already the sun blazed in the sky. Despite the heat, Jim rolled up the car window when he spotted the stranger Luke Spoon over by the entrance to the grocery store. He'd heard about Luke Spoon. He'd moved here from New York City; some of the guys at Flapdogs had mentioned him the other day, and not in a good way.

Spoon was with his young son, and Jim watched them with interest.

"That boy is Felix Spoon," said Alice. "He's the one who peed on the floor during morning prayers last year."

"Peed on the floor? Why?" Jim squinted for a better look. "I wonder what they're doing over there. Don't they know that stores are closed on Sunday?"

The father and son were peering into the A&P, cupping their hands around their eyes and pressing their faces against the window.

"Weird," said Jim. "Best to steer clear of those two."

Alice said nothing.

Soon Spoon and his kid wandered away from the store, hand in hand. They crossed the parking lot and disappeared down the road.

When they were out of sight, Jim got down to the business of this drive. A slender, fair-haired, soft-spoken man with a recently ballooning paunch the size of a basketball, Jim was the kind of father who preferred silence to conversation, but he knew something had to give. *He* had to give. He clenched his hands around the steering wheel.

"Alice, we have to have a talk about Mom." Letting out a long, slow sigh, he chose his words carefully. "Your mother has developed . . . a problem."

"Uh-huh," said Alice, her eyes widening. "I know."

"She has a sort of disease, a disease of the *soul.*"

Jim looked over at his daughter, who sat poker-faced beside him in the front seat. Her orange pigtails were lopsided, one much bigger than the other, a leg of her shorts was stained with chocolate, and her shins were dotted with red mosquito bites.

"Your mother is sick," he said, as if she hadn't heard him.

Alice didn't move a muscle. "Is that why we don't go to church anymore?"

Leaning his forearms on the wheel, Jim put his head down

and wondered why everything had to be so hard. In no time, his shoulders heaved up and down, and he uttered a series of stifled cries that sounded more like sneezes. When he glanced sideways at his daughter, he saw that she was staring at the dashboard where the small plastic statue of Saint Francis, attached by a suction cup, sat atop a coiled spring.

"Don't cry, Dad," she said.

"I'm sorry I'm crying. But it's a relief." As he pulled himself together, Alice picked at a small scab on her knee.

"Alice, honey, it's not your fault and I don't want you to worry about it. This happens sometimes."

"I guess I figured," she said. "You sleep in the cellar; she sleeps on the couch. Is the disease catching?"

Jim put his hand on his forehead and closed his eyes. "It's, well, I'm having a hard time sleeping, worrying about her. She's sick, very sick."

Alice raised her eyebrows, and a ripple of fear crossed her eyes. "Really? Is she . . . could she *die*?"

"No, no, it's not that. Like I said, it's a disease of the soul. You know what a soul is, right?

"It's invisible," said Alice.

"That's the idea," he said.

"How can something invisible get sick?" asked Alice.

Jim had planned this conversation all week, and he'd come up with the phrase *disease of the soul* himself, but he hadn't thought through the basic premise of a sick soul. He was struck by her logic and forced a smile. "Good point, but yes, a soul can get sick, it really can. It's complicated, and human beings don't fully understand it, but the upshot is your mother might be . . . not herself for a while. If I were you, I'd act as if nothing is wrong, and really, don't feel like you have to tell people about it. It's our business. A family matter, okay?"

He pointed his thumb up and winked, but he wasn't a winker, so what he was doing? Alice didn't seem to be buying it. The lengths he would go to for pretense baffled him. He wished he could weep; even those muffled sobs had felt good. Why should he be the only one in the world who never cried?

"Remember, it doesn't mean she's a bad person, and hopefully she'll get better soon."

"She's Mom, and I love her," said Alice in a feeble stab at loyalty, but then she added, "I never thought there could be something *really* wrong with her."

"Well, there's nothing *really* wrong with her," said Jim.

"But you just said there was," said Alice, who was now blotting the blood from her scab with her elbow.

"Yeah, but . . . I don't know, Alice. It's like Mom's made of eggshells. Not tough like you and me."

"I don't think we're tough," said Alice.

Jim wanted to reach over and take her hand, but he didn't do it. The poor kid.

"Look, I'm your father and I'm tougher than you think. I'm going to take care of us," he said. But truthfully, Jim O'Brien didn't know what to do. His wife was a medicated mess.

"Dad," said Alice, "Everybody knows that Mom is sick. The kids on the block are calling her *crazy*. And who's going to take me to school next week? I always walk to school with Mom, but now it's like I'm afraid of her, plus she hardly ever gets off the couch. She used to be great."

"I know," said Jim, and in that moment his heart was gripped with longing for the wife he'd thought he had. When they'd gotten married, he felt like the luckiest man in the world. And years before that, when he first laid eyes on her at the high school talent show—her reddish curls around her shoulders and her soft, smart voice reciting a poem that he couldn't begin to comprehend—Jim knew then that she was *it,* the one he'd love forever. They'd moved to Hanzloo about six years ago, but a few years in, he started to notice changes in her, as if she were allergic to the town itself. He'd watched her turn into her own ghost.

Alice's bottom lip began to quiver now. The kid could break into tears at the drop of a hat, and Jim didn't want that.

"Hey. Second grade is a pretty big deal," he said. "I bet you could walk with Clarisse McCarthy and her twins if Mom isn't quite ready by then. They're starting kindergarten this year, right?"

"No!" said Alice. "Not the twins!"

"Come on. You're bigger than they are; don't let them push you around. I told you before, Alice, you have to put some wind in your sails."

"Puh," said Alice, blowing through her lips.

Jim folded. He was done with this conversation. As a last resort he said, "Alice, do me a favor, I know you do the rosary sometimes, just add in a little something directly about Mom. You know, a little prayer."

"What?" said Alice, looking at him as if he had just suggested she cut herself up with scissors. "Why should God listen to us? Mom said she doesn't believe in God." The car was airless, warm as an oven. Alice wiped the sweat off her upper lip with her finger.

"Let's keep what Mom says between you and me. You see, that's what I'm talking about, her soul is sick. Of course Mom believes in God. She's practically an angel herself. Just try to say an extra prayer that's personal from you. God cares."

"How come *you* can't do it? God doesn't even know my name. There's too many people in the world."

"I think he probably does know your name."

"No. He probably remembers who you are, but since then too many people have been born."

"Alice, it's stupid to argue about God. I'm just saying, pray or don't, okay, or maybe just try. It might be good for you to talk to somebody about Mom anyway, and the best part is God is private. You know what I mean?" Jim wondered what the hell he was talking about. He'd actually rolled around to the same conclusion his wife had; there probably was no God. But you can't tell that to your kid.

Jim reached over and grabbed Alice's knee. "We'll get through this, right?

Alice turned to him, and the look in her eyes spooked him. Seven years old and the map of sadness was already routed in her eyes.

TWO

Summers in Hanzloo, Pennsylvania, could be long and boring, especially in the searing heat. This summer, eight days had crept past ninety degrees. Late on many afternoons, after the laundry was pinned to the line, rugs vacuumed, and the dishes steamed dry in the Westinghouse, a certain group of mothers looked forward to circling their lawn chairs in Clarisse McCarthy's driveway for a pitcher of whiskey sours, an hour or so before the men came home. They shooed their kids away across the lawn, kept an ear out for telephones that rarely rang, and shared puffs from one another's menthol cigarettes, flicking the ashes over the metal arms of their lightweight chairs.

Today was that last lazy afternoon before school began, and the women wiped their faces with ice-soaked napkins. They talked in wonder about Lil O'Brien, who had apparently been acting strange, like nervous breakdown strange.

"What a shame," said Vicki Walsh. "If Hanzloo had a town flower, it would have been Lil." Some of the women nodded in agreement, as if this were her funeral.

"It reminds me of that soap, *The Guiding Light*," said Stephanie Conte.

Few had seen Lil since the beginning of June, when she'd collected her daughter, Alice, on the last day of school. She didn't look good then, thin and pale as paper, and the rumor was that things had slid from there.

Clarisse McCarthy claimed to have the scoop.

"Can't you tell us more?" said Ginny Rice, who had tanned herself into leather. "I mean, something must have happened in the marriage. You don't just fall apart. What exactly is wrong with her?"

"I'm not going to gossip, and please don't ask me to," said Clarisse. "Suffice to say, yesterday when I came home from church, I saw her wander out to the curb to get her mail in a nightie. Like there's mail on Sunday, right? She looked, I don't know, like a ghost. I walked right by with the twins, and I don't think she saw me. No sign of Alice anywhere." Clarisse paused here to blow smoke toward the sky. "Jim's withered by it, he told me so. You should hear him. Can you imagine being married to Lil right now? She's always been a sad little thing."

"Well, she's sweet," said Steph.

Ginny Rice didn't seem convinced. "But what did Jim say? Maybe she's . . . I don't know, I always thought she was artistic, that strawberry blonde hair, those gorgeous green eyes. She's special. Are you sure you're not exaggerating, Clarisse?" Ginny brushed a crumbled pretzel off her lap. "Anyways, I like Lil."

"Yes, Ginny. Everybody likes her," said Clarisse. "But if you had seen her yesterday, all greasy-haired, I think you'd understand what I mean." Clarisse looked to the others for support, and at the same time decided that she didn't want

Ginny at any more of these gatherings.

Secretly, Clarisse McCarthy resented that Lil O'Brien hadn't fallen under her spell like the other women had. It was true, Lil O'Brien stood apart. "Look, let's stop talking about Lil," she added.

Clarisse, a vivid blond, had curves strikingly reminiscent of Marilyn Monroe's. As if to offset the impression that she resembled the film star in any other way, Clarisse leaned toward the demure—shirtwaists and knee-length pencil skirts—though not every pencil skirt was meant for such a full and luscious figure. A highly regarded member of the parish, Clarisse even had Father Bruno, the pastor of Immaculate Conception, wrapped around her finger. She ran every bake sale, clothes drive, and potluck dinner. Still, no amount of good works could keep people from staring at the slow sway of her behind when she walked. It was the one thing in all of Hanzloo that Clarisse McCarthy could not keep an eye on. As one sorry husband had once made the mistake of saying out loud, "It's like a giant juicy peach."

By the second round of drinks, the conversation turned to Luke Spoon and his son, Felix, which was not unusual. Luke Spoon had been a favorite topic all summer. Why would a single man with a kid move from New York City to Hanzloo?

"He walks around town like he owns the place," Ginny remarked.

"He's never at church," said Clarisse.

"I just get the feeling he thinks he's better than everybody," said Stephanie.

"Where's the wife? That's what I'd like to know," said Clarisse.

"Oh please, are we playing 'where's the wife' again?" said Vicki.

"What if there is no wife?" said Ginny. "Wilbur thinks he's *gay.*"

"Gay?" said Steph. "What?"

Clarisse leaned in. "*Homosexual.*"

"Oh shush," said Steph. "Don't say that."

Privately, some of the women thought Luke Spoon was attractive, almost handsome, in an offbeat way. Even Clarisse McCarthy had those moments. His dark hair was a wavy mess, and his face often hid behind a five-o'clock shadow and dark-rimmed glasses. The husbands didn't trust him, but for the wives he provided endless fascination.

"As long as he keeps that creepy kid of his on a tight leash," said Clarisse. "Let's not forget how he peed during prayers."

"Oh yes, wasn't that interesting," said Stephanie, wiping the sweat off the back of her neck.

"I did not find it interesting," said Clarisse. "Peeing on the floor? Disgusting if you ask me."

Across the lawn, a chubby boy had plopped his bottom onto the sprinkler to block the spray of water. The other kids were screaming at him, and Dawn, one of Clarisse's twins, started beating him on the head with her fists.

Clarisse, hearing the commotion, turned toward the group of children and shouted, "Thomas Walsh, get off my sprinkler! And don't make me come over there."

Thomas, who had forgotten his bathing suit and was now in sopping wet underpants, quickly got off the sprinkler, because people did what Clarisse McCarthy told them to do.

"Anyway," Clarisse continued, "That Spoon kid is a menace. Felix the brat, I call him."

Felix Spoon was indeed a scrawny, sullen child, with dark, glistening eyes, like smooth black olives, and long eyelashes that any woman would envy. His mouth curled down in a way that could easily be taken for a scowl.

"I'll tell you what, that peeing incident really rattled Sister Lorretta," said Ginny. "You won't find a sweeter nun in the entire state of Pennsylvania, but she was *mad*." The women suddenly exploded with laughter. Ginny Rice laughed so hard that her drink sprayed through her nose.

"You have to admit, it is kind of amusing," said Stephanie, trying to recover. "Peeing at prayers?" The thought of it set them off again.

"Never a dull moment here in Hanzloo," said Ginny, after they settled down.

The women looked across the lawn at their children and sipped their whiskey sours in silence for a moment. It had been a hot, tedious summer, and by now they had tired of the endless bother of their own children and the constant distribution of Popsicles and bologna sandwiches. Once school began, they'd have a few hours of peace each day.

When five o'clock rolled around, one by one, they glanced at their wristwatches. Husbands had to be picked up, dinners cooked, and kids dealt with. "Well, I'll miss these driveway gatherings. Summer's over, I guess," said Vicki Walsh. The women gathered their children, hungry, and wet in their swimsuits, and went home.

"Let me help you clean this mess," said Stephanie, who lived across the street.

"Thanks, Steph, you're a good egg."

What Steph wanted to say but didn't was, *I'm not an egg, Clarisse.* Nobody envied Steph, in her old slacks, and her brown hair plastered down by two clips. Nor did they listen too closely to what she said, but Clarisse relied on her loyalty and compliments.

Last spring Steph had really come through for her when a couple of the girls went to lunch in the village of Farrow's Corner, ten miles away, to complain about Clarisse being too bossy, this regarding the Let's Adopt Africa tag sale. According to the women, Clarisse had sashayed around the school cafeteria with a black charcoal pencil, crossing out and reducing the prices on other people's items. At the lunch, Steph listened to the complaints while picking onions from her salad with a fork, but once back in Hanzloo she'd relayed the entire conversation to Clarisse.

That evening, when Clarisse's husband, Frank, found her sitting in the dark kitchen with a spoon in a quart of butter pecan ice cream, she said, "Everybody hates me, and I hate them." Frank had buried his nose in her hair, and said it all boiled down to petty jealousy, and she shouldn't let it get her down. Clarisse smoothed her mouth over a lump of ice cream and sucked, leaving an exposed pecan on her spoon. "I can't win," she said. "I just can't win."

Since then, Clarisse and Steph had become even better friends. Now Stephanie gathered her two boys, Dale and Bobby, and headed across the street. "I'll meet you out front tomorrow morning," she called to Clarisse. "You must be excited, the twins' first day of kindergarten."

"I can't believe it," said Clarisse. "Don't be surprised if you hear me sniffling."

That evening, after the dinner dishes were done and Frank

had settled in front of the TV for *Bonanza*, Clarisse headed upstairs to the twins' room to prepare them for bed.

When Clarisse entered their room, she found Fawn standing by her bed, naked, with a blindfold around her eyes and her hands tied behind her, while Dawn jumped on her bed wielding a yardstick.

"What in the world are you doing?" Clarisse said, rushing over to Fawn to untie her hands.

"We're just playing pirates and slaves," said Dawn.

"Stop it!" said Clarisse. "I told you before. You're not to play mean games. Put on your clothes, Fawn, and get off the bed, Dawn."

"I hate you!" said Dawn.

"What?" Clarisse felt as if she'd been slapped in the face.

"I love you, Mommy," said Fawn, throwing her arms around her mother.

Dawn jumped off the bed and ran over to join in the embrace.

"No, no! Not fair! I love you too, Mommy," said Dawn. "I didn't mean it."

"There, there. That's more like it," said Clarisse, but even as she gathered both girls in her arms, and kissed their foreheads, she wondered what demon had taken hold of her daughter. Over the summer, she'd noticed a change in Dawn.

THREE

THE NEXT DAY, as if a switch had been flipped, the air was cooler, and the sun pulsed and glowed in a bright blue sky. Hearts were high as a lazy parade of mothers and children meandered through neighborhood streets, past small blue kiddie pools that had not yet been put away and forgotten bathing suits and towels that still hung on clotheslines stiff and dry. All headed toward Immaculate Conception, the only school in town. The kids wore freshly creased uniforms and brand-new saddle shoes or Hush Puppies and carried leather book bags and brown-bag lunches.

Clarisse and Steph met in the middle of Mundy Lane and walked with their children trailing behind them. They passed the Chinskys' house where Hedda Chinsky was on her knees pulling weeds from the shrubbery.

Old Hedda Chinsky didn't turn to wave. Some months ago, she and Clarisse had had words when Hedda caught Dawn and Fawn burying a dead frog in her garden.

"They killed it!" Hedda cried.

"Oh, Hedda, I doubt that. I'm sure it was already dead when they found it. Little girls don't go around killing things," Clarisse had said, and the two women hadn't spoken since.

Clarisse and Steph walked in silence until they reached the O'Brien house.

"Look at that, Lil's house looks deserted, doesn't it? She never opens the blinds. I wonder who's walking Alice to school," Clarisse said, shaking her head.

"It scares me, like a haunted house," said Steph.

Halfway to school, a spat erupted behind them. Steph's boys, Dale and Bobby, had a love-hate relationship with the twins.

"What's going on? Knock it off!" said Clarisse, turning around to see what the problem was. Dawn was sticking her tongue out at the boys.

"Dawn kicked me!" said Dale Conte.

"He licked his finger and rubbed it on my arm!" cried Dawn, taking a swipe at Dale.

"Oh sweetheart," said Clarisse to Dale. "Don't do that, she'll get your germs.

"I just don't want them getting sick, you know?" Clarisse said, turning back to Steph. "I guess the girls are a little over-excited," she added, under her breath.

As Clarisse and Steph arrived at the school, they exchanged good mornings with the others who were waiting with their kids for the gates to open. The twins, with their long, white-blonde ponytails tightly braided and adorned with colored bows, drew a crowd of other girls around them. It was nearly impossible to tell the two apart, both had light blue eyes, and celestial noses perfectly proportioned on their faces. They welcomed the attention from the others, holding hands, cute as new dolls, and not in the least bit apprehensive about starting school.

Beyond the playground, the old stone school loomed, and next to it, the church. Immaculate Conception was a remnant of the past, built way before the new developments in town.

"Well, look who's here," said Clarisse, elbowing Stephanie.

Luke Spoon was walking down the street holding hands with his son, Felix.

"What the hell does he do all day?" said Vicki Walsh, who was holding a tissue to her boy's nose.

"Well, one thing he doesn't do is mow his lawn," said Ginny Rice, who'd just arrived, glistening in tanning lotion, dragging her daughter Nancy by the hand. "I drove by early this morning after I dropped Wilbur at the bus stop. Have you seen the condition it's in?"

When Luke Spoon had moved to Hanzloo last spring, he'd rented the old Ross house, which was set back on an empty stretch of the Post Road. The dilapidated house was one of the only homes left in town that wasn't part of a development. Luke Spoon's lawn was a low forest of dandelions and other flowery weeds, as if he had something against regular old grass.

"Look at the way they stand off to the side. It wouldn't hurt if he said hello to someone," said Ginny.

"There's something sad about him," said Steph.

"Let's face it, the poor guy needs a wife," said Clarisse, peering over the top of her sunglasses.

"Why doesn't one of us march up to him and ask him what happened to his wife?" said Ginny.

"Now, there's a thought," said Clarisse.

A moment later, the iron gates swung wide, and the

emergence of Sister Annunciata, the one-eyed principal, was both a comfort and a call to attention. With a ragged eye-patch stretched across her face, she stood at the playground gates folding her arms into the sleeves of her habit and surveyed the scene. Spotting two fourth graders who were in a tangle, she grabbed them by the backs of their necks, pulling them apart as if they were light as two kittens in a basket. "Next time I'll bang your heads together," she said, as the boys straightened up.

Last spring (according to Teresa Sepolino, Sister A.'s secretary), when Felix Spoon came to school with his father for the first time, the kid had come right out and asked Sister A. what happened to her eye. The nun, putting her face so close that they were nose to nose, had said, "God plucked it out because of something stupid I did."

Sister A.'s missing eye, like Luke Spoon's missing wife, was one more thing to talk about and not get to the bottom of, like an itch in the middle of your back that couldn't be reached.

When the school bell rang, the women kissed their kids, some who were reluctant to go through the gates of the playground, preferring instead to wrap their arms around their mothers one last time. But others, like fifth grader Mike Fitzpatrick and his gang of five boys, charged fearlessly through the entrance bouncing a basketball back and forth.

Felix Spoon stood staring at the ground until his father pulled him into a close embrace and turned him around with a gentle push toward the playground.

The twins kissed their mother on each cheek and skipped into the playground, followed by a gaggle of adoring girls from every grade.

At the last minute, Alice O'Brien, all alone, darted across the street, right in front of a passing car that swerved in order to miss her.

"Slow down!" said Clarisse, calling out to the driver, with her fist raised in the air. She watched as Alice, with snarled hair the color of carrots, trailed behind the other girls. The pleats of her uniform bellowed. No one had bothered to iron them. Clarisse couldn't help thinking that Lil O'Brien, for all her ethereal beauty, was a lousy mother.

She watched as Alice tried to attach herself to one set of girls or another. It broke Clarisse's heart to see it. She felt it might be time for her to intervene in some way.

FOUR

INSIDE THE PLAYGROUND, kids ran wild, and the loud chatter of their voices rose up over the cement. Mike Fitzpatrick and his gang of five were shooting hoops, their white shirts already wrinkled and untucked. On the other side of the playground, Dawn and Fawn enjoyed invitations to join several different jump-rope games, and Alice O'Brien sat on a bench, scratching her legs and fidgeting.

At exactly 8:42, the church bells rang and every nun, teacher, and child on the playground came to a sudden halt. It was the Angelus, the devotion in honor of the Incarnation —the mystery of the word made flesh—it was expected that everyone would recite three Hail Marys in silence. Father Bruno came out to the balcony of the rectory and stood with his hands clasped over his dark chocolate vestments. In three minutes, the bells rang once more, indicating the close of the Angelus, and the children began to run around again.

It was then that Mike Fitzpatrick gathered his troops over by the trashcans in the corner of the playground. "Let's get Felix Spoon over here," he said. "Give him some of your Chiclets, Joe."

"I don't think he'll come, he's a turd," said Joe Quinn.

"Just get him over here," said Mike. "Tell him I want to see him." Mike stood against the brick wall with his arms crossed, chewing on a toothpick.

"What are we gonna do with him?" asked Jimmy Ginty.

"I got a plan," said Mike.

Joe Quinn brought Felix over to the boys, who had captured five caterpillars that were crawling around in the garbage.

"Eat these," said Mike, thrusting the caterpillars toward Felix.

"What?" said Felix. "No! Why?"

Mike grabbed him by the shoulder and shook him. "I said eat them, dumb-duck."

"Okay, okay," said Felix.

The boys stood in a close circle as Felix picked up the first caterpillar. He held it up to his eyes. It squirmed in his fingers until he popped it in his mouth and swallowed it whole. He ate the other four, too, as the boys groaned with disgust.

"Nice," said Fitzpatrick, "Now, let's get the girls."

Across the playground girls were jumping rope and chanting.

House for sale, move right in
The lady upstairs is drinking gin

The boys set off toward them with Felix at the head of the pack.

"Felix Spoon ate caterpillars! He ate five whole caterpillars!"

In an instant jump ropes were dropped, and squealing girls fled from boys. Some of them ran toward the red church door and huddled together, burying their faces in each other's hair. Felix Spoon headed straight for the McCarthy twins, who stood frozen in the middle of the playground. With his arms outstretched like a zombie, he barreled between them, knocking one of them over. Kids came running from all directions to form a circle around the twins. Dawn had been the one to fall, and she hugged her knee as if it were about to detach from her leg. Fawn sat on the ground beside her sister, crying, with her hair mussed and her uniform askew. Several of the twins' hair bows lay on the ground, and Dawn's elbow and knee were scraped. Children stared, some had their hands over their mouths, and some looked downright frightened, as if a star had crashed to earth. Alice O'Brien started to shake as she stood up to see the commotion.

Felix Spoon pushed through the crowd to see what he had done, and shortly Sister Annunciata bounded across the playground and stepped into the circle. She grabbed the boy by the collar and dragged him off to her office, as Mrs. Pell, the school nurse, rushed to attend to the twins.

ONCE IN her office, the nun latched the door, pulled up two chairs and set them across from each other. She told the boy to sit in one, and she sat in the other, adjusting her rear end on the chair. "So, Felix Spoon," she said, taking a moment to settle herself. "We meet again. Look here, straight into my eye." She pointed to her one good eye, and the two sat face to face in silence for quite some time.

The boy examined the nun closely. The sister's eye was gray as a cloud, and although he found it mesmerizing, he couldn't look at it for very long because the rest of her was so intriguing. She appeared to him like a bad person in a fairy tale, but he was not afraid. Her giant rosary beads, which usually swung from her black woven belt, sat in her lap, and she held its crucifix with thick knobby fingers. Her shoes, poking out from her heavy underskirts, were like black mounds, and their heels were worn on one side. A musty smell emanated from her robes, and her wrinkled forehead seemed pinched under the starched white coif, which sat like a cupcake box under her long black veil. She had a perfectly awful face, lined and puffed with age, an extra-large nose, and the wondrous black eye patch that was frayed on one edge.

Finally, the nun spoke. "I'm glad you're taking the time to look me over, young man, because I've been watching you for quite some time," she said, leaning toward him. "I want you to listen to me very carefully." She pointed at him with her bent index finger. "Who do you think you are?"

After a moment, the boy responded thoughtfully, "I think I'm like you, and one of my eyes might be torn out, or something bad like that."

"Interesting answer," she said, slapping her hands on her lap. "Is that what you're waiting for? Something bad to happen to you?"

The boy looked to the floor. "I'm waiting for my mother." Outside, the church bells rang three times, and Sister Annunciata sighed.

"I see," she said eyeing Felix's untied sneakers. "And where is your mother?"

"I don't know," he said crossly. Then, softening, he looked up at the nun. "Do you know where she is?"

The nun sneezed unexpectedly and took out her cloth handkerchief. She blew her nose with a honk. "Felix, let me tell you something," she said, wiping her nose. "There's no excuse for eating caterpillars and knocking down little girls." She folded the hanky and stuffed it back into the inner regions of her habit.

Tears bubbled up in Felix Spoon's eyes. "I didn't mean it. Sometimes I have to do things. Tell me, what is my punishment?"

She took a moment to watch as he cleared his eyes with his fists. "Well, I'd say that eating caterpillars is its own punishment, wouldn't you?"

The boy seemed surprised. A glimmer of a smile swept across both their faces, as if they shared a certain sense of humor. "I feel bad for the caterpillars," said Felix, and once again his eyes welled up.

"But what about the girls? Don't you feel bad for them? One of them has a scraped knee. Hurting people is a dead end, Felix. Don't you know that? You must apologize. You have to go to them and say you're sorry. And you have to be sincere."

"Not fair," he mumbled, banging the floor with his foot. "They deserve it. I'll tell you what, they killed a frog by stabbing it with sticks."

Sister A.'s nostrils opened wide. "That's gruesome," she said.

"And I saw one of them kick someone in my class. A girl named Alice. She's easy to pick on. Everybody thinks the twins are cute, but they're mean."

The nun considered that. "Regardless. Apologize, Felix, you'll feel better. And do it soon. Much can be accomplished with the words *I'm sorry*. Now, look, here's what I'm going to do. I'm going to give you something, and I want you to be very careful with it." Sister Annunciata once again reached into the folds of her mysterious black robes and pulled out a small gray stone. She held it in her open palm. "Will you keep this for me?" she said.

The boy looked at it and said, "Why? It's nothing but a rock."

"Is that what you think?" said the nun. "Here, hold it in your hand."

Felix took the rock and examined it. "It's warm," he said, looking up at the sister's eye.

"I'm not surprised. It was in my hidden pocket. It comes from God's cave," she said. "Will you keep it for me?"

"God's cave? That sounds bad, I didn't know he had a cave," said Felix.

"You might be surprised. There are some interesting things in God's cave. Now will you keep the rock for me?" said the sister, adjusting the patch on her eye.

"Why should I?" asked the boy, disappointed in the rock.

"That's not my business. I simply asked." The two stared each other down. "So?" said the nun.

"I guess," said Felix, looking at the stone.

"Is that a promise?"

The boy said nothing.

"Don't you know what a promise is?"

"It's something that you say you'll do," he said.

"Has someone made a promise to you that they haven't kept?"

"No difference if they have or haven't," said Felix.

"A broken promise is hard to take," said the sister.

"I don't care," he said, twisting his mouth.

"On the other hand, sometimes you have to wait for a very long time for a promise to be kept." The boy sat without a word. "I wonder who you are, Felix Spoon. Do you know that I'm fond of you?"

"It doesn't help. You're strange. You only have one eye," said Felix.

"That's not nice. Just like you, I know what it feels like to be set apart," said the sister. "The more important issue is that now I've given you a gift, and you can go back to your class. We'll see what you do with it."

Felix shrugged. "Is it magic?"

"No, like you said, it's nothing but a rock."

The boy studied the old nun's face and thought for a moment. "Sister, may I see your empty socket?"

The nun smiled, and Felix was surprised to see that one of her teeth was golden. "Why would you ask such a thing?" she said.

"Because I'd like to see you the way you really are. It must be hard to look at things with just one eye."

"I see things differently is all."

Felix Spoon made a face, like it didn't matter to him, and he got up out of his chair and went to the door. Before he left, he turned to her, and said, "I guess I'll keep the rock." He put it in his pocket, but then thought twice. "What if I lose it?"

"Well, that's worth considering."

"Don't punish me if I lose it, it's not my fault."

Sister A. let out a long breath. "Not everything requires blame, Felix. And here's something to ponder, maybe your mother lost *you* somehow."

"What?" he said. It was the first time during their interview that he seemed rattled, and he looked at the sister with hollow eyes.

"Run along now, you're missing morning prayers," said

27

the nun, as she gathered her skirts to stand. "And I don't know who told you you're allowed to wear sneakers to school, but you might want to tie the laces, so you don't trip and break your arms."

When Felix Spoon went to his new classroom, prayers were already over, and the children were standing with their hands on their hearts, about to recite the Pledge of Allegiance. He stood at the front of the class. All the students were staring at him, with their right arms across their chests like miniature soldiers in a strange cartoon. His new teacher, Mrs. Dickson, tapped her chalkboard pointer lightly on her desk, "Okay, Mr. Spoon, go take a seat, and hurry up." But before he could walk to a desk, a sour taste rose in the back of his throat, and a wave of nausea overcame him. He took a step back hoping to lean against the blackboard, but instead, lurching forward, he threw up all over the floor. The puddle, dotted with chunks of caterpillar, was milky and large, much more than what seemed possible to come out of one small boy.

Through the intercom, a frantic Mrs. Dickson called for assistance from the janitor. "Hurry!" she said.

Felix Spoon, weary and confused, looked at the mess he had made and wondered, as he often did, why he was the way he was.

There was nothing he could do. With stooped shoulders, one hand over his mouth and the other hand in his pocket, he fingered the jagged rock that came from the secret cave of God. As he stood waiting for instructions, it occurred to him that something from God's cave might be worth cherishing.

FIVE

THAT SATURDAY AFTERNOON, King, a white stallion, escaped from Ginty's Stables up on County Road 11. One of the grooms had accidentally left the horse's stall door open, and it fled into the nature preserve across the roadway, eventually emerging from the woods behind the cul-de-sac on Mundy Lane where the McCarthys, the Contes and the O'Briens lived. The huge horse, its long mane flying off its neck like a flag, and its powerful hindquarters beautifully attuned, pounded down the middle of the street. It was gone in a flash, but not until it trampled over the Chinskys' lawn, leaving big clods of grass upended. King continued on to other neighborhood streets, galloped back to the stable, and finally sauntered into his stall as if he'd just been out in the pasture grazing lazily.

Because Mundy Lane was a dead end with a wide circle that butted up against the woods, it tended to be a popular spot for street games, and a game of *SPUD* was underway when the horse came through. A handful of kids from other streets were there to witness it, as well as the Conte boys, Alice O'Brien and the McCarthy twins.

The woods, though only about two square acres, held all the intrigue of an enchanted forest, and when the horse appeared at the edge of the tree line and paused regally, reminiscent of an Apache's horse on the top of a ridge, it was magical, in a frightening way. The kids scattered, taking refuge behind hedges, some hid over by Mr. Conte's brand-new Edsel. King's heavy hooves clopped down hard on the pavement as he thundered past.

After King was gone, the children gathered on the Contes' lawn and replayed the scene to each other; who saw what when, and how cool it was. But the excitement wasn't over. Shortly, Felix Spoon and his father wandered up Mundy Lane. Nothing out of the ordinary ever happened on Mundy Lane, and now, two strange events in just a few minutes. The conversation shifted and kids whispered wisecracks to each other about how weird the Spoons were.

"Here comes cootie-bag, caterpillar-eater," whispered Dale Conte.

Upon seeing Felix, Dawn, who still wore Band-Aids on her elbow and knee from the incident in the playground, jumped up from where she sat cross-legged amidst the other children, and ran across the street to their house. Fawn trailed dutifully behind her.

Mr. Spoon stopped halfway up the street and sat on the curb. He sent his son to continue up the street alone. Fathers didn't usually sit on curbs. His long legs were bent at the knees, and his hands, clasped between them, made it seem like he was praying.

Felix Spoon stopped in front of the McCarthys' white house and paused to observe the other children across the way. They stared at him in silence, and he stared back. He made his way up the McCarthys' driveway and rang the doorbell.

Clarisse McCarthy opened the screen door. Her hair was fresh out of curlers and she wore a flowery shirtwaist dress with a soft leather belt.

"What the heck are you doing here?" she said.

"Can I talk to the twins?" said Felix, looking up at her.

"What? No. Absolutely not," she said.

"But Sister A. told me to," said Felix.

"That's absurd. Sister schmister. You're a bully."

"But I'm not," said the boy, shrugging.

"Yes, you are. And don't get fresh with me."

"I'm not being fresh. What did I do to be fresh?" he said, looking around.

Clarisse McCarthy felt her voice rising into a high pitch, and before she knew it, she reached down and slapped the boy in the face. "That'll teach you to pick on my girls. You're bad, Felix Spoon. We don't behave like that here in Hanzloo."

Felix ran down the driveway, holding his face, while the children watched from across the street. When Luke Spoon saw his son running toward him, he rushed to meet him half-way, and scooped him up in his arms. "What the hell happened?"

"Mrs. McCarthy slapped me in the face," said Felix.

"You've got to be kidding."

With his son in his arms, Luke strode up the street to the McCarthy home, left Felix standing in the driveway, approached the house and rang the bell.

Clarisse's heart was still racing from the slap. When she saw Luke Spoon at her front door, she tried to keep her cool.

"Hello, Mrs. McCarthy. My name is Luke Spoon. I live

on the Post Road," he said, stretching out his long arm, and pointing down the street. "Pardon the intrusion, but did you actually slap my son?"

"Of course I know who you are, Mr. Spoon, and, look . . . yes, I did slap your son. But I can explain," she said. "Please come in."

Luke Spoon at her own front door—ha ha—what a happy accident. She ran her fingers through her hair. "Forgive the mess around here, Saturdays are always hectic. But please, don't stand in the hall. Come on in."

Towering over her like a fun house shadow, Luke Spoon seemed oddly benevolent, considering she'd just slapped his kid. He wasn't wearing his black-framed glasses, and she saw that he had hazel eyes. Clarisse hoped she could smooth things out with him. She straightened her dress.

"Look, can we start over? I don't believe we've formally met. I'm Clarisse McCarthy, you've probably seen me around," she said, offering her hand.

"No, I really haven't." He shook her hand, which Clarisse took as a good sign. She ushered him into the living room where he stood uncomfortably.

"Can I get you a coffee or something?" she said.

"Um, I don't like coffee." He looked her in the eye, holding her gaze for a moment. His eyes narrowed. "I find it outrageous that you slapped my boy."

Apologies did not come easily to Clarisse, but she knew she had to formulate something. "I really didn't mean to. It's just, well, did you see the stallion that ran down the block?"

He smiled the slightest bit, and Clarisse wondered if he was finding her charming, and so she let herself get animated in the telling of the story.

"A big white horse came out of the woods and galloped down the lane. Can you imagine? I got confused and nervous when my daughters ran home. They were scared. Between the horse and your son walking up the street." Here she paused and was more careful with her words. "You understand that the incident in the playground the other day left its mark. But, hey," she added, raising her hands in surrender. "That's no excuse. I don't normally go around slapping children. I don't know what came over me." Clarisse was quite sure that he'd forgive her. "Why don't you come in and sit for a minute?"

"My son is waiting outside."

Clarisse went to the window and pulled the curtain back. "I'm sure he's fine, see? He'll be playing with the others in no time." The children had resumed their game of *SPUD* and Dale Conte was throwing a big brown ball in the air.

Luke looked out the window to see his son.

"Please. May I call you Luke? Let me make it up to you. I really am sorry," she said, gesturing to the couch.

Luke sat down and ran his hand through his hair. "Actually . . . I'd prefer chocolate milk to coffee. Do you have any? With a shot of scotch."

"A shot of scotch. In milk? For real?"

"For real. I have an ulcer, so I drink a lot of milk."

Clarisse worried that Frank, who was at the hardware store in Silverton, would pull into the driveway soon, and not be pleased to discover Luke Spoon drinking whiskey in his living room.

"Okay, sure, let me . . ." As she turned toward the kitchen, she noticed that the twins were sitting at the top of the staircase, and she clapped her hands in rapid succession. "You girls get your behinds upstairs. I'm having a private conversation with Mr. Spoon." They scurried away, their hands and knees thundered up the stairs on the way up to their attic room.

Clarisse looked back at Luke and rolled her eyes. "They may be girls, but they're twins. Double trouble," she said, as she ducked into the kitchen.

With shaky hands, she poured herself a coffee, though the pot had been sitting there since breakfast. She grabbed the Bosco from the cupboard and squirted chocolate into a glass of milk, stirring it quickly with a long-stemmed spoon, all the time feeling excited, about what she wasn't sure. Glancing at the kitchen clock, she realized that now it was past two and Frank really could come at any moment.

She worried about the whiskey. Should she have said no? She carried the drinks into the living room and sensed him looking her over as she set the milk and coffee on top of the liquor cabinet. She knelt down to get the bottle of Canadian Club.

"Allow me," he said. He walked over and took the bottle out of her hand, poured a hefty shot into the milk, and stirred it slowly. The two of them stood closely for a moment, and Clarisse was painfully aware that she had a reddish pimple on her chin. Luke stared at it. "Oh, did you cut yourself . . . shaving?" He chuckled and swallowed a gulp of his drink.

Was that his idea of a joke, or was he making fun of her? *Shaving?* The remark seemed way too intimate, but also absurd. What woman shaves her chin?

"I don't shave," she said, softly, realizing it was a stupid thing to say. Luke crossed back over to the couch. His green shirt, halfway tucked into his slacks, looked expensive, and she liked his strong, sloping back and graceful gait. There were no men like Luke Spoon in Hanzloo. He was rudely cute, in his New York City way, but there was something else; he moved like an *animal*. And now that he had his chocolate milk, he seemed to relax.

"So, you were saying something. What was it, about a stallion?" he said, as he sat back down, settling in with his drink. She sat, too, across from him on a slat back chair.

"Yes, there was a stallion . . . I didn't actually see it but . . . but the kids did. It came out of the woods." She put her cup down on the coffee table and took a risk. "Why are you looking at me like that? You seem bored."

"I'm not sure what you mean."

She laughed, but Luke didn't.

"Luke, I hope it's okay that I call you Luke, I'm sorry I slapped your boy. I know I shouldn't have done it. But obviously you heard about how he pushed my girls down in the playground, and I'm a mother, it's unbearable to see harm come to my kids. I'm a tiger that way. You know, girls are more delicate than boys," she said, crossing her legs.

"I understand the way you feel," said Luke. But he didn't seem particularly interested in what she was saying and instead glanced around the living room as if he'd never seen furniture before. Clarisse tried to play it cool.

"Do you mind if I smoke?" she asked.

"No," said Luke.

Clarisse pulled out a cigarette and a book of matches from the pocket of her dress. "I'd offer you one, but I'm afraid I only have the one, my husband doesn't like me to smoke."

"What does your husband do, if you don't mind me asking?" asked Luke.

"He's an executive with Henkel Paint."

"Big company," said Luke. "You're nicely cared for."

"Yes, Frank does pretty well for himself."

"Lucky to have you, I'm sure," said Luke.

Clarisse crossed her legs the other way and lit her cigarette. Her shoe dropped off her heel and was now dangling from her toes. "And what about you, Luke, what's your business? I know you're from New York City, everyone in town knows that," she said, feeling confident that she was on the verge of securing some very valuable information.

But instead of answering her question, Luke said, "You know, Clarisse, don't take this the wrong way, but I could swear you're flirting with me."

Time stood still as she absorbed what he'd just said. He had balls. She reached over to flick her ashes in the ashtray, but the ashes missed the tray and fell on the coffee table. "Uh . . . actually, I believe I was talking about my girls."

Luke smiled, and took another swallow from his drink. "I don't mind when a pretty woman flirts."

Clarisse pulled a strand of hair across her mouth, a nervous habit she'd had since childhood, and she felt herself slow down, aware of her nipples against her bra. "I'd hardly say I'm flirting." She took a deep inhale from her Salem menthol and then hastily snuffed it out.

"Oh, forgive me, then. I guess I'm way off base," said Luke, but he stood up and, strangely, so did she. He carried his drink across the room until he was a foot in front of her.

"What are you doing?" Clarisse began to shake ever so slightly, desire creeping up in her like mercury in a thermometer. He was a good six inches taller than she was, and he stood looking first into her eyes and then down at the buttons of her dress. She raised her finger to the tiny crucifix on her necklace.

"Clarisse, I get the picture, you're a sexy woman," he said.

"Oh, well," she whispered.

He moved closer to her face, and she could smell the mixture of chocolate and whiskey on his breath. He raised his hand to flip her hair off of her cheek and whispered in her ear. "If you ever touch my son again, I'll kill you." And with that he dropped his glass on her flowered rug. Chocolate milk and whiskey flew across the floor, and the glass landed sideways on the rug.

Clarisse had the unlikely thought that they were in a movie together, and she pressed her palm across her hammering heart as he slammed the door on his way out.

WHEN LUKE Spoon emerged from the McCarthy house the sun was bright, and he raised his hand to cover his eyes. He saw his son standing exactly where he'd left him on the driveway, with his hands by his sides. Felix's thin frame and wide eyes belonged to his mother, but his perpetual melancholy he'd inherited from both his parents.

"Did you tell them I was sorry?" Felix asked.

"Something like that. Mrs. McCarthy is sorry too. So now we're all sorry."

"Are the twins sorry?"

"Who knows? Try to forget about them," said Luke, wearily.

"Okay. The nun will be glad."

"Good." Luke Spoon hoisted his boy onto his shoulders, and from across the street the neighborhood kids watched as the two of them walked back down Mundy Lane.

Clarisse McCarthy stood frozen in the dim light of her living room. The humiliation she felt was equal to her desire. It had been forever since she'd felt that kind of hunger.

Replaying the scene with Luke in her mind, she went into the kitchen, filled a bucket with soapy water, and lugged it back to the living room. Luke Spoon's empty glass lay like an insult in the middle of her rug, and yet it was something that he'd left behind, an offering of some kind. She set it on the coffee table next to her snuffed out cigarette.

On her knees she scrubbed the rug, wondering what it would be like to have his hands all over her body, what his kisses would feel like between her thighs, what pleasure he might unleash in her. But she cursed him at the same time. Didn't anybody know how sensitive she was? There were limits to what she could take. No one screwed with Clarisse McCarthy; and Mr. I'm-from-New-York-City was going to have to find that out.

S ! X

WHEN ALICE O'BRIEN woke on Monday morning, her pajama top soaked through with sweat, she realized she'd had a nightmare. It had something to do with the horse galloping down the street, but Felix Spoon was featured, too. The dream left her with a feeling of dread. She buried her face in her pillow and whimpered.

Shortly, her cries seemed pointless. So she dressed herself and tried to drag the brush through her hair, but there were snarls she couldn't manage. She tied the whole mess into a thick ponytail with a rubber band and ventured out of the bedroom. From the hallway she saw the bony outline of her mother's body curled under a sheet on the couch in the darkened living room. The blinds were drawn.

One of Lil O'Brien's arms hung like a rubber kitchen glove off the side of the couch, while the other was bent at the elbow over her eyes. Her light red hair, unruly as a trashed Barbie's, lay around the pillowcase, which had yellowed over the last few months.

Alice's mother didn't do the laundry anymore. Her father had taken over, but he rarely got around to folding, and a basket of wrinkled clothes overflowed in the middle of the living room. Alice hoped to find a matching pair of socks without disturbing the silence.

"Alice," said Lil, waking. "Come here for just a minute, would you?"

The area around the couch had a smell now, like some sweet and rotten thing. Alice approached her mother with a gray knee sock in her hand and pushed the pill bottles and poetry books aside to make room to sit on the coffee table. There was a time when Lil had read those books to Alice. The poems were mysterious, even magical, and Alice didn't worry about her mother then. Now the books and the pads of paper she scribbled on were scattered on the table. "Somewhere in those notebooks is a poem, and the words in that poem will describe this . . . situation that we're in. You and me, Alice, we're in a situation, and it ought to be told, but it's hard to describe in regular words. I think it has to be a poem." Lil had said this to Alice with urgency, just yesterday, and Alice had said, "Sure, Mom." But Alice remembered that her entire class had to write a poem in school last year, and all the kids seemed to manage it, but she doubted that her mother could do much of anything anymore.

Lil grabbed Alice's arm with both her hands. "Don't get married," she said.

"Mom," said Alice.

"Don't do it. Promise. Please."

"I promised you yesterday," said Alice, wiping her hand across her forehead.

"Okay, good," said Lil. She closed her eyes again and let go of Alice's arm.

Before Alice could sneak back to her room, her father

bounded up the basement stairs and emerged, holding a briefcase in his hand. He wore a suit and tie. When he saw his daughter, he stopped short, as if she'd caught him stealing.

"Honey, what are you doing over there? Is she up?" He put his briefcase down.

Lil turned her face into the pillows of the couch and pulled the sheet and her arms over her head.

Hi Dad," said Alice, still holding her sock.

Her father sighed. "Sweetheart, I'm late, I have to go. Maybe Mom will get up and make you breakfast."

"Yes, Mom will," said Lil from under the sheet.

"It's okay, I can get my own," said Alice.

"Mom will wait for a minute," said Lil, curling into a ball.

Alice watched her father glance at his watch. He smiled— it was a pressed together smile—as if he was trying to say something, but his lips were glued shut.

Alice shrugged.

"I'll try to pick up a pack of baseball cards on my way home tonight, okay? We can sort the last batch, too." Then, another one of those smiles. "Come on, give me a hug."

Alice crossed the room and leaned into his embrace. "Do good today," he said, patting her on the shoulder.

"Okay, Dad."

Jim O'Brien stopped by the front door and swung an imaginary bat before hurrying out. Alice didn't catch his invisible ball.

Once her husband was gone, Lil sat up on the couch, reached for one of her bottles and, uncapping it quickly, popped two pills, no longer needing water to wash them down. She leaned back with her eyes closed and massaged her head with her fingers.

"Go get me a fork and a bowl and an egg, love," said Lil. "I'll mix it up here."

When Alice returned with the egg, Lil said, "Look at that poor little thing."

"Mom, it's just an egg," said Alice, putting the bowl on the coffee table.

"Alice, this could have been a baby chicken." She held the egg in front of her face. "How smooth."

Lil turned the egg from side to side. She placed it back in the bowl, picked up the fork and thrust it into the egg, cracking it. She stabbed at it repeatedly until the shell mingled with the slimy white and the yoke oozed yellow into the bowl. "Do you see that? It's like I killed it!" she said.

"Mom, you're scaring me," said Alice.

"Oh, honey, I'm scaring myself." Lil lay back onto the couch with a thud. "Can you make yourself something to eat? I don't feel quite right. You can do it; I know you can."

Lil put her arm over her face.

"I told you I could," said Alice.

"Alice," Lil whispered. "You're going to do great things someday."

Her mother saw something in Alice that she couldn't see for herself. Ever since Alice could remember, her mother had told her she hadn't just been born but *broken off the moon*, which didn't sound great to Alice. "You're not ordinary, which is good, because the world can't bear another ordinary girl." She told Alice that someday they'd run away to New York City, and all their friends would be writers and painters, they'd stay up all night long and watch the stars and go to bed when the sun came up. "I've been to New York City. You'll see."

All Alice really knew about New York was that the Yankees played there, and she would have been happy to go to a game someday. Her mother said that by the time Alice grew up, she could *be* a Yankee because girls would be allowed to do whatever they wanted. "Dream monstrously, Alice. Don't just be some girl, be a man." But Alice didn't want to dream like a monster, and everyone knew a girl can't be a man. The things her mother said embarrassed her, and often she allowed herself to wonder what it would be like to have a more regular mother, but she loved her mother more than anyone, and she hoped her father didn't know that because his feelings might get hurt.

Lil fell back to sleep and Alice sat for a moment, watching the thin sheet rise and fall with her mother's breath. What if she *did* die? There was a girl in Farrow's Corner named Penelope Frost, whose mother had died of the flu. Her picture was in the paper, and Alice had seen it. She thought about what her father had asked her to do—say a prayer for Mom—but Alice doubted anything would work.

She went to the kitchen and took a powdered donut from the bread bin. She sat at the table looking out the kitchen window, her feet dangling from her chair. It was there that she communicated with Sneedler.

Back when things were normal, Alice used to tell her mother about Sneedler, and his peculiar ways.

"It's okay to have a good imagination," her mother had said.

But Sneedler was not imagined, he was real; he often lingered in the tree outside the kitchen window. Why couldn't anyone else see him? Soft around the edges, and like a ghost, he bounced around, weightless, his head changing shape and color depending on his mood. Sneedler didn't use words, but somehow, he communicated in a way that pleased Alice so much she would find herself smiling, and her mother would say, "What's so funny?"

The problem was that Sneedler had no other friends, and it fell to Alice to keep him company, which could be a burden when she had other things to do.

"Now look, Sneedler, it's time to go to school. You can walk me there, but you can't come in."

Sneedler's face turned purple, and it crumpled, like it always did when things weren't going his way. But tough. It was too nerve-racking to bring him into her classroom, and he'd just have to live with that.

When Alice's donut was gone, she wiped the sugar from her mouth with the back of her hand and placed her glass beside the kitchen sink, where last night's dinner dishes were still soaking. Baked beans and small squares of pork floated in the cool, soapy water.

She organized her book bag and left for school, careful to close the front door silently. Sneedler and Alice walked to school side by side through the quiet streets of Hanzloo. They had taken to leaving the house late in order to avoid seeing other children walking to school with their mothers.

It was a bright, cool day, and Sneedler's colors were constantly in flux, as if every leaf and shadow affected how he felt. When they reached the school, they stood before the iron playground gates and a wordless goodbye passed between them. She watched him fly into a tree and disappear into the leaves.

As soon as he was gone, nerves gathered in her stomach.

This being the second week of classes, Mrs. Dickson had determined who the troublemakers were, and she was anxious to split them up. Alice had been relocated in front of Felix Spoon, who sat in the last seat of the third row. Now she had a hard time concentrating during the math lesson, and worried about what he was doing behind her. She could feel the rim of his desk bump into her chair. Why couldn't he sit still? Twice she thought she felt him poke her with his pencil.

Midmorning, between math and reading, Mrs. Dickson gave the children two minutes to stretch their legs, and Felix tapped her shoulder. "Can you have a private meetup with me?" he whispered. She turned to look at him. It was the first time she'd seen his face up close, and her eye was pulled to a tiny freckle on his nose. Alice considered telling on him, but she realized he hadn't done anything wrong.

"Huh?" she said.

"Wait till you see what I have. I'll meet you in the cafeteria after school. Will you come?" said Felix. Alice slipped back into her desk without a word.

Fears of meeting Felix Spoon in the cafeteria consumed her, and she made a mistake in her English workbook. The word of the day was *kitten,* and though she spelled it correctly, she colored the kitten bright yellow.

When Mrs. Dickson bent down, surrounded by a perfume cloud, her gold locket knocking against the face of the desk, she frowned and told Alice that cats were not yellow. With her ballpoint, she made an X beside the kitten, and continued on her way. Alice tried to erase the yellow, but the eraser ripped the page. She made matters worse by trying to cover up the rip with her black crayon. The cat, in its confusion of yellow and black, was a perfect expression of the way she felt, but when the teacher came by for a second look she didn't bother to lean over. "I can't give you a sticker for that," she said. Alice watched her move down the aisle and stop at Cathy Lawrence's desk. She licked one of her coveted silver stars and put it on Cathy's page, with a flourish. Cathy had colored her kitten pink, but everyone knew that kittens weren't pink, and Alice's feelings were hurt.

After lunch other bad things happened. Mrs. Dickson stunned the whole class by dumping the contents of Felix Spoon's desk on the floor.

"You are a human garbage pail! How can you think straight when you're so disorganized?" Mrs. Dickson's gleeful rant rang out as she turned his entire desk on its side.

The class watched as Felix got down on his hands and knees and crawled around. Slowly, and with great care, he put his things back in his desk. He seemed interested in the things he found in his own desk, as if he'd never seen them before. Among his books were a small net bag of blue marbles, several crushed figures made of pipe cleaners, and a plastic statue of a gorilla. Alice's cheeks blushed with shame, as if her own desk had been poured all over the floor.

After school she lingered on the playground, hiding by the church wall, arguing with herself about whether to go to the cafeteria to look for Felix Spoon. She searched the trees for Sneedler, but he wasn't there, so she waited until the other kids made their way out of the gates in groups of twos and threes. The sun slipped behind a cluster of dark clouds, and the wind picked up, as if rain was on the way. Alice hugged her sweater to her neck. When the playground emptied, she edged along the wall of the church to the side door of the school.

The door was heavy, and she pulled it open with both hands. Her saddle shoes clicked on the floor as she made her way down the deserted hallway where she caught sight of Mr. Lorton, the janitor, who smelled of cigars, and had a hump on his back. He was cleaning out one of the fourth-grade classrooms, his broom leaning up against the big gray garbage can that rolled around on wheels. He didn't notice Alice sneaking by.

In the cafeteria, one dim light was on, and the room, still and empty, had the scent of sour milk and old ham sandwiches. The long, smooth tables and benches, which at lunchtime were jammed with children, now vibrated in stillness.

"Alice, over here," called Felix Spoon in a loud whisper. She spotted him underneath a bench over by the silver steam tables, where each day nameless, aproned ladies in hairnets, who were somehow *less than* their mothers, heaped macaroni and cheese and soupy meat on children's plates.

"Felix Spoon?" she said.

"Shhh! Come on over."

"I can't. I'm . . . scared." The word popped out before she had a chance to stop it.

"Cripes' sake, what are you scared of? Nobody's here but me," he said, poking his head out from under the bench.

"What do you want to show me?"

"You have to come here."

Alice hesitated at first, but when she reached the bench, Felix said, "Come on, get under."

"I don't want to," said Alice.

"You *have* to. Come on, don't you want to see?"

Alice put her book bag down and crouched down to join Felix under the bench. Her heart was thumping.

On all fours, Felix crawled down the length of the table, like a raccoon. "Hurry," he whispered, looking back at Alice.

She followed him, her knees hard against the floor. Her socks fell into bunches around her ankles. By the time they came to rest, both of them were breathing hard, their clothes were mussed, and Felix Spoon's face was rosy with sweat. He tore open the collar of his shirt and a button fell off. He looked at her and smiled, and she couldn't help but smile back.

"Okay, you ready?" A harsh but silent flash of lightning came through the windows. "Whoa," said Felix. Seconds later, thunder growled in the distance.

They sat cross-legged facing each other with their hands folded in their laps. He pulled a red velvet box from his backpack and held it in his palm. Come on, close your eyes and give me your hand."

Alice hesitated. "Where did you get that box?" she said, thinking he might have stolen it. It looked like something that a rich person would own.

"It belongs to my mother," said Felix.

"It's really nice." Alice closed her eyes and allowed Felix to draw her hand across the top of the box. Alice concentrated, letting her fingers feel the soft velvet.

"Well?" he said.

"Feels like the fur of a tiger," she said.

"You felt a tiger before?" he asked.

"No, how could I have felt a tiger? Who has ever felt a tiger? Not anyone in Hanzloo, that's for sure."

"I like you, Alice."

"What?" she said.

"That's why I chose you out of everybody in the whole school. You'll understand. But first, you have to put one hand on your heart and swear. Say, 'I—Alice—won't tell a soul.'"

Alice had never sworn.

"OOOOJOOO!" said Felix, pointing two fingers at her. His eyes seemed to double in size, and she snapped to attention.

"Why are you saying that?" she asked, pulling away.

"I'm pretending I'm Houdini. Don't you know who Houdini is? He can control the world! You have to swear because it's *important* to keep this promise."

"I—Alice O'Brien—won't tell a soul," she said, with her hand on her heart.

Felix opened the box and held it out for her to see. "This . . . is from *God's* cave."

The jagged gray rock sat on a small pillow of tarnished satin. To Alice it looked like something you'd find in a parking lot. "Really? Are you sure? Where is God's cave? I never heard of it before."

"I don't know. You don't believe me." Felix lowered his eyes, and Alice felt bad.

"No, I do. I guess."

"I haven't been able to find out where the cave is yet," he said.

Alice stared at the rock.

"Want to touch it?" asked Felix.

Alice opened her hand, and Felix placed the rock in her palm.

"It's *beautiful*," he said. "And don't pretend you think it's an ordinary rock."

Alice couldn't remember a boy ever saying the word *beautiful*. Closing her eyes, she tried to feel something from the rock, half hoping that it did come from God, that it might protect her from getting into trouble, because now she had a creepy feeling that she was doing something wrong.

They heard footsteps, and the florescent lights in the cafeteria clicked on in a harsh, uneven succession. Teresa Sepolino, Sister Annunciata's secretary, peered into the room.

"Who's there? Who's under the tables?"

As she neared, Felix grabbed the rock from Alice and put it back in the velvet box. He scurried out from under the table, and snatched his book bag, leaving Alice. "Run!" he yelled, as he raced past Mrs. Sepolino toward the door of the cafeteria. He turned before he left the room. "Don't be stupid, run!" But Alice froze.

Teresa, despite her bad back, got down on her knees and pulled Alice out from under the table. She took her by the arm and shook her. "Alice, what was he doing to you! Tell me, dear."

"Nothing. He showed me something is all."

But Alice, rigid as a board, wouldn't say what, and Teresa eventually sent her home, suspecting that the *something* Felix had shown her was his penis. First, the peeing on the floor, and now this. Did the boy have a compulsive need to expose himself?

SEVEN

TERESA SEPOLINO FRETTED for hours. Reporting this incident to Sister Annunciata was unimaginable. She didn't think she could utter the word *penis* to the nun; it was that simple. And forget about the priests; out of the question.

But Clarisse McCarthy would know what to do. Approaching her would entail putting pride aside, as Clarisse had never given her the time of day. Teresa decided to call Clarisse for the sake of the child.

"I'm sorry to bother you at night," said Teresa. And she unburdened herself.

"In the cafeteria? That's disgusting," said Clarisse. "You can't be serious. Oh my God."

Clarisse, Stephanie, and Teresa sat in Clarisse's kitchen the following morning around a tray of Fig Newtons. Clarisse didn't waste any time with small talk.

"Here's what I think. Felix Spoon is demented. Little Alice, good Lord, what next?" Clarisse was saying.

Steph noticed that Clarisse often referred to Alice as "little" Alice, and to Lil as "poor" Lil. She suspected that her diminishing adjectives had less to do with compassion and more to do with the fact that Clarisse had no jurisdiction over Lil O'Brien. Steph took it upon herself to play devil's advocate, knowing that Teresa might not be so inclined to stand up to Clarisse. She put her cookie down.

"Okay, I agree this is disturbing, and, yes, the kid is an oddball, but what did you *actually* see, Teresa?"

Teresa bit her bottom lip, and concentrated, as if it were a trick question on a quiz. "Well, I walked in . . . the two of them were under the table . . . very, very close," she said, putting her hands together like a prayer. "The boy ran . . . shouting to Alice, 'don't be stupid' and by the time I fished her out from under the table, she was . . . you know . . . shaking, and speechless. And when I asked her what they were doing, she wouldn't tell. She just said, 'he showed me something.' So, I don't know, but it didn't feel right."

"That's an understatement," said Clarisse, who shuddered as if she had just pictured a car crash in her head. "Poor Lil is in no condition to handle something like this," Clarisse said.

When further pressed by Steph, Teresa said she couldn't quite be sure about what actual touching had occurred, and that's when Clarisse jumped in.

"Please, Steph. We get that it was something sexual, no need to mince around. We have to move on this. That boy is trouble. I mean, come on . . . he's already hurt my girls and now this. Honestly, I don't care much for the father, either."

The women got quiet.

Steph crossed her arms and smiled ever so slightly at Clarisse. "Really?"

"Look, Teresa, thanks for telling us about this. We'll think about a plan of action." Clarisse stood up, putting an abrupt end to Teresa's visit and ushering her to the door as fast as she could.

"I thought you said Luke Spoon was the perfect gentleman when he came to apologize," said Steph after Teresa left.

Clarisse pursed her lips and took a moment to pull at an eyelash. "I don't know. I've had a few days to think about it, and, so what, he can turn on the charm. Something about him gives me the creeps," said Clarisse. "You can't just do *nothing* in a case like this, Steph. Come on. I feel I should step up."

"Yeah, but I don't really think there's enough evidence here."

"Oh, so we should wait until he goes further than showing? How about touching?" said Clarisse.

"Clarisse, he's seven years old!" Stephanie Conte didn't buy it. Clarisse had done a flip-flop. When Clarisse had called her saying that Luke Spoon had paid her a visit, you would have thought he was Paul Newman or something. But she was on the warpath now, and Steph was reminded of the time Clarisse had almost driven the Witters out of town with her campaign to ostracize them because they'd painted their house red, which according to Clarisse looked like *something you'd find on a whore's lips*.

"Well, what are you going to do?" said Steph.

"I'm going to think about it, Steph. I'll figure something out. But I really wish you'd be with me on this. I could use your support."

EIGHT

WORK WAS SLOW. Callahan was out of the office. Hallelujah. Jim O'Brien despised Callahan, and the feeling was probably mutual. Callahan—Joseph C—had waltzed out of Rutgers into the executive spot that Jim had been bowing and scraping for the last five years.

Gleason Brothers Department Store: Wow, Callahan, he sometimes thought, you really made your parents proud. These snide remarks he kept to himself, though they rolled around in his mind all day.

Taking advantage of the fact that his boss was out for the day, Jim meandered down the hall for a third cup of coffee.

"I'll be right back, Dinah," he said to the secretary he shared with Mike Wilson.

"That's fine," said Dinah, as if he'd asked for permission. It often looked to Jim like she'd just gotten out of bed. Who wears a hairnet to work? She was efficient, but also fond of pointing out Jim's sloppy mistakes. "Are you sure you want to phrase it this way?" she'd say, exuding disbelief.

He made his way down the aisle. Those secretaries who were not at their metal desks were in their boss's offices; he could see them through the windows, sitting with their legs crossed, holding dictation pads. Others were at their typewriters, the tick, tick, tick of their fingers on the keys reassuring everyone in a numbing sort of a way.

"Hi Sue," he said to a young woman who looked up from her work up as he passed. She wore glasses on the tip of her nose.

She smiled at him, but just barely.

The office, on the fifth floor of Gleason's, had a hardwood floor, and its gray walls, as if to inspire and encourage *nothing*, were bare. At the end of the hall of desks, a small lounge for coffee had an orange, pseudoleather couch and a couple of mismatched chairs.

Jim stirred sugar into his coffee, picked up a copy of the *Reader's Digest* that was sitting on the coffee table, and idly thumbed through the magazine, when an article caught his eye.

Explaining What A Husband Is

In the first place, make your husband feel that you like him. Well, hey, thought Jim, what a concept. *The look on your face when your husband comes home from work may be the most important expression in your marriage. There are women who do all their chores and fulfill every household responsibility and yet their husbands don't feel liked. Chances are that, when you marry, you may have to give up some career or ambition. If you're going to make your husband feel guilty because he robbed the world of a great talent—don't marry.*

Jim couldn't believe what he was reading. Whoever wrote this article had really tapped into something. He skipped down a few paragraphs.

A man may want to make love because he is romantic, happy, sad, frightened, angry, cheerful, in despair, or restless. Don't resent it. You can be happy with this browbeaten beast, this vulgar bozo, this oversensitive tyrant. Make an effort to understand him.

Jim could just hear Lil making fun of something like this, but he felt like erecting a statue to the author. What ever happened to respect for your husband? Wasn't there *something* you could expect from your wife? Maybe he was too easy on her.

Jim marched back to his desk and called Doctor Garufee. At first the doctor was reluctant to talk to him. "Look, there's confidentiality between a doctor and his patient. You understand that, right Jim?"

"I know, but these drugs she's on, they're just not working. She's acting crazy. Last week I found her standing in the walk-in closet in the dark. My daughter needs a mother, and frankly, I need a wife."

"I understand," said Dr. Garufee. "This kind of thing is tricky, though. Sometimes it takes time to find the right combination of pills; women can be extremely sensitive. You have to be patient, but firm. She's been through a lot."

What had she been through, Jim wondered? She'd barely been off Mundy Lane.

"Let's wait until the appointment and see how things go. Hang in there."

Jim had hung in, but he had a hard time believing his wife couldn't just snap out of it. And forget about sex. Whereas he couldn't say they'd ever had a raucous sex life—he'd always had to approach Lil on tenterhooks—now it had completely gone out the window. He had needs. For God's sake, he was reduced to sleeping in the cellar like a dog.

Ten minutes after his conversation with Garufee, he picked up the phone again and dialed Kay Book's extension. Kay worked in the billing department.

"Howdy, Kay," he said.

"Hello, Mr. O'Brien," said Kay.

"I was thinking about Flapdogs after work. You free?

"I guess I'm free," said Kay.

"You don't sound so sure," said Jim.

Kay sighed. "No, okay, that's sounds fine."

"No pressure of course. I mean, if you've got something else to do."

"I'll be there, Mr. O'Brien," said Kay.

Jim hung up. She seemed tired of him already. How did that happen?

What the hell, it wasn't against the law to have a drink. Jim had absolutely no interest in Kay, a pudgy twenty-year-old with a loud annoying laugh, who sucked on Salem cigarettes, leaving red lipstick on their tips, sometimes filling up a whole ashtray during happy hour.

Jim told himself he wasn't going to call her anymore, but increasingly, around four o'clock in the afternoon, his hand, as if it had a mind of its own, reached for the phone, and in an hour, he'd find himself shoulder to shoulder with Kay Book at good old Flapdogs. Listening to her complain about the other girls in billing wasn't so bad as long as he could sail away down Martini Lane. Sometimes he'd watch the cigarette smoke bellow out of her mouth and think, just wait until your life really falls apart. You have no idea what lies ahead, little girl.

No one seemed to realize what was happening to him. If he'd cracked into a thousand pieces and fell underneath his desk, he suspected they'd say, "Hey, is that a pile of dirt on the floor, or is it Jim O'Brien? And by the way, who cares?"

Interestingly Clarisse McCarthy was the only human being who had asked him how he was doing lately. Over the last few weeks, she'd taken to calling him; drawing him out, telling him he could lean on her if he needed to.

It was tricky because Lil didn't like her, but he had to admit it felt good to have the feeling that someone cared, and Clarisse McCarthy was *Clarisse McCarthy*. Jim slipped the *Reader's Digest* into his briefcase and headed over to Flap-dogs.

He had to pass by Dinah's desk when he left, and she looked up as he snuck by. "It's only ten to five," she said, glancing at her watch.

"Well, *whoop-de-do*," said Jim. "You know, Dinah, you might want to think about the fact that I'm the boss, not the other way around."

She looked away as if he were an annoying five-year-old who had just said, "Poop."

NINE

SINCE LUKE SPOON moved to Hanzloo, correspondence with the world had thinned considerably, but he still ventured out to check his mail. Outside the parameters of the recently built developments, the Ross house, weathered and drafty, stood alone on the Old Post Road, back from the street. Spoon had loved the place immediately. He liked to think of himself as the kind of guy who would live in a house like this; one without a manicured lawn, one that sat smack in the middle of a chaotic field.

Still relieved to get out of the city and its galleries full of red-faced, wine-swilling bigmouths who blew smoke from cigarette holders in each other's faces, Luke was in no hurry to leave Hanzloo. He'd had enough of the art scene for the time being. Nature was the real art gallery, and all his old friends would have to agree, although none of them would be caught dead here.

His stretch of the Post Road was deserted, though a quarter mile away the strip mall loomed, complete with an A&P. Still, he didn't have to worry about neighbors looking in the windows. He could walk around in nothing if he wanted to, but, somehow, he never did.

Midmorning, the mailman came by in what looked to Luke like a toy truck for a man; it had big wheels and one door, with just enough space in the back for the mail sack. Luke waited until the mail truck pulled away and drove down the road before walking out. He wondered what that must be like for a grown man to wear a uniform. Luke hadn't worn a uniform since his school days at Holy Angels for Boys, in Indiana, where he was born.

The sun slipped behind a passing cloud as Luke stepped on to his porch. Autumn was nearing, a shadow moved across the lawn, and a few yellow leaves scurried over the grass, like crabs on a beach. He pulled the collar of his jacket up like a guy in a magazine might do. Who was he posing for? Solitude was supposed to bring peace, but he tortured himself about everything. Still, today he congratulated himself on staying out of trouble in Hanzloo. So far. His run-in with Clarisse McCarthy on Mundy Lane the other day swerved danger-ously close to reckless. Maybe he shouldn't have thrown his drink on her floor.

At the curb, along with some forwarded mail from his manager—invitations to art openings that he'd just toss out—Luke was surprised to find an actual letter in the box, and he pulled his glasses out of his shirt pocket to get a better look. The address, comprised of letters cut from maga-zines and newspapers, had been pasted on a plain white enve-lope. He ran his fingers across the letters and felt where the glue had crusted. No return address. Weird.

Sliding his thumb under the flap of the envelope, he unfolded a single sheet of paper. The words on the page, also glued, letter by letter, bore no relation to each other in size and style; some were larger than others, some in script, some lowercase, and some were bold and capital.

The sticky, crooked sentence on the page resembled a child's art project, and briefly he thought Felix had managed to send it, but as he read, it was clear that someone else had cooked this up.

The message was ominous:

Your son molested Alice O'Brien at school.
Get out of Hanzloo.

Luke stared at the letter with his mouth open. What the hell? Was this somebody's idea of a joke? *Get out of Hanzloo*?

He walked back from the mailbox and sat down on the stoop with the opened letter in his hand, paranoid that he was being watched. Lowering his glasses to the tip of his nose, he looked up and down the street but saw no people and no cars either. One lone bird flew in the distant sky, small as a dot, and the stillness of Hanzloo, which moments earlier had seemed comforting, now spooked him. He went back into the house and closed the front door, even turning the lock— something he hadn't done since moving in—and sat at the kitchen table with his chin in his hand.

The word *molested*—he had to think for a moment—what did it actually mean? No way it could be true. Could a child molest? What a mess this could be.

For one brief moment, Luke allowed himself to consider the possibility that it was true, that somehow what he'd always recognized as Felix's singleness was instead a kind of trouble that had twisted in a deeply disturbing way. It seemed inconceivable that Felix could hurt anyone, but maybe he was wrong.

He moved over to the kitchen sink, intending to wash out his coffee cup, but instead put his hands on the edge of the counter and stared out the kitchen window beyond the tree-tops, to the clouds that rolled back in the sky, and thought despairingly of Joni, as if he might find her there. Where the hell *was* she? He allowed the longing to wash over him, hope-fully to pass quickly. His nightly dreams were full of her. He missed her, and the boy must, too. But at the moment, he was pissed at her all over again.

THAT NIGHT, in their tiny Greenwich Village studio, he'd found it amusing, the way she stood in her bra, and the man's trousers she'd been wearing lately—her black hair cropped short as a boy's—smoking a Camel through a red and gold cigarette holder. Sweat glistened on her forehead and above her lip; her cheeks were ruddy from the whiskey and the heat. Joni put her glass to her lips and threw her head back, taking a big gulp that ended in an openmouthed *aaaah.*

"The way people are in those little towns? They'll squash Felix." She flicked her ashes on the floor, one hand on her hip.

"I spoke to your mother—"

"My mother! Spare me! I don't want to hear about my mother. You think my mother is going to solve this? You really are stuck in the Catholic crap, aren't you? It's like you're still an altar boy. How could you even think about put-ting him in a Catholic school! Is this what you want?" she said, hitting her chest with her palm. "Cause this is what you just might get!"

Old Ruth Plough, in the apartment below them, banged

on her ceiling with a blunt object, and without thinking, Joni grabbed the broom from where it hung on a nail on the wall and pounded the handle on the floor three times.

"Come on, Joni," said Luke. "Knock it off."

"Mark my words, Felix will not survive Hanzloo. I know what kind of town that is."

"You don't know, you really don't. Look, I need to get away from New York for a while. I'm sick of it. We need to regroup, settle down a bit. I'll get down to work. And Joni, you're out of control."

"You're not listening to me, Luke. I'm not going with you. What I have to get away from is *you*. You can keep pretending that you're not who you are, living this starving-artist myth. You're successful, Luke. Why can't you get that into your head? You think just because you live in a little dump in the Village means you don't have to admit you have money? You can't run away from New York. Be who you are! But I'm not successful. I'm just a bigmouthed nobody, and I can't hang off the end of your arm forever.

"That's not true. What about Felix? You're a mother, Joni. A mother doesn't leave her child." I thought we were a *family*."

"What's a *family*?" she said under her breath. "Maybe a mother does leave, maybe a mother should leave from time to time. I'm going to Paris with Mariana, and that's that. I'll never have this chance again." She pointed at him. "But I love my boy, you know I love my boy. And don't you tell him otherwise."

"Mariana is an accident waiting to happen."

"She's an *artist,* Luke, she actually spends time painting. You should try that. Ever since you became a hotshot, you haven't picked up a brush."

That was true, and that alone was a good enough reason to get out of New York.

"You need some time away? *I* need some time away," said Joni. "We'll assess things when I get back. Besides, Felix has you. You're as much of a mother as I am. Why does the woman always have to be the mother?"

LATER THAT afternoon, having obsessed about the anonymous letter for hours, Luke buried it under some pants and shirts in the back of his dresser drawer, as if it were a dirty magazine, and left the house to pick up Felix from school.

He leaned against the trunk of the giant elm tree across the street from Immaculate Conception. Luke didn't always meet his son at school, but when he did go, he parked himself at a distance, and kept his arms crossed. Today he wore sunglasses, as if that made him less visible. Now, because of the letter, everyone in Hanzloo was a suspect, and Luke found himself scrutinizing the crowd.

At three o'clock, Sister Annunciata unlocked the gates and stood with her hands folded into the long sleeves of her habit, overseeing as children charged out of the playground.

One girl, whose arm was in a sling, burst into long sobs at the sight of her mother, while a group of boys grabbed a smaller boy's sweatshirt and tossed it around. A few kids wrestled, and some jumped around the sidewalk as if communing with some inner demon. Others took hold of their mother's arms and pulled for attention while a few whined and begged for something intangible, like a break from their own existence. Felix was no different from these children, thought Luke. They all seemed insane, and no different from the kids in New York City, whom he'd often watched at Washington Square Park, while Felix fingered through the sand, searching in vain for magic pennies.

The mothers were harder for him to observe directly, and he resisted the urge to look at them too closely. They doled out plastic bags of snacks, their slender arms expert at maneuvering strollers, grabbing tissues, or tending to toddlers.

The other day Luke had painted a quick study of tulips in a field. (So, now he painted *tulips*.) He'd made each one a different color, but they seemed all the same, and afterward he suspected that what he'd actually done was an abstract of the mothers. He supposed that was his way of keeping them at bay. He never liked tulips. As he eyed his finished sketch, he laughed out loud, wondering why he would ever think that a woman was like a flower.

He looked for Clarisse McCarthy in the crowd. Her body was an open invitation. He'd found her at once irresistible and repulsive in the crudest way; there was something about the cultivated curls in her hair, the small crucifix around her neck, the cloth-covered buttons on her cotton dress, and that marvelous *ass*. She'd be so easy to wreck. He wondered where he got the nerve to think like that. When he spotted her, he quickly looked away.

He had to watch his step. Those kinds of scenes with women he'd hoped were in his past. There had been so many of them: poor Maria Zoble, on a bench in front of the bakery on Fourth Street, in tears in the middle of a thunderstorm, asking him how he could have taken her virginity without loving her, and all he could do was watch the raindrops fall off her ponytail. Or that crazy Clair What-Was-Her-Name, who threw a beer in his face at the White Horse Tavern and wound up getting them both kicked out on the street, because the drink had gone right past him and landed all over another guy's jacket. It made him sick to think of it. Part of the deal he'd struck with himself when moving to Hanzloo was that he'd live like a country priest. Besides, he was hoping that Joni would come back.

Felix came out of the playground with his schoolbag dragging on the sidewalk. It was heavy with books, and he wasn't able to close it. His shirttails hung over his trousers, and his shoelaces were untied, as usual. Luke often thought that Felix looked like he'd been beaten up when he emerged from school. There'd been a runt of a kid at Holy Angels— Rusty Ixter—and Luke and his friends used to rough him up under the stairwell by the gym. Luke was pretty sure that kids were picking on Felix—and he felt that if he'd somehow managed to make amends to Rusty Ixter, his own son would have been spared a similar fate. You don't get away with anything, really.

Luke waved and Felix crossed the street to meet him.

"Hi Luke," said Felix. His hand rose to shade his eyes.

"Hi son."

They shuffled along in silence for a while. Felix kept stopping to put his book bag down and lift it up again.

"Want me to carry that for you?" asked Luke.

"Yeah, it's a little too heavy for me," said Felix.

"Got tree trunks in there again?"

"Naw, just books." It was hard to get the boy to lighten up, and they meandered home in silence, past the front yards where leaves had been raked into small piles, and the garbage cans had been dragged to the ends of driveways for pickup.

Felix occasionally crouched down to look for four-leaf clovers in the cracks between the sidewalks. It didn't take long to make their way home, and as they stepped onto the stairs of the porch Felix pulled at his father's shirt and pointed up. "Look," he said.

Luke saw that a skywriter had drawn a message in a blue patch of the sky. He got down on one knee and put his arm around Felix while they watched.

"What does it say?" asked Felix.

"I don't know. I can't make it out." Luke squinted.

"As soon as they make the letters, they disappear," said Felix.

They watched together as the rest of the word was written. "Why bother if it's only going to disappear? I'd like to write a message in the sky, one that wouldn't go away," said Felix, waving to the message as if it were a friend of his.

"Yeah? What would you write?" said Luke.

Felix raised his hand and moved it across the expanse of the sky. "Rock . . . of . . . God," said Felix.

"What the hell?" said Luke.

"Nothing," said Felix, and Luke did not pursue it further.

"You know . . . speaking of messages . . . I got a message in the mail today," said Luke, and he sat on the steps of the porch. "Do you know a girl named Alice O'Brien?"

Felix was still gazing up at the disappearing letters in the sky.

He blew a big sigh through his lips. "Yeah, I know her, she sits in front of me." He climbed up to the next step. "Can we go inside? I'd like a glass of milk."

Luke followed Felix inside the house. The boy sat in his little red rocker in the middle of the living room. Aside from the rocker and Luke's big easy chair, there wasn't much else in the room. Beside Felix's rocker, a cold grilled cheese sandwich sat on a plate on the floor. A TV, up on a card table, sat against the far wall, its antennae reaching up toward the ceiling in a V. On a whim, Luke had painted the walls light green, and now they were covered in Felix's drawings.

The sketches, like hieroglyphics in a cave, were drawn directly on the wall, and they puzzled Luke. By now, spread over two of the four walls was a mountain range, and stick figures walked up and down the hills in an endless procession. It had all started a few months back. One night, out of the blue, while Luke watched the evening news, Felix had carried his bag of colored pencils up from the basement and outlined the first mountain directly on the wall, as if it were just another piece of paper on his art pad.

Luke had been torn between delight and concern. Too curious to interrupt him, Luke watched as Felix put the first tiny stick figures on the mountain; each had a different face and hairdo, some carried swords, some held hands.

That the boy had no inkling he might be punished for doing such a thing made Luke envious. If Luke had drawn on a wall, his father would have knocked him upside the head. To be so free. How radical. How simple. What a great idea, but he didn't want to spoil the kid with praise, so he didn't say a word about it. Neither of them did. But since then, Felix had settled into a nightly ritual of drawing his masterpiece, usually when Luke read or watched the news. And it was always the same thing, mountains and meticulously detailed stick figures on an endless trek to no obvious destination.

Luke brought two glasses of chocolate milk out from the kitchen.

"Here you go, tiger," he said. Felix took his glass, sipped the milk, and rocked back in forth in his chair. "So, who is this Alice O'Brien?" said Luke, pulling his easy chair around to face Felix.

"Just a girl. She lives on Mundy Lane. Remember that lady who slapped me? She lives over there. You know, there's the twins' house, then those old people, the Chinskys, and Alice lives right next to them. Her house is yellow."

"Oh, yeah? So, she's a friend of yours?"

"I don't know." Felix sat rocking on his chair for a moment and then looked squarely at his father, as if bracing him for the news. "Kids don't seem to like me too much."

Luke's heart sank. "What do you mean? That can't be true. Why do you say that?"

"Nobody likes her, either," he said, as a matter of fact. Felix wiped chocolate milk away from his mouth with his sleeve.

"How come?" said Luke.

"She's always crying. She's practically a crying machine. Or it might be her hair. It's really orange, like a pumpkin. People make fun of her. You know what, though. I'd like to invite her over, someday."

"Really? Well," said Luke. "She must be special, then."

"I'd like to show her the paintings in the basement, and all my stuff, the marbles and the soap dolls, and even maybe some of the things inside the wood chest. It might cheer her up." Felix finished the last gulp of his chocolate milk and handed the glass to his father. "Can we stop talking now?"

Luke let it drop. Ridiculous. Felix was not a child molester; the whole notion of it was absurd, and he felt somewhat relieved.

The next day, though, the poison letter lingered in his mind, and after dropping Felix at school, he walked up Mundy Lane and stood in front of the O'Briens' yellow house. The place looked shuttered up. He had the letter folded in his shirt pocket, but once in front of the house, he thought twice. *Uh, excuse me, but my son might have . . . might have . . . what?* Should he handle it through the school? Speak to the old nun instead? That would be awkward too.

He rang the bell twice before Lil O'Brien opened the door a sliver. Her eyes squinted in the sunlight.

"What," she said.

He thought he'd woken her from a nap.

"Are you Mrs. O'Brien?"

She moved her hand over her mouth as if to wipe something away, and her fingers lingered on her lips. "Who are you? Do I know you?"

He wondered if she'd been drinking, or maybe she was ill. "It seems I've disturbed you. I can come back another time," said Luke.

"Sure," she said, wearily. "Go away if you want." With that she tilted her head back and closed her eyes, letting out a sigh.

"Are you all right?" he asked.

The woman was thin; the delicate bones of her clavicle were visible through her skin. Her reddish hair fell around her face, untended. She wore a white nightgown, and Luke followed it down to the outline of her breasts, but stopped himself there, returning to her eyes, which were a striking green. She grabbed the neckline of her gown to cover herself.

"Forgive me, I'm not dressed," she said.

"I'm sorry, I'll go," said Luke.

70

"Are you from the doctor's office?" she asked, opening the door further. "I don't feel good."

"No, I'm not a doctor. Look, do you need help?"

"Yes. Yes. I do. Can you come inside?"

Luke glanced back at the street, uneasy, but he entered the house. Identical to Clarisse McCarthy's, it was also its opposite. Unlike Clarisse's spic-and-span living room, Mrs. O'Brien's had disintegrated into chaos. Pill bottles, magazines, books, and laundry. But even in the dim light he could see that this woman liked colors. The pattern on her rug was a collage of cubes, and her furniture, dark blues and reds.

"Did something happen here? You are Mrs. O'Brien, right?"

She stood before him, barefoot, swaying slightly, with her lips parted and her eyes lowered. Her nightgown, so threadbare, he could see the slender outline of her body. She looked to be about thirty, but something about her was ageless.

"Yes . . . something has definitely happened here," she said. "Wait a second, who are you?"

"My name is Luke Spoon. My son is in your daughter's class."

"What do you want?"

"I'm not sure," he said.

"Not sure," she repeated, as if distracted by another thought. But then she snapped at him. "Alice? What happened?"

"I don't really know." He pulled the letter out of his pocket and debated whether or not to show it to her.

Lil stared at the folded paper and tears welled in her eyes. "Are you being sent here by the doctor? Did something . . . did I do something?" she said.

"No, of course not. I told you, my son . . ."

"Right . . . that's . . . but . . . you're playing with me," she said, and backed away.

"No. Your daughter is fine . . . I mean she's not hurt. She's at school, I'm sure." Luke put the letter back into his pocket.

"Okay, then what?" She pulled her hands into fists and laid them aside either cheek, as if it were all too much for her.

"I'm not well." She stumbled, about to fall over.

Luke rushed over in time to catch her, and she collapsed in his arms. She was light as a child. As he carried her, he felt his hand inadvertently brush against her breast.

"You're touching me," she said, as he laid her on the couch.

"Jesus, what's wrong with you?"

"Mrs. O'Wrong," she said, pressing her face into a pillow. Luke stood over her, bewildered. This was not the visit he'd imagined.

"Listen, do you want me to call your husband?" he asked.

"No!" she wailed, turning toward him. "Can't you stay, can't you just sit next to me for a while. What's it to you? A couple of lousy minutes."

He didn't want to stay but sat down on the edge of the couch anyway. She curled into a ball, rocking gently back and forth.

"Mrs. O'Brien," he said, but no words came, so he sat with her, watching her breath rise and fall. Her gown was like a translucent second skin. It was the closest he'd been to a naked woman in some time, and he took her in. He felt something akin to arousal, but it wasn't that. The curve of her hip, the pale skin on her legs and feet, helpless and exposed, stirred a kind of desire in him that he couldn't pinpoint, as if he envied her proximity to complete despair; as if he'd only been dancing around its periphery, and, until this moment, he hadn't even realized it.

"Tell me something," she whispered, with her eyes closed. "Tell me something good."

"I'm not sure what you mean," he said, staring blankly at the basket of laundry in the middle of the room.

"Yes . . . anything. Please. And then you can go."

He glanced at his watch, torn between wanting to get out of her house and feeling that he couldn't leave her in this condition. He thought about calling an ambulance, but that seemed extreme, and being discovered in a house with somebody's wife, who was obviously doped up on something, didn't seem wise.

"Look, Mrs. O'Brien, I came here to talk about our kids."

"Yes, the kids. Okay."

"I can come back another time." Luke stood to leave.

"No, please, let's talk about the kids," she said with her eyes closed. "You know what I wonder? When is it, that precise *moment* when you're not a kid anymore? You are suddenly grown. You know how to act; you do things right. I forget. When is that moment?"

Luke looked down at her.

"Why are you in such a hurry? Can't you sit for a minute and talk to me? Is it really that hard?" said Lil, wiping her mouth, again, as if there was something sticky on her lips that wouldn't come off. "Something has happened to me." Lil drew her knees up to her chest.

"I can see that," said Luke. He felt bad for her. "I've actually wondered about that very same thing, you know, about kids turning into adults . . . it seems arbitrary."

"Huh?" Lil rubbed her eyes as if she had a headache. "Everybody loves kids. Kids, kids, kids," she said in a whisper.

"Okay, well . . . ," he said.

"Could I trouble you for some orange juice? Maybe there's some in the kitchen. And then I promise, you can leave."

"I'll see what I can find," he said. A warm sweat broke on the back of his neck as he rushed across the room toward the kitchen.

In the kitchen, the smell of garbage was strong. He spotted an open can of tomato juice on the counter, and poured some in a glass, grabbing a packet of saltine crackers from the table.

When he returned to the living room, he was relieved that she had covered herself with the sheet and propped herself up somewhat. "Have this," he said. She took the juice and drank in small hurried sips while rocking gently back and forth.

"You seem so irritated. What have I done? I didn't mean it, whatever I did." She nibbled on a cracker.

"I'm not irritated," he said, though he was. Against his better judgment, he sat down on the couch again.

"We were talking about the kids," she said. "Soon Alice and I will pack it up and go to New York."

"I live in New York City," he said, blankly.

"Really?" Lil's eyes brightened. "Have you ever gone to Madison Square Park in the rain, and met a young man called Matthew?"

"New York is a big place. There are a lot of people there," said Luke.

"He dies at the end. But first he sits on a bench in the rain."

"Oh, I see," said Luke. "He not a real person."

Lil looked at him sadly. "I guess you're right. He isn't real. Are you real? Am I?"

"I don't know what makes the world go 'round if that's what you're driving at, Mrs. O'Brien. I ought to get going."

"Yeah," she said, wiping her lips again. Then, with startling clarity, she added, "Why did you come to my house?"

Luke thought now might be the time to show her the letter. He reached into his pocket. "Like I said, it's about the kids."

A rapid pounding on the door and several sharp trills of the doorbell interrupted their conversation, and they sat up straight on the couch. Lil grabbed her sheet and pulled it up to her neck.

"Lil? Lil? Are you in there? Your door is open!" The front door swung wide, casting a triangle of light across the room. Clarisse barged into the room, trailed by Stephanie.

"Good grief, what's happening here?" said Clarisse, gripping a tin pie plate of brownies on either side. "What in the world . . . ?"

Luke stood, and shoved the letter back into his pocket. "Nice visiting with you, Mrs. O'Brien," he said. He started toward the door, but his shin knocked into the coffee table, and he winced in pain. "Damn! Somebody ought to open the shades in here."

Stephanie rushed to the window to turn the blinds, but Lil cried, "No!" shielding her eyes with her hand.

Luke proceeded toward the door, coming face to face with Clarisse, who did not move aside.

"This is not funny," said Clarisse, her voice shaking with righteousness.

"I didn't say it was." Luke flicked his thumb across his

lips. "You know what? You're a real pip, Mrs. McCarthy. If I were you, I'd tend to your friend, 'cause she needs help."

Luke stepped around her and hurried out the front door, slamming it shut behind him.

After he was gone, Clarisse looked at Stephanie, who stood by the windows gripping the string of the blinds.

"What are you looking at?" Clarisse said.

"Nothing," said Steph.

"You see? I told you. He's *rude*."

TEN

MR. NEW YORK CITY hightailed it out of there in a hurry, guilty as a rat. Clarisse rushed to set the brownies on the coffee table, ignoring the mess around her. She pulled up a chair and sat across from Lil.

"Can't you get a seat from the dining room?" Clarisse said to Steph, who stood paralyzed by the windows. Clarisse then turned her full attention toward Lil. "Honey, what was that man doing in your house?"

"I have no idea," mumbled Lil.

"Well, what was said?"

"Nothing. All these visits today. I'm not up to it," said Lil shutting her eyes.

Stephanie dragged a chair in from the dining room.

Clarisse gathered her thoughts. Her reason for feeling qualified to handle a crisis like this was due in part to opportunities she'd been fortunate to have while attending St. Agnes for Women, a small Catholic college in central Missouri. Though Clarisse showed little aptitude for academic scholarship, in her senior year she had been chosen, because of "excellence of character," to spend a month at St. Lucy's, north of Boston, a Catholic charity that transitioned found-ling children into foster care. Though it was hailed by the col-lege as a great honor to be chosen, the work was grueling, and little more than an unpaid internship. The facility was basic, and beds were filled with children making their way through a relatively unsupervised system that hung precariously on the kindness or unkindness of the nuns who ran it. One of the most intriguing aspects of the program for all the girls who applied was that they would be housed in the basement of a convent in close proximity to the nuns. It gave the girls a rare glimpse into the *real* lives of the nuns, and it proved to be a life-changing experience for Clarisse.

One thing the nuns drummed into Clarisse was that the first step in any difficult situation would be to search for the eyes of Jesus in the face of the unfortunate. Clarisse folded her hands in her lap and took a moment to try to find Jesus in Lil's face.

"Lil, please look at me."

Lil opened her eyes toward Stephanie, "Can you tell me what's going on, Steph?"

Though Clarisse could not find Jesus in Lil's face, she saw that Lil was changed. Her eyes had lost the spark that once dazzled everyone in town, and Clarisse felt a ping of satis-faction.

"I wish you would tell me why Luke Spoon was here. You're hardly dressed, honey. It's tempting. And who is he? No one knows." Clarisse couldn't help it. She heard the strain of falseness in her own voice, but if Luke Spoon and Lil O'Brien . . . well, it galled her.

"Who is *Luke Spoon*?" asked Lil, and she closed her eyes again, pulling her fists against her chest.

"Oh, come on Lil. The man who was here," said Clarisse, getting tense.

Unlike the round-faced, gentle nuns of her youth, the nuns who ran the Boston home were tough as old boots, and though Clarisse failed to follow in their path, she learned there were certain advantages to that kind of toughness.

"This is not a game, Lil. You are playing with fire," said Clarisse, aware that something about Lil's condition disgusted her. "I'd like you to sit up and listen."

Lil pushed herself up and sat before Clarisse and Steph, like a child.

Truthfully, at the home, Clarisse had found it almost unbearable to be around the strange, disturbed children. Many of them rocked incessantly in their cribs, and some never smiled. The smell of the place alone was enough of a reason to be traumatized.

"Honey, look at this mess," said Clarisse, glancing around the living room.

"I can't seem to clean it up," said Lil.

"It's not your fault," said Steph, frowning.

"Have you eaten anything today?" asked Clarisse. "And what are these pills?" she reached for one of the bottles on the coffee table.

"They're for crummy mothers, Clarisse. Not like you. They're mine. You shouldn't get involved with that."

Lil seemed drunk.

"You're not a bad mother, Lil," said Steph.

Clarisse squinted at the label on one of the pill bottles.

Lil reached for a used Kleenex that lay crumpled on the coffee table and wiped her mouth with it.

"Oh, Lil, that's dirty! Take a fresh one," Clarisse said,

screwing her face up in genuine disgust. She pulled a tissue from the box and offered it to Lil, who didn't take it.

"I like dirt," said Lil.

"It's unsanitary!" cried Clarisse, and a sharp memory exploded in her mind.

Clarisse had endured many rough days at the home, but a particular incident stood out. One night, it fell to Clarisse to care for a toddler named Ennis, who had a facial disfigurement that made his lower lip droop nearly to his chin, cursing him with a steady thick drool. He always had a cold; his nose was a faucet of snot, and from the congestion in his chest he suffered a perpetual cough. It was heartbreaking. The child had the sweetest disposition, despite his medical problems, but he was hard to tend to under the best of circumstances, and especially since he'd contracted a parasitic disease. Though he'd been treated by doctors, much of the time it was left to the nuns (and the girls) to care for him. Feverish, he screamed, his little body alternating from rigid to limp. Though his diaper was soiled, and tears streamed down his face, Clarisse couldn't bring herself to pick him up, even as he gasped for breath from exhaustion. She sat by the crib terrified, unable to care for Ennis, worried that he might vomit on her, or that she might catch whatever he had.

Upon discovering Clarisse next to the crib with her palms over her ears, a fierce nun, Sister Clotilde, scolded her: "Mother of God, you heartless bird. Stop the fuss and pick that baby up." But Clarisse had used the very same words. "It's unsanitary," she'd whimpered. Sister Clotilde, her eyes iced over with rage, lifted her arm and smacked Clarisse's cheek with the back of her hand. "You'll never be a nun! You have no idea what goodness is!" Clarisse was stunned. The sister scooped up the boy, held him in her arms until he quieted, and whisked him away for a diaper change, leaving Clarisse to slink back to the dormitory. She rocked herself to sleep on her narrow cot, feeling her holy calling slip away.

This was not the story Clarisse retold about her glorious stay at the home. In fact, she had a completely different version, and the women of Hanzloo had heard it often, after a cocktail or two. The revision made much of the harsh conditions at the home, and Clarisse's tireless devotion, but Sister Clotilde's name was never mentioned. Still, the nun's words popped up in her head even to this day—sometimes in dreams, sometimes while wide-awake. Here in Lil's living room, as Lil slid herself back down on the couch and buried her face in her pillow, the memory of Ennis came back, and Clarisse softened her tone.

"Oh, sweetie, talk to me," Clarisse begged.

"Don't sweetie me," whispered Lil.

And it went back and forth like that for a while.

Stephanie, feeling like a third wheel, snuck off into the kitchen to put on some coffee. She shoved aside dirty plates and sponged off the counter, and turned on the Westinghouse, crammed with food-streaked dishes, partly to muffle the sound of Clarisse's voice. You can't barge into people's lives and start pushing them around like checker pieces on a board.

Steph carried a tray with the coffee pot and cups into the living room, and was sorry to see Clarisse smoking a cigarette, which only meant that she was feeling insecure.

"Maybe we should tell Lil why we're here," said Steph. "Lil, please have a brownie." Stephanie peeled the tinfoil off the pie plate.

"Okay, fine, let me handle this," Clarisse said, holding her hand up to Steph, like a traffic cop. "Lil, we're concerned about you . . . and Alice."

"Nothing's wrong with Alice," said Lil.

"We want to make sure about that, right Steph?"

Stephanie noted that Clarisse had a way of treating everyone like a three-year-old, but at least Lil was listening now.

"We think it might be a good idea if Alice came to stay at my house for a while," Clarisse continued.

Stephanie couldn't believe what she was hearing. The suggestion that Clarisse take Alice home was not something that they had ever discussed.

"Are you crazy? No!" Lil sat up straight. "*No!*"

"It's because we love you, Lil," said Clarisse.

Tears spurted from Lil's eyes, wetting her face all at once, and then dripping off her chin. "You don't love me! You couldn't love anything! How could you suggest such a thing, Clarisse?" Lil wiped her eyes and nose with the palms of her hands, trying to recover her composure.

Clarisse bristled. "This wouldn't be forever," she said, tapping her cigarette into the empty juice glass on the coffee table. "We have a cot and we'll move it into the twins' room. Alice loves the twins, you know that."

Lil kept shaking her head no.

"Sweetheart, frankly you're in no condition to take care of Alice. If you had pneumonia, I'd suggest the same thing. There's no shame here."

"You can't take her!" cried Lil. "What is this?"

"Honey, I'm trying to help you. If too many people find out about what's going on here, there could be serious consequences. Forgive me, Lil, but you're not well. I know you want the best for Alice. She'll be two doors down. Right Steph?" Clarisse turned to Stephanie, urgently.

"Oh, Lil, we care about you, *and* Alice. That's all it is," said Steph. "It's a suggestion, no one is forcing you."

"I can't believe you're in on this too, Steph. Where's your decency? Where's your—" But Lil lost her train of thought and stopped. "Am I crazy?" she said, afraid, as if they knew something that she did not.

"You're tired, Lil. You're very tired," said Steph.

"Medication gets in the way of thinking," Clarisse added. "You don't seem right."

"I'm all right," Lil mumbled, but her mind was jumping from point to point. "Who is involved? The school, the police?" Lil turned to Steph in a panic.

"No. I swear to you. We're your friends. You know we wouldn't talk behind your back," said Stephanie, who, in general, was not a deft liar.

"That's just it. We're trying to avoid involving anyone else." Clarisse picked up the coffee pot and poured three cups. "Have some coffee," she said to Lil. "Now, don't get mad, but I've talked to Jim, and he likes the idea of Alice coming to stay with us."

Lil's eyes narrowed. "Jim? No!" she yelled, banging her palm on the coffee table.

"Please, calm down." Stephanie rushed to the couch and sat down beside Lil. "No one is taking Alice away from you. You must believe that," she said, putting her arm around her.

"There's something else," said Clarisse. "And you better listen to this. You can blame me all you want, and go ahead, act crazy, but Alice is in danger. That Spoon boy—the son of the man who was just here sitting in your house, on your couch, with you half dressed—has been caught molesting your daughter. Whatever it is you've got going on with Luke Spoon, you have to shape up and think of Alice."

Stephanie was horrified by Clarisse's icy tone. No one knew what had occurred in the cafeteria, but Clarisse had jumped on the molestation horse and was halfway to kingdom come with it.

Lil, quiet now, turned to Stephanie and said, "Steph? What is she talking about?"

"I don't know, you have to ask Alice about it," said Stephanie, pushing a strand of hair behind Lil's ear.

Lil tried to think back on the last few days, but she couldn't remember seeing Alice this morning, much less last week.

"Here's what we've been able to find out. Teresa Sepolino found Alice and the Spoon kid under the tables in the cafeteria and the boy ran, leaving Alice trembling and so upset she couldn't speak," said Clarisse.

"This could be a big trauma for Alice, you know?" added Stephanie.

Clarisse leaned forward on her chair. "You may not have heard that Felix Spoon pushed my girls down on the playground, and they still haven't recovered fully. He ate caterpillars, for God's sake! Something's wrong with him."

"No, I don't remember, I don't. You spoke to Jim, Clarisse? He's my husband," said Lil, resting her head in her hands. "How awful. I never liked you."

"What?" Clarisse went silent. "Listen, somebody has to step in. Like it or not, Lil, we're a community who cares. The truth is, Jim doesn't know how to help you. You have to take a little responsibility here. I'd hate to have to bring this story to Sister Annunciata. I'd hate to have her think she needs to call child services."

BY THE end of their visit, Lil had disappeared behind her eyes. "I guess you're right," she said, as if she didn't care.

After seeing the extent of Lil's condition, Steph had rolled around to thinking it might be for the best. Maybe they were a team, pulling together.

Lil agreed—zombielike—that she had to get off the pills; she admitted she'd been taking too many.

"Jim's the one who wants me on the drugs. He wants to keep me quiet."

"Oh, please, don't say things like that, Lil. You'll work it out between you. Jim is a good man," said Stephanie. She didn't feel it was right to get between husband and wife.

"Alice will have a blast with my girls," said Clarisse. "Don't you worry about a thing. Alice should come tonight. I also called Mrs. Tanker, and she agreed to clean your house after she does my place tomorrow. How does that sound? See? Things will get better now."

Lil just sat there.

"I'll pick up Alice from school today. I see her walking home alone and I don't know that it's such a good idea."

"No," said Lil. "I'll go."

"Are you sure you're up to it, honey? It's no problem for me."

"Yes, I'll take a shower and comb my hair," said Lil, blankly.

"Oh, Lil," said Stephanie.

"Oh, Lil," said Lil.

Clarisse and Steph left her in the darkness of her living room, saying they'd see her at the schoolyard.

LATER, BACK in her own home, Clarisse's thoughts turned once more to the home in Boston, and Ennis, the poor sick child. She was unsettled. Sometimes she thought she was better than everyone—unless she happened to be having one of those days when she thought she was worse than everyone—and fluctuating between the two extremes made her life a violent zigzag of congratulation and flagellation.

When Lil said, "I never liked you," Clarisse's seesaw tipped from high to low.

I'm trying to help, she thought, and no one seems to understand.

ELEVEN

LIL STOOD UP and the room swirled. She focused on a spot on the wall until the dizziness subsided. In the kitchen, she threw on the light and glanced around at the condition of things, as if for the first time. Out of an open cupboard, a waterfall of brown paper grocery bags had tumbled to the floor. Grabbing one, she headed back to the living room and with one swipe, shoved the pill bottles, magazines, used tissues, plastic spoons and sugar packets into the bag. Carefully she closed her tattered books and stacked them on the floor by the couch.

The thought of taking a shower made her yearn for one more nap. In the bathroom, the mirror above the sink was spattered with dried water drops, as if someone had spit at it. There she examined herself in the speckled glass. Fingering the dark circles around her eyes she moved her hand over her cheeks and down across her chapped lips. Something had happened to her; she was oddly disconnected, hardly alive. She pulled her nightgown over her arms and threw it on the floor. The garbage pail was a small, repulsive mountain of cotton balls, used tissues, and soiled sanitary napkins. Lil stepped into the shower, holding her hand against the wall. The water rained down hot and steamy as she turned her face into its stream and let it pour across her body. She washed her hair with a vengeance, as if her scalp, her head, her brain, needed a serious talking to. Reaching for the razor, she spoke out loud, *Stupid*. How silly it seemed to shave a leg.

NOW SHOWERED and dressed, she braced herself for the long walk down Mundy Lane toward the school, making sure the coast was clear before she ventured out.

Her outfit, a wrinkled blouse polka-dotted with coffee stains, and blue slacks that fit clumsily below her waist, fell far below the standards of her former self. All she'd been able to find for her feet were terrycloth slippers. Who cared? Luckily, sunglasses appeared on the dresser, and she snatched them at the last minute, grateful to have something to put between her and the world.

Outside, her hair blew wildly in the wind. Putting one foot down, and then the other, she walked as though the sidewalk might dissolve beneath her feet and swallow her. The world was a liquid wonderland; the edges of houses were soft and fluid. By the time she reached the end of her street, the journey to school seemed nearly impossible. This was her town, her neighborhood; it was where she lived, but now it frightened her and looked absurd. Why did everyone have the same exact house?

Lil kept going, past the little squares of cherished green lawns, the identical gray garbage cans, and the mailboxes on wooden poles, some leaning, some at strict attention. She steadied herself on a car that was parked by the curb, and looked down at its bumper to see her face in the chrome, distorted, her cheeks stretched sideways like a clown's.

On Pine Street, she encountered a small figurine on the Rices' lawn—a bird (was it a dove?) made of stone—and she stopped short. She thought it spoke to her. Her ears played tricks. All she had to do was get to Immaculate Conception, and then find Alice in the sea of children.

Once she arrived at the playground gates, a momentary sense of accomplishment faded quickly. As if everything had its own personality, the gates stared back at her, hard and angry. She crossed the street to where the huge elm tree stood and there she leaned against its trunk.

Soon a procession of mothers and baby carriages came from all directions. How strange, like the coming of the kings at Christmas or a slow march toward death. As the women got closer, Lil knew they must be talking about her. It was clear from the way they stopped and stared. Ginny Rice cupped her mouth and leaned in to whisper to a woman whose name Lil couldn't remember. Lil longed for her living room, her little friends, the pills, now buried deep in the garbage. Perhaps she shouldn't have thrown them all away.

If she could see Alice's face, things would normalize, and all these women would fade away. She and Alice could walk home together, like they used to do. She'd tell Jim that no, Clarisse could not take Alice, and she would also tell him that she's done with the pills.

But when Clarisse and Stephanie came down the street toward the school, for a fleeting moment, Clarisse, in a bright yellow shirtwaist dress, looked to Lil like a gigantic ball of fire. This terror had no end.

Clarisse crossed the street and walked right up to her, taking charge. "Lil. You made it. Very good. But you don't look so steady," she said. "Why don't you come stand with us?"

"No, I want to stay here," said Lil.

Clarisse patted her on the shoulder and said, "Okay, we'll keep an eye out." She noticed that Lil was wearing slippers, and wondered if Lil wasn't trying to be nuts, just to get attention. The slippers particularly enraged her, because as pathetic as it was for her to wear them, they somehow looked elegant on Lil.

Clarisse left Lil beside the tree and returned to her friends.

The mothers, clustered in front of the playground gates, threw sideways glances while tending to their toddlers. Lil, crazy? It all seemed true. For most of them, it was the first glimpse they'd had of her for months. Who knew how to behave in the face of this?

And now, as if this moment was not interesting enough, Luke Spoon came sauntering toward the school. When he saw Lil O'Brien at his usual spot by the elm, he stopped in the middle of the street.

"Oh my. He's lost without his tree," said Ginny Rice, who found the whole scene amusing.

"He does look lost," Clarisse noted.

"This is beyond awkward," said Stephanie, glancing at her watch. "I wish the kids would come out."

When the playground gates opened, the children ran wild. Dawn and Fawn skipped over to Clarisse, who knelt down to embrace them. As she buttoned Fawn's sweater, she spotted Felix Spoon and Alice O'Brien in the crowd of children. *Were they together?* It was hard to tell. Alice, lost in thought, squinted toward the sky, and Felix stopped to rummage through his book bag, as if he had forgotten something.

FOR ALICE, the sight of her mother set off such a panic that she began to look for Sneedler in the trees. Now she worried that something might have happened to him. She began to turn around in slow circles with her eyes toward the sky hoping to find him, but he was nowhere.

Dawn and Fawn pointed at Alice, and they too began to turn around, as if it was all a funny game, but Clarisse put a firm hand on their shoulders, and dug her fingernails in.

Felix Spoon dragged his book bag over to Alice and pulled at her sleeve, which stopped her circling. "Alice, why are you turning around like that? Isn't that your mother over there?"

"I saw her," said Alice, "But I seem to have lost my friend."

"You have a friend?" said Felix.

Alice didn't answer.

"Come on," he said. "Godsakes." He took her hand and walked her across the street.

Lil had slid down the tree trunk and was crouched with her arms around her knees. When the children approached her, she looked up, shading her eyes from the sun.

"Mom, please don't sit on the ground."

"Just resting here," said Lil. "Can you help me up?"

The children each took hold of an elbow, and with their help, Lil steadied herself on her feet.

"My father's over there, he's good at this kind of thing," said Felix, addressing Lil directly.

"Maybe not such a good idea," Lil half-heartedly protested, but Alice and Felix escorted Lil down the street to where Luke Spoon was standing. "Can we walk them home?" asked Felix. Alice took hold of her mother's hand, and Felix took hold of his father's. As they turned to leave, he grabbed hold of Alice's hand, and the four of them made their way.

Clarisse McCarthy felt the world go silent as Lil, Alice, Felix, and Luke Spoon walked away from the school amidst sunlight and shadows on the brilliant autumn afternoon. Red and yellow leaves blew like charms around them. They looked like a perfect family . . . like the Kennedys, like royalty, like love itself.

Jim should be made aware of this. Clarisse flipped frantically through her options. Something must be done. This had to stop.

And then, there they were, Sister Clotilde's words, all the way from north of Boston, trampling across her brain like a band of tiny, mean nuns.

You heartless bird. You heartless bird. You heartless bird.

TWELVE

The unlikely quartet walked in silence through the streets of Hanzloo.

Luke Spoon could not relax. His eyes darted around as if the bushes were stuffed with accusations aimed at him and his son. It would make sense that in this town you could get arrested for walking down the street.

It didn't help that Lil O'Brien, a complete stranger until a few hours ago, was now physically attached to him through the chain of their children's held hands.

Sadness hung off of her like an oversized dress, and he couldn't help but wonder what had gone so wrong with her. But he didn't want to wonder too much. Two encounters with this woman in one day were two more than he needed.

For Lil, the problem was more basic. *Foot, foot, foot, foot.* Keeping one in front of the other proved to be a formidable task. Her heart leapt in her chest. At the moments when she felt faint, she concentrated on the simple task of holding Alice's hand, while sunlight and shadows once again played with her balance. Her mind zoomed around from one problem to the next: what the boy may have done to Alice, the encounters with Luke Spoon, Clarisse, and Stephanie. Her life seemed to have slid into a rushing river that she could not control. No thought was bearable. Feelings stirred, but they were hard to access. Just one thing was clear: Clarisse would come for Alice soon, probably tonight.

At the mouth of Mundy Lane, Lil and Alice stopped and Felix tugged on his father's sleeve, "This is where they live, Luke."

"Of course," said Luke, and he faced Lil for the first time. Gone was the loose-tongued sloppiness of this morning's visit. Her eyes, dull and tired, were the color of light green marbles, and, in spite of his resistance, he found himself moved by her all over again. It wasn't attraction; it was recognition. Her disconnectedness was something he knew in himself. She was unreachable, and so, he thought, was he. As they stood in a cluster at the base of the lane, she fell to thoughts he couldn't read. "Mrs. O'Brien, will you be all right?"

"Yes," she said, momentarily looking into his eyes. "Thank you for walking with us."

"Maybe someday they can come over," said Felix.

"Yes, that would be nice." Luke smiled stiffly at the boy.

"Can you?" Felix asked Lil.

"I have no idea," said Lil, trailing off. She was thinking about how long the short walk up Mundy Lane might be. She reached for Alice's hand.

"Is something wrong with her?" Felix asked his father.

Lil and Alice had already started up the street. Luke and Felix watched briefly, and then walked on toward the Post Road until Felix said, "Luke? Do you know where the cave of God is?"

"What?" said Luke.

"God's cave," said Felix. "Do you know where it is?"

"No. Cripes, Felix, where do you come up with this stuff? There's no such thing."

Sensing the unusual irritation in his father's voice, Felix dropped it. It hadn't occurred to him before that he might know about something that his father did not.

THIRTEEN

BECAUSE OF HIS recent habit of stopping off at Flapdogs for a martini or two after work, Jim O'Brien had gotten accustomed to making a beeline down the dark and narrow staircase that led to the basement as soon as he walked through his own front door. He'd come to think of the low-ceilinged, dank room that he shared with the washing machine, dryer, rakes, and shovels, as his own personal dungeon. A short nap helped him face the dreary trek back up the stairs to scrape together dinner, or scarf down what Lil had thrown on the table.

But today, before he'd left work, he'd had a phone call from Clarisse McCarthy, and as a result he cut his drink with Kay Book short, fearing things on the home front might be more volatile this evening. Fueled by the drink and the article he'd read in the *Reader's Digest*, he felt ready. No more Mr. Pansy.

Sure enough, when he walked through the door, instead of sprawled on the couch asleep, he found his wife sitting on a chair with her hands folded in her lap.

"Hello Jim, I need to speak to you," Lil said. She was not in her frayed nightie.

"Okay," he said. "You got dressed, I see."

Ignoring that, Lil said, "Clarisse McCarthy was here today. She wants to take Alice and said she's spoken with you, and that you think it's a good idea. Is that true? You and Clarisse McCarthy are now deciding what's best for Alice?" Lil's hands were trembling slightly. She spoke without emotion, but that didn't fool Jim.

Jim pulled his tie loose and set down his briefcase. It was unfortunate that his eyes seemed perpetually stuck in an expression of slight surprise, as if to say, *Who, me?* He'd been relieved when Clarisse had contacted him again today, but now, face-to-face with his wife, this business of colluding with Clarisse made him uncomfortable, and he could see in Lil's eyes that he'd hurt her.

"What am I supposed to do?" he said.

"We're doomed," said Lil, barely audible.

"Come on, Lil, let's not get all dramatic. The fact is that Clarisse says Alice has been molested by that weirdo boy. Don't you care?"

"I care, Jim. I care, I care. But it's Clarisse who said it." Lil was not up to a fight, and she paused to collect her thoughts. "We have to ask Alice. Will you sit here and talk to her with me?"

"No!" said Jim. He always came back at Lil too hard, and immediately regretted his tone, feeling like a shit. Lately he had come to think she brought out the worst in him. "What I mean is it might be too embarrassing for her. It's not something a father ought to do. It's a mother's job. You should do it privately."

"Have you been drinking?" asked Lil, surprised.

Jim looked away.

"I'm sorry," said Lil. "Sorry for all of it." She drew her hand across her eyes and pressed her temples with her thumb and forefinger.

"You're mentally ill, Lil."

"That's a poem," she said.

"Oh, Christ. Look, I'm tired, and I don't want to talk stupid with you. I'm glad you got yourself up and dressed. Welcome to reality. You'd better speak to Alice because Clarisse will be coming soon. And yes, I did talk to Clarisse, and I do think Alice should stay with her for a while. She's *responsible,* Lil. She gets up in the morning. She bathes and feeds her children. And I bet she's even glad to see her husband when he comes home at night.

By the way, Clarisse called me at work and told me all about the little appearance you made at the schoolyard today. Really, what the hell? Now you're walking hand in hand with the kid's father?"

Lil looked up. "That never happened."

"We've got an appointment with Dr. Garufee for tomorrow."

"What?"

"Lil, I'm not a mean man, and I love you even if you've given up on me, or yourself, or whatever the hell it is with you. But Alice, good grief, Lil, she deserves a better mother."

And that was it. Jim went downstairs to the basement, stripped to his jockey shorts and socks, and took a moment to scratch at the scars on his dry, eczema-afflicted legs. He lay down on his cot, exhausted from having come as close as he could come to yelling at his wife.

He'd always had the feeling that she surpassed him in every way. Beautiful Lil Carmichael, why she'd married him he'd never know. At the time he thought he'd hit the jack-pot, but he should have realized then that a woman like that needs to fly.

The Carmichael family was a big deal in their small home-town, outside of Cleveland; the older brothers divided up into lawyers and doctors, and the older sisters married well. Any of the Carmichael girls would have been a step up for Jim. They were all smart and gorgeous in the most unusual way. Lil was the quiet one, but just because she was quiet didn't mean she wasn't screaming inside, he knew that now.

In her senior year, she'd won a regional poetry prize; a trip to New York City for a poetry reading, and she came back full of pipe dreams about moving there and being a writer. Jim thought the dreams would blow over. But now he suspected those dreams had driven a wedge between them. But when? And why? Who really wants to live in New York City?

He courted her vigorously. He took her to the Cleveland Zoo; they had a favorite elephant, and an ape they named Samson, and they'd watch him swing from the bars of his cage. The zoo fascinated her. Sometimes she'd be moved to tears by the tigers, as they lay flat and limp on bare cement floors.

It took every ounce of courage for Jim to put his arm around her for the first time, and then two years before he got the courage to kneel before her, at a bus stop, and ask for her hand in marriage. She threw her head back and laughed. "It could never happen," she'd said. But it did, and they eloped because oops . . . along came Alice. They were happy for a while. He'd endured Lil's mushy meatloaf and burnt pork chops with patient laughter, and the sex, which if he were honest, half the time felt like a game of Marco Polo, a blindfolded groping in the dark. Neither one of them had an inkling what to do in bed. But to his great relief, Lil seemed to accept Jim, eczema and all, even rubbing greasy ointment on his legs and back without complaint. They made a life together.

When Alice came, Lil seemed overwhelmed by motherhood. The baby cried day and night, and Lil could not soothe her. Clearly, she loved her daughter, but she couldn't ease what she perceived was the baby's innate sorrow, and she blamed herself.

"Babies don't have sorrow," Jim said. "They just cry. It's no one's fault."

"You don't see what I see," Lil said.

Over the past few years, Lil's sweetness had turned to a dull sadness. It started out with her sitting for long hours in the living room with the blinds drawn. There were little scraps of paper all over the house.

"Those are my poems," said Lil.

Jim had no idea what that meant; one word here, another there.

I'm a simple man, he thought, just trying to do the best I can. But nothing about him interested his wife. And now she had a screw loose. He supposed he'd let her down, but he couldn't begin to figure out how. He flashed on the end of a movie he'd once seen; two shipwrecked people, hanging on to pieces of a broken boat, drifting apart in the vast ocean as the credits ran down the screen.

But the worst of it was Alice. He couldn't even allow himself to think of her. And lying on his bed, with his arm over his eyes, mercifully, he fell into a deep sleep.

Lil walked down the hall to Alice's bedroom and knocked lightly. Alice peeked out.

"May I come in?" Lil hardly ever came to Alice's room anymore, and when she entered, she was surprised to find that the bed was perfectly made. Alice's worn stuffed monkey and a baby doll with no legs were neatly placed across the pillow. Not a sock or shoe was on the floor, all her things had been tucked away, except for her baseball mitt, which was on top of the dresser. Her small, wooden desk was neatly organized, a math book lay open, and a pencil was sideways on a sheet of lined paper beside it.

"Am I in trouble?" asked Alice.

"Trouble? No. I just . . . wanted to ask you about something."

Lil sat down on the bed, and then lay down. She picked up the legless doll and cradled it in her arms. "I can't believe you still have her."

"Yeah, I do," said Alice, and she stood beside the bed, her hair falling below her shoulders. Lil took Alice's hands and lifted them to her lips. "You're really something, do you know that? Where in the world did you get those eyes? I've only seen that color once before. In a painting of an old woman—"

"An old woman cutting pears," said Alice.

"Yes! She had eyes like yours, the most amazing emerald green."

Alice wondered what her mother's question was.

"Oh, Alice."

"What is it Mom, what's wrong?

"That boy. That boy," said Lil. "Tell me something, love . . . did you go to the school cafeteria with . . . you know, the one we walked home with today?" Alice pulled her hands away and looked down at the floor, where she'd left her zebra slippers tucked halfway under the bed.

"Felix Spoon."

"Yes. What happened there?" said Lil.

"Nothing."

"Something must have happened."

"No," said Alice.

"Why can't you tell me?" asked Lil, sitting up. She lifted Alice's chin with her palm and looked into her eyes.

"I promised," said Alice, and her bottom lip quivered a bit.

"What do you mean?"

"I had to swear I wouldn't tell," said Alice.

"But I'm your mother, doesn't that count for anything?" asked Lil.

"I guess." Alice thought about Felix Spoon and how he'd pointed at her eyes. It could be that something bad would happen if she told about the rock.

Lil pulled Alice into her embrace and Alice allowed herself to rest there for a moment until Lil took her by the shoulders and looked into her eyes. "You can tell me things, you know."

"I can't Mom . . . please don't make me."

"Did he hurt you? Or threaten you?" said Lil.

Alice raised her eyebrows. "Felix Spoon is nice to me. Nicer than most kids."

"I don't want him to hurt you. Did he?" Lil veered off on her own train of thought.

"He didn't. He just . . . Mom, believe me, it's okay. He asked us over to his house today, remember?"

But Lil didn't recall, and she couldn't bear to think of how many moments of Alice's life had fallen away, without anyone's attention. Even now, Lil's mind, like a foggy day, was thick and dull; she couldn't focus. She thought about sleeping, wanting to lie down on Alice's bed again. She'd already forgotten the name of the boy, though Alice had just mentioned him a minute ago. Everything tired her out. But molesting? That she did not forget. What if it were true? Maybe staying with Clarisse for a few days wouldn't be so bad. Just a couple of days, until she could straighten up.

Lil held Alice's two hands in hers.

"Alice, listen to me. Something is going to happen. Mrs. McCarthy is coming over here in a few minutes. You are going to spend some time at her house," said Lil.

"What?" cried Alice, her mouth went slack.

"You know that I'm not well, right? I have to get better so I can take care of you."

"No, I don't want to," said Alice. "The twins? Mom! No!" Alice raised her fist to her mouth and closed her eyes. "Please don't make me. I won't be any trouble, please. You don't even have to cook."

"You aren't trouble, Alice."

"But I like *our* house, and *you*, and *Dad,*" said Alice, fingering the bumps on her bedspread. "I've never even been in their house. What if I do something wrong?"

"You won't, Alice, believe me. I know it may seem scary now, but maybe it will be a little bit fun, too. I'm sure they have a lot of toys . . ."

"But how long do I have to stay?" asked Alice, desperately trying to wipe tears from her eyes.

"I don't know, I just don't know. You have to be strong.

You *are* strong. Oh, Alice, this is not your fault, it's mine."

Alice stopped listening; she stopped feeling or hoping for something different. There was nothing to be done. The sound of her mother's voice became muffled, her face blurred. Alice's thoughts turned into slow soft somersaults of resignation.

Jim O'Brien had drifted off on his basement bed and was jarred awake by multiple doorbell rings. "Shit," he said aloud.

Clarisse had arrived. He pulled on his pants and shirt, slipped into his loafers, and trudged up the stairs to open the door. "Clarisse, hold your horses."

"I was worried when no one answered," Clarisse said, untying the flowered kerchief that was tied under her chin.

"Come on in," said Jim.

"So, how are things?" she whispered, unbuttoning her coat.

"Lil is talking to Alice now," said Jim and then he called down the hallway. "Lil! Clarisse is here!"

Clarisse looked around the living room. "I told you Mrs. Tanker is coming to clean, right? She'll straighten this mess."

"It's really not necessary, Clarisse," said Jim. "I'll take care of it."

"Nonsense."

Alice came out of her room holding a small red suitcase in one hand and her book bag in the other. She walked down the hall toward the living room.

"Alice!" said Clarisse, clapping her hands together. "I hear you're up for a little vacation at my house! The girls are so excited!"

Alice looked blankly at her father. "Mom said I should

wear my coat." Jim was relieved to see her hold herself together with a poise that seemed beyond her years. He got her coat out of the closet and helped her into it, buttoning each button slowly.

"So, Alice, this'll be fun, right?" he said.

"Uh-huh," said Alice.

Jim put his arms around her and gave her a hug. Alice held onto his neck and whispered urgently into his ear. "Please Dad, don't make me go."

Trying to avoid a scene at all costs, he unhooked her arms from his neck. How could he convey apologies for the mess they found themselves in—the mess that seemed to fall directly upon Alice? He felt his face contort into an absurd grimace, then he turned to Clarisse. "Well, all set then."

Lil came down the hall and stood at the entrance to the living room.

"Lil," said Clarisse, frowning. "How are you feeling, honey?"

"Great," said Lil. "Like a million bucks."

"Oh, come on, Lil," said Jim. "She's only trying to help."

Lil crouched down and opened her arms to Alice, who walked slowly over to her mother and received a kiss. "Remember what I said, okay?" she asked.

"Yep," said Alice. "When can I come home?"

"I don't know," said Lil.

Alice turned to Mrs. McCarthy. She'd never needed to look at her before. How can you switch mothers? Mrs. McCarthy had a face she didn't want to touch or smell, a face with eyes that Alice didn't recognize.

"You have your toothbrush, honey? Clean underpants?" said Clarisse. The mention of underpants embarrassed Alice and she turned back once more to her mother, but Lil had left the room.

"Come on, now, sweetie," said Clarisse. "Let's not make a big fuss."

Alice picked up her bag and walked out the door with Clarisse.

It was dark outside, almost cold as winter. The wind rustled through the treetops, and leaves scraped across the pavement. On Mundy Lane, blurry yellow lights shone from the windows of the living rooms and bedrooms. She could feel that Sneedler was trailing them, and he wouldn't stop throwing rocks to try to catch her attention. She turned back but couldn't make him out in the dark. What a pain he could be. Alice hadn't had a chance to explain things to him, and she had her own problems now. It was serious to be walking down the street in the dark. Her bag was getting heavy, and Mrs. McCarthy didn't seem as nice as she'd been a minute ago.

Alice wondered if they'd have any good food in their fridge, and whether it would be okay to ask for some. She wished she could have some spaghetti. It seemed that everyone had forgotten about dinner, and she was so hungry her stomach ached.

ONCE THE front door to the McCarthys' house closed behind her, Alice knew that Sneedler would never visit her here. There was an awful smell of fish, and Sneedler hated fish almost as much as Alice did.

Dawn and Fawn appeared in the hallway zipped up, neck-to-toe, in pink, footed, furry pajamas. Their hair was damp and freshly braided. They turned around and wiggled their behinds at Alice.

Alice smiled. They *were* cute. For an instant she felt lucky to be in their house. Other girls would want that.

"Hi," she said.

The twins collapsed into cascading giggles.

From the living room came the low bark of Mr. McCarthy. "Keep it down! I'm watching a program!" he yelled.

Alice peeked in to see him nestled in a big black chair, his bare feet propped up on a footstool. Aside his chair was a small table, and a lit cigarette leaned in an ashtray, its smoke spiraling toward the ceiling in gray curlicues. The TV squawked with laughter from a variety show. Alice had forgotten that he'd be there. He was wide as a small wall, and his sandy-colored hair stood up like a flat square of grass. She didn't like to think it, but he was fat. It was one thing to have a new mother, but a new, fat father who yelled was even worse. Despite his scolding, the twins carried on, paying him no mind, but Alice worried that he might explode in anger.

"Let's go into the kitchen," said Clarisse, not at all concerned about her husband's tone. "Come on, girls."

The McCarthys' kitchen was exactly the same as Alice's, but the striped wallpaper and red cabinets made it look different. It was orderly and clean, just the way Alice wished that her kitchen at home could be.

"Do you want a snack, Alice?" asked Clarisse.

"Thank you, Mrs. McCarthy. I'm pretty hungry," said Alice.

"Didn't you have dinner?" she said.

"No, I guess we forgot about dinner tonight," said Alice, trying to be older than she was.

Clarisse leaned her head out of the kitchen, "Did you hear that, Frank? They forgot to feed her!"

107

The girls sat around the kitchen table while Clarisse pulled some dishes out of the refrigerator, and set a place for Alice, pouring her a glass of milk.

"Who do you like better," said Dawn. "Me or Fawn?"

"I like you both," said Alice.

"I like you both," mimicked Dawn, and again the twins laughed wildly. Clarisse set down a chocolate chip cookie in front of each of them.

"That's not fair," said Dawn. "I want two. She can't have ours; not fair!"

"Listen, missy, Alice is now like a sister to you both. You'll share everything with her," said Clarisse.

"She's not my sister," said Dawn, grabbing hold of Fawn's arm. "*This* is my one and only sister."

"Nonsense," said Clarisse. "We're all brothers and sisters in God's family, you know that. Now Alice, honey, eat some food first. I have something left over from our supper."

When Clarisse set the plate before her and Alice realized that it was *real* fish, a kind of slab of fish, not like the fish sticks that her mother served her, she didn't think that she'd be able to eat it. But neither did she want the tomato-y thing, which seemed more like jelly than tomatoes. She managed to swallow a tiny piece of fish, but it was cold and rubbery, and she gave the tomato a try, but the gelatinous square felt as though someone else had already eaten it, and, gagging, she spit it out into her milk glass.

"Look what she did!" cried Dawn.

"Alice!" said Clarisse, staring in horror at the blob of tomato aspic floating in the milk.

"I'm sorry," said Alice, as she fought back tears and disgust.

"I told you, Mama," said Dawn. "She's always like this!"

"Can we have her cookies now?" asked Fawn quietly.

"Go up to your room, girls. Now!" Clarisse pounded the table and the twins promptly hopped off their chairs and thundered up the stairs.

"You told me you were hungry Alice."

"I'm sorry, Mrs. McCarthy. I just . . . don't like that."

"You don't like it?" Clarisse's jaw clenched.

She'd fixed the foldout cot up in the attic room, even bought Alice a small stuffed rabbit for her pillow. She wanted things to be perfect, and had taken this burden on, with grace and conviction, but within a half hour of Alice's arrival, things had already soured. In the face of a sniffling Alice, she had no pity. Clarisse grabbed the plate off the table. "You don't know what hunger is," she said, under her breath.

But Alice's stomach growled and twisted. As she climbed the stairs led by Clarisse's firm hand, Alice thought about spaghetti and meatballs, the kind her mother used to make, before she'd caught the disease of the soul.

FOURTEEN

LUKE AND FELIX waited for the butcher at the counter of the meat department in the A&P. When Auggie emerged from the meat freezer and wiped his hands on his blood-stained apron, Felix's face came alive.

"Hello fella," he said, reaching over to shake Felix's hand. Auggie's bushy moustache erased his top lip.

Felix reached up to touch the butcher's hand. He'd lost the top of his fourth finger in a slicing accident and Felix liked to feel its flat edge.

"I guess I know what you want," said Auggie. "Pig's feet, right?"

Felix stepped away.

"All right, all right." Auggie grabbed the cylinder of bologna from the meat case and hauled it over to the big silver slicer. A few slices of bologna fell onto wax paper and Auggie handed them across the counter to Felix.

"That ought to keep you for a week," said Auggie.

Felix put a piece of bologna in his mouth.

"Thanks, Auggie," said Luke, and as they turned their cart toward frozen foods, they almost rammed into Clarisse

McCarthy, who was with the twins and Alice O'Brien. Clarisse held a box of Maypo in her hands and was studying the ingredients on the package.

The twins held on to either side of an overflowing shopping cart, filled to the brim with boxes of cereal, a milk carton, bags of cookies, eggs, and other groceries. Alice stood awkwardly to the side, her hair tied in high pigtails wrapped with pink bows.

"Oh!" said Clarisse, locking eyes with Luke Spoon. She showed him the box of oatmeal. "I suppose it's worth a try."

Gone was the hostility she'd spewed at him in Lil O'Brien's living room. What he saw standing before him in the A&P were her large, round breasts, barely held together by the buttons of her blouse. Clarisse had retained her girlishness. She reminded Luke of a cunning Marilyn Monroe, one without the tragic eyes. Clarisse's eyes had a yearning to them, but the yearning suggested appetite, not loss. She'd figured out how to get away with bright red lips—not something every woman could pull off—especially in the supermarket on a Saturday morning.

A single thought stood up in his brain like one remaining bowling pin after a blowout.

I need to get laid.

LUKE'S MOTHER had wanted him to be a priest, but he'd let her down. His younger brother had been the one to take the vows.

Father Peter—driving drunk after the Christmas Eve meal at the Fin and Claw, with Mom and Dad in the back seat of the car—had slammed head on into a tractor trailer, and—poof—there went Luke's family. It was a gruesome tragedy, and though his brother held on the longest, by the time Luke landed in the Indianapolis airport, they were all dead. The nurse at the front desk had handed Luke his brother's priest's collar and said, "God bless." Peter had been the golden son. But Luke had to wonder, had Peter resented his choice? Was the accident a ferocious, sublime act of unconscious hostility?

The death of Luke's brother and his parents transformed his life instantly. He went from being the estranged son—the starving ne'er-do-well artist—to being a wealthy orphan. Even through the Depression, Luke's father, Dirk Spoon, had been a successful businessman. Spoon, Inc., sold small hardware—screws and bolts—to the military during the war.

The last time Luke had seen his parents, on a rare visit to the family home, he'd had words with his father, and ties were broken forever. It happened at Holy Name Church. Luke had not received communion during Sunday mass, and afterward, on the way out of church, his father confronted him about it.

"Too good for communion? What kind of crap was that?" the old man said.

"What?" said Luke, pulling back as if he'd expected a hit in the head. "It's personal."

Standing in the parking lot of Holy Name, his father's voice bellowed as the argument escalated and ended in a threat to exclude Luke from "the will."

"You're a goddamned waste of skin," the old man yelled.

Other parishioners mulled around in earshot, discreetly folding up their church bulletins. Luke had driven off—pissed—skipping out on his mother's much-anticipated brunch at the family home, and it broke her heart.

Eventually she must have interceded on Luke's behalf because upon their deaths the entire fortune dumped directly into his lap, much to his surprise and embarrassment. He kept the news to himself, and his friends thought Luke Spoon was just like them—a broke *artiste*.

In the wake of the tragedy, Luke found himself grieving deeply for his mother. Dear Eleanor. He feared though, that somewhere inside, he, too, resented her. Haunted by her, she'd left him with the strangest affliction: Why couldn't he have been the priest? She would have loved him most. A strange brand of sibling rivalry.

Without his mother's cloud of purity hovering over him, he wondered if he might have lived a less-tortured life. It seemed so easy for others to forgo the Catholic faith, but he felt ensnared in its questions, which were like a tangle of rosaries, impossible to disassemble.

After the accident, Luke's paintings changed.

During that time, he went back and forth from his apartment on Sullivan Street to a small work studio he'd rented near the Hudson River and hardly saw a soul. He digested his grief and survivor guilt in such a way that braided his mother's Catholicism, his inability to embrace it in the way she had wanted him to, and his own desperate desire to believe in something. Somewhere along the way, Luke Spoon decided he'd paint life instead of living it. During that period of frantic creativity, he kept to himself, and lived what he secretly imagined to be a priest's life. With a newly fueled devotion to his work, he achieved a modicum of peace.

His work caught the eye of a prominent gallery owner, Seth Olsen, a man with a preference for horizontal stripes and the color red. He ferried Luke into prominence rather quickly. Luke's work was taken seriously. His initial show, *My Mother*—which he'd hoped offered up a fair serving of self-parody (completely missed by most)—was well reviewed, hailed by the *New York Times* as "fascinating, dark, and almost holy." This, and every other remark about his work, threw him into a state of crippling embarrassment and a vague sense that he was a fake. The price of success quickly became apparent to him, but his friends thought he was being insufferably arrogant by his refusal to embrace his good fortune. Luke fell back into his old ways, ended his bout with celibacy, and launched into a long string of girlfriends—one crazier than the next—until he came face to face with Joni, and that's how sex and love convened for Luke, really for the first and only time.

Now, standing in the middle of an A&P, in the small, forgotten town of Hanzloo, Pennsylvania, with an empty, restless heart, he wondered what had it all been for?

Clarisse McCarthy was smiling at him, noticing the stains on his shirt.

"Looks like you've been painting the house," she said. The twins moved closer to their mother.

"My dad's an artist," said Felix.

Luke cringed.

"Oh, really?" said Clarisse.

Felix kept at it. "Remember when you slapped me?" he said, looking up at her, as he popped the last piece of bologna in his mouth. Clarisse shot the boy a look, and Luke remembered all over again how much he didn't like her. What the hell.

"Mama, let's leave," said Fawn, pulling on her mother's skirt.

Luke noticed Alice then, and was struck once again by her simple beauty, of which she seemed totally unaware. Even with her hair tied up in frilly pink bows, her features were serene, and ordinary, but like her mother, a second look revealed more; something otherworldly, and Luke thought he'd like to paint her. Paint a child? Why not? Paint whatever you want.

"So! I finally found out," said Clarisse. "There's a little game going 'round town, it's called What Exactly Does Luke Spoon Do? I guess I win."

"Painting is a hobby of mine," said Luke. He pushed his cart a few inches forward, thinking he might be able to move on.

"I bet you're being modest," said Clarisse, wishing the children weren't there.

"Hi Alice," said Felix."

"She's our sister now," said Dawn. "And my mother said we're not allowed to talk to you, and neither is Alice."

Alice stood mute.

"Really. Is that what your mother said?" Luke said, addressing Dawn, who recoiled, not used to being addressed directly by an adult who wasn't a teacher or one of her parents. "And why would your mother say that?"

Clarisse shushed her daughter and tried to relocate herself in the center of his attention.

But Luke stayed focused on the girl. "There's no need to be afraid of Felix, he's a wonderful boy," said Luke, resting his hand on Felix's shoulder. "But your mother might want to watch out for *me*." Then he turned and smiled at Clarisse. "Mrs. McCarthy, you ought to come over one day and watch me paint the walls. It's interesting, I do it with my tongue."

Luke wheeled his cart forward, leaving Clarisse in frozen foods, with that mixture of longing and indignity that was typical of their few encounters. Somewhere underneath his rather snide remark she could have sworn he'd just invited her over to his house.

As they made their way to the checkout Felix said to his father, "I never saw you paint with your tongue." Felix was disappointed that his father told a lie.

FIFTEEN

"WE APPRECIATE YOUR seeing us on a Saturday," said Jim, reaching over to shake the doctor's hand.

Doctor Garufee sat down behind his desk and offered Mr. and Mrs. O'Brien a cigarette.

"She doesn't smoke," said Jim, taking one.

"So." The doctor glanced at his chart and turned toward Lil, "Your husband said you're refusing your medication, is that right? Why don't you tell me about that." Lil had forgotten how completely bald the doctor was, and it made her smile.

"This isn't funny, dear," he said. "It's dangerous to stop the medication."

"No, I know, of course, it's just . . . that I feel better," said Lil.

"You don't look well, you're too thin, for one thing," said Garufee.

"I don't want to be . . . drugged anymore," said Lil.

"Playing with medications is no joke. If you do what I say and stick to the rules, I'm sure we can figure out how to adjust your medication, so it suits you better. There's nothing unusual about that."

Jim jumped in clumsily. "Yeah but wait a minute. She's on the drugs for a reason. We don't want to go backward here."

Garufee leaned back in his chair and took a long look at Lil. "Mrs. O'Brien, why are you so sad? Shall I take a guess?" he asked.

"No, please don't," said Lil. "I'm feeling better and the medication makes me too tired. I don't like it; I don't like it."

Garufee shook his head. "I wouldn't put you on a drug that wasn't good for you. I thought you and I had a good relationship."

"Of course, I trust you. Yes, I think we do have a good . . . Listen, doctor," said Lil. "They've taken my child." She leaned forward in her chair, trying to bypass Jim.

"Who are *they*? I understand your daughter is only two houses down and the McCarthys are a very responsible family." Garufee continued carefully, "You do realize this is a result of your behavior. I'm not being unkind, but no one has done this to you. You've made certain choices, right? I think it's fortunate that your neighbors have stepped in."

"I don't like the way this is going," said Lil, having a hard time speaking up. She felt the room tilt.

Jim listened to their conversation, confused. There seemed to be a subtext. What were the certain choices Lil had made?

The doctor rubbed the edge of his mouth with his thumb. "Don't misunderstand. You're unwell. You need to settle down and follow the advice of people who are thinking more clearly. If you listen to me, I'll help you out of this. Why fight? It's a waste of time, believe me. Everyone is on your side; your husband is on your side; your neighbor is on your side. You need help. And we all want the best for your daughter."

Lil eyes wandered to a photograph of Dr. Garufee and his family; it stood out among others on his desk. She had noticed it before on other visits. The doctor's wife was seated on a red velvet chair. Her hands rested on its arms, and her nylon-stockinged legs were thick and crossed at the ankles. Her face was cocked to the side, and she smiled, ever so slightly. The doctor stood behind her with his hands on her shoulders, his head, bald as the moon. Beside them, in a wheelchair, was a child, smiling brightly. His arms were bent and crooked, and his legs were encased in silver braces.

Lil closed her eyes. "Yes, okay, I understand."

"Good," said the doctor and he scribbled a prescription onto his pad, tore it off and handed it to Jim. "She'll get through this. We'll try reducing the dosage. Things are not as bad as they might seem." As he shook Jim's hand and led them out the door of his office, he said, "Be kind to each other. Life is hard."

JIM AND Lil drove out of Farrow's Corner toward home in icy silence. Lil watched the clouds and treetops speed by, wishing she could open the car door and tumble to the side of the road. When they entered the limits of Hanzloo, she said, "Please drop me at the church."

"What?" said Jim. "Why?"

"Please, don't argue, just let me off, and I'll walk home."

"Church? All of a sudden you want to go to church? By the way, Alice told me you don't believe in God. Nice one. Who tells a kid that? You're dangerous, Lil," he said.

"Either stop the car at the church or I will open the door while the car is moving," said Lil, calmly. Jim pulled over by the entrance to the church and banged his hands on the steering wheel.

Lil paused before getting out of the car. "I'm sorry, Jim. I keep saying that, and it doesn't help, I know. I'll make my own way home," she said, opening the door. "And I'm not taking the pills. I don't tell you what medicine to take."

"Please. Lil. Let me help you!"

Lil ducked out of the car and shut the door behind her, not looking back. She heard the rumble of the muffler as Jim drove away.

THE OLD church, a cool chamber of lacquered pews and marble floors, was empty. Her footsteps echoed down the side aisle as she slowly approached the altar and the huge cross that hung on the wall behind it. An enormous arched ceiling of dark wooden beams capped the church, and the vague smell of incense hung in the air. Even before she had spiraled out of the orbit of her life, Lil rarely went to church on Sunday, preferring to visit in the weekday afternoons, when the church was quiet and dark.

She stopped to admire the reds, blues, yellows, and greens of the stained glass windows, made more vivid by the sunlight streaming in behind them. Her favorite window depicted the Good Samaritan as he stopped to care for a man who'd been left by the side of the road, ignored by passersby. The sight of one man cradling another in his arms and lifting a cup to his lips while others watched always caused her to pause and take a second look. She thought all the figures, bad guys and good guys, looked alike. There was something irresistible about their square hands and feet, their muscular legs, and it was funny, in an appealing way, how they all had perfect noses and big full lips.

Lil passed the Stations of the Cross, stone etchings framed in ornate gold. The familiar sight of Jesus carrying his cross pulled her in. As a kid she had stared at this image, trying to grasp its meaning. Her childhood impression of the crucifixion had never evolved: because you are a sinner, when you grow up, you must carry your instrument of torture on your back and then be nailed to it at death. Lil used to make up sins to tell the priest in the confessional, and then tack on the end of the list, that she had lied.

But now she understood. Now she had a sin, a real whopper, and Dr. Garufee knew all about it. She felt Garufee was an inch away from telling Jim, and maybe the fact that he'd been the one to give her the information was all that had stopped him from breaking the confidence. He hadn't tried to talk her out of it, either. He'd explained that for him it was a medical choice, not a religious one.

Lil never anticipated how much her decision would haunt her. The trip itself had not been so bad; the early morning Greyhound bus ride from Farrow's Corner, where she'd sat anonymously with only a handful of other passengers, almost seemed like the start of an adventure. It was a gray December day, two weeks before Christmas. She had the money in the back fold of her purse. The stash she'd been saving for the trip to New York City. Twenty dollars here, ten dollars there.

She leaned her head against the window, and watched the bare, brown hills go by. Her feelings were as frozen as the ground. Where was the guilt?

LIL HAD been a small girl, the last under a pile of nine children. According to the nuns, girls could suffer, like saints; they could hurt themselves for the sake of others, and if they

121

were lucky some of them were blest with the ability to absorb the pain of everyone around them. A little girl's greatness lay in her ability to be last in line, to be invisible.

She wasn't afraid, even after hearing Dr. Garufee's warnings of the dangers of aborting, even after sneakily looking it up in the library. Awful things could happen. You could die. You could bleed to death on the table. But what was worse than being buried under another pile of children? With Alice she felt there was a chance that they might get out of Hanzloo, but once the babies started to form a line inside her, she knew she'd never get free.

Lil lied to Jim about going to visit her sister in New Jersey, and as if possessed by an inner demon she'd never met before, she rode the bus with a cool resolve.

The Philadelphia Greyhound station was alive with commuters, travelers with suitcases—all strangers—and she was a stranger, too. She stood in line at the taxi stand. No one cared who she was or where she was going. The cab ride was tense; the driver smoked a cigar, and barely acknowledged that she'd gotten in the cab. Lil worried that he'd take her to the wrong address. He dropped her at a small five-story building in a remote part of town.

She pushed the tiny button: 4H, and a loud buzz startled her. She opened the door and took the tiny elevator up.

The doctor's door was ajar, and once inside, Lil saw the room looked more like a small apartment than an office. It was clean, but shabby. A black couch with flattened cushions sat against the wall, and grey carpeting covered the floor. Nothing hung on the cream-colored walls. A young man sat behind a small desk, wearing large glasses wound in the middle with tape, and his face was dotted with acne. He extended his hand warmly, as if he'd been expecting her for quite some time. "Hello Lilian, I'm Carl."

It was only when Dr. Ella came out of a back room that fear crept up her arms. The doctor, her face loose with the sagging skin of middle age, had gray-streaked hair—wound tightly in a low bun. She wore a white coat, like any other doctor might, and she extended her hand for a shake. Perhaps sensing Lil's nervousness, Dr. Ella asked about her trip. There were no other personal questions; the word *husband* never came up.

Doctor Ella called it the procedure room, and she led them in. There, Lil went through the doctor's checklist of medical history attentively, nodding yes or no, and undressed quickly when left with a scanty robe.

In one brief moment, Lil panicked, and could not catch her breath. The doctor pulled away from the cold silver table and said, "Are you sure you want to do this? It's not too late to stop."

"I'm sorry. I'm nervous."

"You're lucky you came to me," said the doctor. "I know what I'm doing."

"If I die—"

"You won't," said the doctor, emphatically.

"Okay. Yes. Do it."

"All right," said the doctor, with a quick, decisive nod. "You're going to fall asleep," she said. For a moment she laid her hand on Lil's forearm, and then she poured liquid onto a palm-sized square of gauze and placed it over Lil's mouth.

"So easy," Lil whispered, as she drifted off.

Lil O'Brien, a good Catholic girl, who had lived a life of little white lies and venial sins, committed her gigantic mortal sin in a deep, deep sleep. When she woke up and looked around, she knew exactly where she was, and the young man with the broken glasses said, "Welcome back." He'd been sitting on a chair in the corner of the room, reading a paperback. No complications, no lightning strikes from heaven. Just some cramps in the abdomen and some deep dreaming on the night ride home.

Back in Hanzloo, Jim never suspected, and no one cared. "I know what I'm doing. Lucky you came to me," were the words she remembered from the doctor. But with the first warm days of spring, shame curled up inside her where the baby once grew.

Now, SLIDING into one of the pews not far from the altar, neither genuflecting nor making the sign of the cross, Lil sat staring at the crucified statue above the altar, that was nailed—nailed!—to the wooden cross. She kneaded the palms of her hands with her thumbs and imagined what kind of unbearable pain a nail would cause, and who would even think to thrust a nail into a person's hand?

She felt that if someone nailed her to a cross, and hung her in her underwear, in the middle of Hanzloo, it wouldn't take three days and nights for her to expire. She would die immediately. Surely Clarisse McCarthy would be there to witness it, Jim, and all the others, too. Would the children be allowed? Would Alice stand stone-faced, holding on to Clarisse's hand?

From high up, behind the shadows of the confessionals, a large black crow hiding in the rafters of the church swooped across the ceiling and landed on the tilted head of the Jesus that hung on the cross above the altar. Lil called out to the bird, and her words rang throughout the church, "Shame!" Her voice came back at her. She cried again, "Shame! Shame! Shame!"

The bird took flight again and disappeared into the upper beams in the church ceiling, the flutter of its wings resounding.

From the small alcove where the red vigil candles flickered peacefully, Sister Annunciata stomped across the dimly lit church.

Lil stood up abruptly.

"Hold on!" said the sister, and she hobbled down the center aisle, her heavy rosary beads rattling as she cut across a middle pew to block Lil's exit. The old nun leaned, out of breath, with her hand on the pew. "Shame," she said, considering the word. "Oh, there's a heavy load" The sister's voice was low and gruff.

The women spoke in urgent whispers.

"Sister, I'm . . . I," said Lil, flustered.

"Oh, never mind, I don't care. Let me sit, and I'd appreciate it if you'd stay here so I don't have to run around this church after you."

"Of course," said Lil, her head throbbing. The last thing she wanted was a lecture.

The sister tried to settle her breath; she sat down with her legs wide apart underneath her heavy skirts, placing her palms on her knees for support. To Lil, her face, with its frayed eye patch, large nose, and hanging jowls, seemed attached to her habit like a Halloween mask that could be peeled right off. "Sister, are you okay?"

"I'm better than you are," she said. "At least I'm not screaming at a crow."

"I thought I was alone," said Lil.

Sister Annunciata gave a hoarse laugh. "I must admit, though, you really got me. I thought I'd been visited by one of these figurines," she said, pointing around at the statues in the church. "I had a real moment there. I said to myself, 'One of these things has finally come to life.'" Sister Annunciata chuckled as she reached into her deep pocket, pulled out her handkerchief, and gave her nose a honk.

Lil had never had a conversation with Sister A. before. She'd only observed her from a distance at school functions, in church, and at the playground.

"I'm sure I shouldn't have screamed in church," said Lil, picking up her purse. "I'll be on my way, as long as you are okay."

"I assume you came here for a reason."

"It's not what you think," said Lil.

"I don't think anything," said the sister. "What should I think? I'm curious, why are you calling out 'shame, shame, shame' in the church in the middle of a Saturday afternoon?"

"I didn't mean to be heard. It was nothing."

"Two lies, right in a row."

"I've been having difficulties," said Lil.

The nun narrowed her eyes and peered at Lil. "Aren't you Alice's mother?"

"Yes, you know who Alice is?" said Lil.

"I know all the children. And I know you, too, Lil O'Brien."

"Well, they've taken Alice. If you knew me better, I suppose you'd think it was for the best, but it's not right."

"Who took Alice? I saw her in the playground yesterday."

"Clarisse McCarthy has taken her because I'm sick."

"You look okay to me," said Sister A.

"I'm not okay." Lil lowered her head. "I've been on drugs and I can't think straight."

"Clarisse McCarthy? The good-deed-doer? That would worry me. Why are you on drugs?"

"The doctor prescribed them. I've been depressed, unhappy, angry!"

"I'm sure you're not the first person in Hanzloo to get the blues. Why does that mean Alice moves in with Clarisse McCarthy? Where's your husband in all this?"

"They say that the boy Felix Spoon, I don't know, molested Alice in the cafeteria and Alice won't tell me what happened. I fear it may be true. And maybe it's my fault because, look at me. My husband says Alice deserves a better mother." Lil looked at the nun urgently to see what she would say.

"Felix Spoon did what?"

"I don't know. Maybe he did nothing, but who can tell?"

"Has anybody asked him about it?"

"I haven't, I don't even know the Spoons."

"But didn't I see the four of you walking away from the schoolyard together yesterday?"

Lil sighed. "I'll be explaining that for decades. It was an accident, nothing."

All she wanted to do was go home now.

Sister A. fell silent for a minute. She took hold of her rosaries, idly fingering them. "Do you even know what's bothering you?"

Lil turned away.

"I never understand why people in this town won't talk to me like I'm a human being. It's frustrating," said Sister A.

"I'll tell you why. It's just . . . that you live in a vacuum," said Lil, raising her voice slightly. "You have no idea what it's like to have a child, a husband, a real life. The church may be run by the priests, but you nuns do the dirty work, making sure the kids stay frightened and ashamed so they will grow up and follow in their scared and ashamed parents' footsteps."

Lil feared she had gone too far. Sister A. dug into her pocket and lifted her handkerchief to her one good eye, dabbing what looked like the wetness of a tear. Just a few harsh words were all it took.

The nun shook her head. "These crummy allergies. My eye is like a waterfall," she said, as she stuffed her handkerchief back down into her pocket. "That was quite a mouthful, but don't presume to know me. Don't be fooled by the fact that I only have one eye. I see things, believe me."

"Look, I shouldn't have said what I said. You haven't done a thing to me."

"Don't be sorry. You might wind up thinking you're lucky you met me. If you find yourself wanting to talk, I suppose you know where I'll be. The convent receives visitors, you know." The nun stood up. "I'd advise you to take care of yourself. Your daughter is an interesting child. How do you think she feels?" The nun pulled out her pocket watch. "In the meantime, I'll find out what happened with Felix Spoon and Alice."

"But you won't tell the priest, will you?" asked Lil.

"I'll do what I have to do," said Sister A. "And let's hope that it's a good idea."

"But if something like that, well they could take her from me forever. They might, you know!" Lil's eyes filled.

Sister A. seemed to lose her tolerance. "Who do you care about, Lil? You have to ask yourself that."

Lil had no response, in part because she wasn't really sure what Sister A. meant. She watched the old nun make her way back across the pew and up the center aisle. Sister Annunciata stopped momentarily in front of the altar. She reached her hand to the railing and, with difficulty, knelt and bowed her head. Shortly, she stood again and called over to Lil. "Yes, I suppose it feels good to yell in church." Her voice rose way above a whisper, breaking the silence. With that, Sister A. disappeared behind the baptismal, into the inner sanctum of the sacristy.

SIXTEEN

EARLIER, WHEN LIL entered the church the sun had been bright and high, but now, as if it were an entirely different day, a cold rain poured down on Hanzloo. The sky had turned purple and, in some places, black. Making her way toward Mundy Lane, she stepped through puddles in flimsy flats, now as wet as sponges. Wind tore through the trees, blowing off the autumn leaves. In the distance, thunder rumbled, and flashes of lightning stabbed the horizon. As gusts blew at her from all directions, she headed home, and though it wasn't far, it might as well have been a million miles away.

By the time she passed Pine Street, her thin coat was soaked through. Leafy branches, ripped off by the wind, were strewn across front lawns and sidewalks, and small rivers rushed down the pavement and slithered into the sewer drains like silver snakes. Lil passed two small bicycles leaning by a curb, perhaps abandoned in haste by kids who had been caught by surprise when the storm broke.

The streets had the eerie feel of a deserted town.

In the wind and rain, Lil became fearful. Sister Annunciata would go to Father Bruno about the children—of course she would—that's what nuns do. And the police would come, and someone from the government, and they would take Alice, and their lives would be like dominoes falling upon each other.

Lil made a split-second decision to turn right on Pine and headed toward the Post Road to Luke Spoon's house, determined to find out what had happened to Alice. Alice had said it was nothing, but then why couldn't she tell what happened? Lil had to know the truth and had to take charge of things before the nun could intervene.

She ran down the street, with the rain stinging her face, and when she finally reached the old Ross house, it stood before her, dreadful and forbidding.

With the full force of her fist, Lil pounded on the front door, and Felix Spoon, as if he'd been standing there waiting for her, opened it wide. He was sucking on a lollipop, rolling it around in his mouth so that his cheeks bulged, and he looked up at her, surprised.

He called over his shoulder, "Luke! Alice's mother is here. She's sopping wet!"

"May I come in?" said Lil.

Felix stepped away from the door and backed into the hallway. He was wearing a white man-sized T-shirt, spattered with paint. The T-shirt reached below his knees and his feet were bare. He went over to the staircase and yelled again. "Luke, I think you better hurry. Something's happening down here."

Lil took a good look at the boy. He was spindly, skinnier than she'd remembered, and his eyes were hollow and deep. What had he done to Alice? The question made her mad, and she stepped to the side, losing her footing slightly.

"Mrs. O'Brien. Maybe you should come in here," Felix said, gesturing toward another room. "I guess it's okay if you sit in Luke's chair," he added. Felix showed her to his father's chair, and Lil sat there, looking around. Her teeth chattered like someone in a cartoon.

Felix went over to the staircase and yelled again, "Alice's mother is all wet down here!"

"Who?" Lil could hear Luke's voice from the top of the stairs.

"Look," Felix said, pointing. "She's just here. I don't know why."

Luke bounded down the stairs and into the living room. He came face to face with Lil, who had the dubious honor of being their first guest.

A woman is in the house, he thought.

Luke approached her cautiously, as if she belonged in a museum, not a chair. "Mrs. O'Brien, what happened to you?"

"I was walking in the rain," she said, clutching her arms around her. "I'm cold." Once in the house, she'd lost her nerve. In her dripping clothes, aware she might seem crazy—and she couldn't be sure she wasn't—it felt fruitless to confront them.

"Can I get you a towel?" Luke said.

Felix, interested, sucked on his lollipop, but Luke ran his hand through his hair, nervously.

"A towel? Yes," said Lil.

Luke left them alone in the living room. Right away Lil noticed Felix's peculiar drawings on the light green walls, and she followed the trail of stick figures as they made their way up and down the hills and valleys that wound around three of the four walls.

Felix took his lollipop out of his mouth. "You're not like other people, right?" he said, closing one eye and looking at her.

Lil could have said the same thing about him. He didn't speak like other children. The little molester.

Luke came back into the room with two folded towels, and laid them on his easy chair, quickly stepping back.

Even this late in October, Lil O'Brien wore a thin blue summer skirt, and her blouse was blotched with rain. She tilted her head to one side and toweled her hair between her hands, and then laughed a little.

"This is so absurd."

Luke smiled a little. He watched her like a movie.

"Do you have a hair dryer?" she asked, wringing out the hem of her skirt, creating a small puddle on the floor.

"No, but I do have a clothes dryer in the basement."

"No. I should go. I'd need to change . . . I really should go. I don't . . . know why I'm here, exactly."

"But she's all wet," said Felix, to his father.

"Uh, you can go upstairs and change. I'll give you a robe."

A robe? She couldn't put his robe on, could she? Too cold to think it through, she followed Luke Spoon up the creaky, narrow staircase.

"I warn you, I'm not the best housekeeper."

Luke emerged from his bedroom with a thick, blue terrycloth monstrosity, and gestured down the hall toward the bathroom.

She closed the bathroom door behind her and fiddled with the doorknob, realizing it had no lock. The freestanding bathtub on stubby curved legs had a thick ring of rust around the inside of it. The toilet seat was up, dust balls had collected in the corners of the floor, and an elaborate spiderweb spread across the top edge of a shelf. Her headache pounded, as rain pelted against a small foggy window.

Lil let her clothes fall to the floor and wrapped herself in Luke Spoon's thick warm robe; the vague smell of sweat rose up from the underarms.

"Might as well dump it all in here, and I'll throw it in the dryer," said Luke, when she returned downstairs. "Some tea?"

"Okay," she said.

Felix stared at her, his bare feet pushing his rocking chair gently back and forth. He sucked and slurped his lollipop, clutching its thin white stick in his hand.

"The walls," said Lil, almost to herself.

"You mean the drawings? I did them," said Felix.

"Really? Why?" asked Lil.

"I don't know," he said, shrugging. "You're the first person to notice them. Father doesn't seem to."

Luke returned and set a mug of tea on a small table beside Lil.

"Listen, I've got to get home. You really have to give me my things," she said, as if he'd been keeping them from her.

"But I doubt if they're dry."

"It doesn't matter if they're dry," said Lil.

THE SIGHT of her underwear on the top of the pile of clothes unsettled her, and the fact that Luke Spoon had picked them out of the dryer disturbed her even more. "I have to hurry," she said. Luke handed her the basket, and she made her way quickly up the stairs.

Once again inside the privacy of the bathroom, she grabbed her damp bra and snapped it on, then pulled on her underwear, her socks, and her skirt. All of it clung to her, hot and clammy against her skin. As she buttoned her blouse, she stopped briefly to examine her reflection in the mirror that hung above the sink. Her hair was still wet from the rain, and her green eyes looked back at her. She spread her fingers on either cheek. "Get me out of here, of everywhere," she whispered.

Luke and Felix were waiting for her at the bottom of the stairs, like two schoolboys, and a wave of fatigue poured over her. The effort of meeting their eyes seemed too much to bear. She had nothing to rely on, no hellos or goodbyes, no language.

"Can I drive you home?" asked Luke.

"No, no."

"But it's pouring. She'll just get wet all over again," said Felix looking up at his father.

It was true. Outside, the rain fell steadily against the windows, and it didn't make sense for her to venture out in it again. Reluctantly, she agreed to the ride, anything to get home.

Felix wanted to stay behind, and the two adults took the short car ride from the Post Road to Mundy Lane.

Luke drove slowly through Hanzloo as the rain pounded the car. Visibility was poor, and he repeatedly cleared the inside of the windshield with the palm of his hand as it fogged. When he pulled up in front of the O'Brien house, the wipers were swinging back and forth in a steady *zoop, zoop.*

"You never said why you paid us a visit," said Luke.

"Thank you for the ride," said Lil.

"You're very beautiful," he said. It jumped out of his mouth.

Lil turned her head sharply toward him.

"What I mean is I'm a painter and . . . so is your daughter . . . beautiful. You are both so—"

"They've taken her from me."

"What do you mean?"

"My daughter. Alice. Because I'm not well. I guess you've seen enough of me to figure that out by now." She paused, and the sound of the wipers on the windshield amplified inside the car. "And because of your son," she added flatly. "They say your son did something to Alice, molested her. Did you know about that?"

Luke rubbed his eyes under his glasses.

"When I asked Alice, she wouldn't tell me what happened." Lil searched his face. "Did he? Did he do it?" she asked.

Luke leaned into the steering wheel. "Look, my son may be unusual, but I can't believe he'd do something like that."

"How do you know?" asked Lil.

"Who told you this?" said Luke.

"Clarisse McCarthy, and now she's finagled my husband into thinking that Alice would be better off staying with her."

"Clarisse McCarthy? Oh, ridiculous! She's the one who's saying this? She seems to have a lot of power over people in this town," said Luke, and without thinking, he reached out and put his hand over Lil's, as if she were a trusted friend. "I don't believe it," he said.

When she saw his hand on hers, she pulled away.

"You're not coming on to me, are you?" said Lil, fear darting across her eyes. "That's not right. I'm trying to tell you that my family, my daughter, this is awful. If you for think for one minute that I would ever—"

136

"I'm not coming on to you!" he said, raising both his hands. "It's just that I received a letter in the mail—as I'm sitting here, I realize, of course it was Clarisse McCarthy who sent it—I came to your house the other morning to show you the letter, but you were, well, I couldn't."

Lil looked out the car window and wiped her nose. "I hate her."

"You do?" Luke couldn't contain his smile. "You're funny. Who are you?"

"Oh, come on, how the hell do I know? Who are *you*?" she said, buttoning her coat in a hurry. "I'm a housewife, just like the rest of them, and you are asking for trouble here in Hanzloo."

Luke took a firm hold of the steering wheel with his hands.

Lil peered out the window toward her house, which was being pelted by wind and rain. "Snakes come out in the rain, did you know that? If I were you, I'd move away from here." She got out of the car, but before she closed the door she turned and poked her head back in. "What *did* happen between our children?"

Luke raised his voice over the rain. "Probably nothing! That's what I think. Look, maybe *you* should get out of this town. You don't seem to belong here, either."

Lil slammed the car door and Luke yelled after her, "I know you're lonely!" He watched her run up the driveway, as the rain pummeled the roof of his car.

SEVENTEEN

AFTER SIX DAYS at the McCarthy home, Alice was badly constipated, not even knowing what that meant. She'd been holding on to every inch of herself and couldn't get comfortable at their house, most especially in any of the family's bathrooms. Making even a tiny stink or tinkling noise was unbearable. It seemed that whenever she snuck away to try to use one of the bathrooms, the door was closed, and she worried it would be impolite to knock or wait in the hallway. She feared that from behind the door Mr. McCarthy might emerge in his boxer shorts, with a newspaper under his arm, having just flicked a cigarette into the toilet bowl as it flushed, with a bad smell lingering. It had happened once, and upon seeing Alice, he'd walked past as if she weren't there, but then turned back abruptly, and said, "Boo!" He laughed so loud it seemed more like a roar, and though Alice had the sense that he was trying to be funny, she didn't like it at all. Mr. McCarthy's size alone was beastly, but his hairy back and chest made him seem like something that belonged in a zoo, not in someone's home.

"Mom," she kept saying to herself. "Mom!" she called out one night, waking herself up, but no one else.

Alice hadn't seen Sneedler all week, and she pictured him shivering in the cold woods that lay beyond the McCarthys' at the end of Mundy Lane. When no one was paying attention, she peeked out the windows on that side of the house, but there wasn't a trace of him. She knew she should search for him, but sometimes at night the trees looked like they might become uprooted and run around.

And what if Sneedler died?

Before bed, her dad would call to say goodnight. Most of the time, Clarisse McCarthy stood beside her in the kitchen as she talked to him, but one night he called while Clarisse was tending to the twins.

"How's it going?" said her father.

"Not good," Alice whispered.

"Not good? Why?"

"Dad, can I come home?" said Alice, clutching her hand around the receiver.

"Not quite yet, sweetie. Soon."

"Is Mom there?"

"She's asleep. She loves you. We both do."

"Dad, please."

"Very soon."

But Clarisse came back into the kitchen and gestured for the phone.

"Jim," she said. "We're having a grand old time. Don't you worry. Alice is settling in, and we adore her."

After the call, Alice stood in the kitchen staring at the wall phone wishing that instead of the nightly good night from her father, her mother would call. Clarisse seemed to think she was still hungry.

"No more food for you! You must have a tapeworm. Come on, go play with the girls."

But playing with the girls was not that easy. Her initial hopes that her stay would be fun had dwindled quickly. Behind their mother's back, they teased her relentlessly, just like in the playground, excluding her from their private games and making jokes at her expense.

At lights out, she lay straight and still in her foldout cot, rubbing her lips on the edge of the wool blanket, reciting times tables one after another, until the numbers scrambled. Petrified in the tiny bed, afraid to move a muscle, Alice barely breathed listening to the radiators clank all over the house. As the night progressed, her thoughts went wild with visions of thieves sneaking through the downstairs; she thought she could hear them banging into tables and chairs, and what if one of them discovered her beneath her blanket?

Things would brighten with the morning light. The twins' attic bedroom, cluttered with every kind of stuffed animal and board game, had more toys than the five-and-dime, and Dawn and Fawn were not expected to keep their things in order. Alice loved the ruffled butterfly-speckled bedspreads that matched their curtains, and secretly she wished she could have a room like theirs at home. It wasn't so bad to be around those pretty things.

But trouble loomed everywhere. Several days into her stay, the girls were together getting ready for bed, and the twins were engaged in a game they called *KILL*. It involved leaping from bed to bed and jumping up and down as if the beds were circus trampolines. Fawn pretended to be a flamingo, and Dawn, a rabid wolf on the chase.

"Don't watch us!" ordered Dawn. "Face the wall!"

Alice felt bad about this, but did as she was told, turning toward the wall, and she didn't even cry.

Dawn, especially, disliked her, and it only got worse whenever Alice received attention from Mrs. McCarthy. But Fawn could be more kind when pulled away from her sister.

One night, when Dawn was taking her turn in the bathtub, Alice and Fawn played a game together. Alice got down on all fours and let Fawn ride her around like a horse. Fawn held on to the collar of Alice's pajama top shouting *Woo-hoo!* and they both had a good time. When they tired of that they started a round of old maid.

"You're funny!" said Fawn when Alice made a face like Flirtina Fairytoe, one of characters on the cards. "Do it again!" cried Fawn. Alice made the face three times and Fawn laughed louder each time. They settled into the game and Alice was relieved that Fawn played so nicely, but as soon as Dawn came back upstairs in her monkey pajamas, she kicked the card game that they had arranged on the floor and it scattered into a mess.

"You're not allowed to touch our cards!" said Dawn.

"I didn't mean it," said Alice.

Dawn got a stick horse out of the closet and poked Alice in the stomach.

"I'm telling Mom if you don't stop it," said Fawn. "You're being mean."

"No, it's okay," said Alice, sensing there'd be further consequences from Dawn if her mother got involved. "They're not my cards."

Alice couldn't get mad at the twins. They were special and everybody knew it. They had to be pardoned for any bad behavior, an unspoken rule that no one questioned.

By Wednesday morning, when Alice was in the kitchen having breakfast with Mrs. McCarthy and the twins, her stomach felt so bad, she had to do something.

Alice raised her hand as if she were in school. "May I go to the bathroom?" she asked.

"Yes, of course, and you don't have to raise your hand. Really, Alice! Do you have to ask at home?" said Clarisse.

"Stupid," said Dawn, crunching down on a piece of toast.

"Dawn, stop it already," said Clarisse. "Can't you be nice?"

"Uck," said Dawn. "Who raises their hand at breakfast? It's dumb."

"Mom," said Fawn. She hopped off her chair and whispered into her mother's ear. "She doesn't seem old enough to be in second grade."

"Just eat your egg, will you?" said Clarisse.

Alice rushed to get to the bathroom, but as she started up the stairs, she saw Mr. McCarthy standing on the top step. Frank McCarthy had just been passing from the bathroom to the bedroom, figuring the kids were eating breakfast. He paused to inspect a burnt-out light bulb in the ceiling, and when he looked back down the stairs he came face to face with Alice.

He stood in a white T-shirt, naked from the waist down, and what Alice thought she saw was something like a toy elephant trunk hanging between his legs. He immediately pulled his T-shirt over himself and yelled, "Whoa!"

"What now?" called Clarisse, as she hurried out of the kitchen to discover Alice at the bottom of the stairs. Clarisse looked up at her husband and shrieked, "Oh, for heaven's sake, Frank! Put some clothes on!"

IT CONTINUED to be tougher than Clarisse had expected. Alice didn't seem to be happy. The twins were showing their worst side, and Clarisse realized that she had underestimated the strain of having Alice in the house. She didn't really care for the girl, who was plain in a way that irritated her, polite to the point of annoyance.

On Sunday at church Clarisse thought she sensed a judgment from some of the other women. Ginny Rice didn't say hello. So what. But it wasn't just Ginny; she had the feeling that conversations stopped when she approached, that public opinion had shifted, as if she was somehow showing off by taking Alice in.

Alice wasn't used to going to Sunday services, and although Clarisse bought her a shiny blue dress—for which Alice hadn't thanked her—Alice looked sullen as they filed into mass. Upon seeing her, Steph Conte got down on one knee and whispered into Alice's ear, giving her a hug, which infuriated Clarisse. "We're good people!" Clarisse felt like screaming.

She'd already tired of the constant vigilance; all she wanted to do was put her feet up on the couch and take a nap. Alice's presence had made her grumpy and amplified her annoyance about other things as well. Those little green eyes peering all over her home revealed things about her life that under normal circumstances she could ignore, like the fact that her girls lacked . . . *what*?

It pained her to see how they ganged up on Alice.

And then there was her husband. That Frank was successful, having climbed up to a high rung at Henkel Paint, always seemed like part of a bigger plan. If you want to be charitable you have to have money. She wondered if she'd fooled herself into believing that their two cars, her elaborate wardrobe, the high-end appliances that hummed so smoothly, were meant to set the stage for respectability, not envy. "Get the most expensive one," Frank always said. She and Frank shared a certain sensibility about success; people had to respect you, otherwise how would they be inspired to follow your example? The Kennedys were wealthy. They had wonderful and expensive things. They had taste and style. Nothing to feel bad about. Not that she compared herself to the Kennedys, except that she did.

And, of course, there was nothing wrong with Frank. Everybody loved him. He had a joke for each occasion; he shook hands and slapped backs. He'd do anything for anyone. He threw his money around, buying too many Girl Scout cookies, giving extra in the church envelope.

Frank, larger than life. Powerful. But the way little Alice O'Brien looked at him, as if he were a bad, repulsive man, made Clarisse feel unsure. She sunk into a private, hellish mood of hating herself and her family, questioning every choice she'd ever made.

These nights Clarisse dreaded getting into bed. She'd skip her nightly ritual, no more dabbing either side of her neck with perfume as she slipped into her nightgown. Instead she preferred her flannel pajamas.

Thoughts crystallized, like, face it, it had been years since she actually desired him. Frank was a huge man in every way. There was a time, before the twins were born, when she'd enjoyed their remarkably athletic romps in bed, the way he'd lift her up and pin her down.

In other ways, Frank's *largeness* worked for her. He was a good, kind man, and theirs, a healthy marriage. Right? She called him her *big galoot*; his raunchy laugh shook the house and made her smile affectionately. His solid, square body beside her, her hairy bear, often afforded her a sense of safety, and of course his fat wallet was a plus. Anything she asked for she got. But nothing came without a price. It wasn't that she didn't want sex; she just didn't want it with him. Sometimes, when he was all over her, she felt as if an entire wall of the bedroom had fallen on top of her, flattening her like a pressed flower. She *wanted*, and *wanted,* and *wanted*, but what she wanted wasn't Frank.

Clarisse found herself daydreaming about Luke Spoon. He wasn't a nice guy; but the heat between them was hard to ignore. She toyed with a little idea for a couple of days. At first it was a pinprick in the back of her mind, until it ballooned into a physical ache.

On Wednesday morning she dropped the kids at school, skipped coffee with Steph, and went home to take a long, luxurious shower. Standing naked in front of the closet, she rifled through her dresses until she found the brown silk one that she'd hardly ever worn. She'd laid it out on the bed, deciding that—no—it wasn't too much. From her underwear drawer she fished out some panties, a bra to match, tinted nylons, and a garter belt. After inspecting herself in front of the mirror from every angle, she sat on the bed and smoked cigarettes for an hour.

THE DRIVE over to the Post Road was short. She pulled her car into a small abandoned turnaround, and made her way to the Old Ross house, staying just behind the tree line. Her heels sank in the dirt, and when the road was clear, she hurried across the street, and up to the front porch, her heart jumping crazily.

Luke Spoon came to the door. He held a coffee cup and looked as if he'd just gotten up. He wore a loose, wrinkled shirt and pants, and a curl hung over one of his eyes. Without his glasses he squinted, and then smiled, as if he knew why she'd come.

"Why, look who's here," he said. "A pleasant surprise."

"I . . ." She began to speak but thought better of it.

"You came to see how I paint with my tongue?" asked Luke.

"Something like that."

"Come on in," said Luke.

Clarisse was nervous now. The house seemed empty, as if he'd just moved in or out. Peeking into the living room, she had a moment of doubt. It was weird in there, but sensing her nerves, Luke put his hand up to her chin and turned her face toward his. He moved his fingers over her lips, and she closed her eyes, letting out a small sigh. Her mouth opened and she felt the tip of his finger against her tongue.

She pulled back. "What are you doing?"

"I'm getting ready to adore you," he said, amused.

Clarisse crossed her arms and looked away. "Oh, come on," she said. "It's not like that."

"It's not?" he said.

"No, I thought you might show me a painting. You said . . . at the A&P . . ."

"*You* said . . . at the A&P."

"I said?"

"Your eyes and lips talk up a storm, Clarisse."

"Well, that's . . . sweet."

"Shhh," he said, touching his forefinger to his own lips now. "Why don't we . . . I know . . . come upstairs."

Clarisse thought about protesting, about feigning outrage, but Luke took her by the hand, and she followed him up the stairs. They seemed to move in slow motion, and once in the bedroom, Clarisse was relieved that the shades were drawn. Some pants, shoes, balled socks, a couple of wet towels were strewn across the floor, and a big blue terrycloth robe hung on the door. An unmade bed took up most of the room as if Luke and his house existed for this purpose alone.

He led her over to the bed and sat her down. "Is this what you had in mind?" he asked. "Sorry I forgot to make the bed today. It's not easy to be all alone with the family chores."

Clarisse was silent.

"I like your red lips," he said.

She trembled as he knelt down in front of her and slipped off her shoes, taking a moment to rub his hands along the edges of her feet and then move his hand slowly up her stockinged legs. He spread her legs slightly to unhook her nylons from the garter belt under the skirt of her dress, and she leaned back a little, her hands behind her.

He began to kiss her knees. "Oh God," she said. "Let me . . . my stockings . . ."

"No, let me," he said. He rolled them off one by one and flung them on the floor. Once her legs were bare, she lay back on the bed and Luke stood over her, unbuttoning his shirt. His torso was smooth and fit. He quickly stripped to naked and lifted her legs onto the bed. Climbing on top of her, his knees on either side, he reached under the skirt of her dress to run his palms along her hips. "That's what I'd call an ass," he said. "Holy shit." He put his fingers between her legs, feeling the moistness on her panties.

"Why, Clarisse McCarthy," he said, and moved up to kiss her mouth, leaning into her. She felt his hard penis rest against her, and her breath quickened. He reached his hand into her dress, and felt for her breasts, and she cried out.

"Let's get rid of this dress," he said, and they wriggled it off together. He smelled of soap and coffee, and as his hands explored her further, he growled, which embarrassed her, but pleased her, too.

Luke pulled off her panties, and her body felt big and exposed in a way she was not used to. "Do you like me?" she said, breathless.

"Sure," he whispered, and then he nipped her ear, and kissed her cheeks, and moved down, pulling her bra to expose the nipple of her breast. There he lingered, sucking and exploring. Clarisse felt herself relax deeply. This was what she wanted, his tongue all over her. He moved up to her lips again. She put her nose against his chest and took deep, long breaths. The smell and taste of his sweat, salty and real, made her ache with some kind of hunger that she'd never had before, and she surrendered. Finally, finally, finally, it was what she needed, what she wanted, what she had to have. He handled her carefully, with authority, allowing her no hesitation or fear.

She opened her legs around him and arched her back. "Please, please . . . ," she begged. She was *coming* . . . She was really . . . *coming* . . . and then, so was he. Clarisse McCarthy had never, never, never . . . "Yes," she said, holding onto him tightly. They lay there for a short while. Clarisse's bra was twisted halfway off her left breast and he idly ran his fingers over her nipple. She felt reassured by his long slow breaths and wondered if they might drift off to sleep. Oh, the exquisite laziness of lying in bed, the shattering of her dull routine. Something had happened, really happened.

Soon, though, Luke rolled over and sat up on the bed, facing away from her. "Yowza," he said, amused. "That was one fast fuck."

Clarisse was stunned. She drew her arms tightly across her breasts and curled her legs into herself. She stared straight ahead at the small of his back. *What?*

He stood up and pulled on his pants. As he buckled his belt, he reached over and grabbed hold of her ankle, and gave it a gentle shake. "Hey. Not bad, right?"

Clarisse closed her eyes.

"You've got one hell of a body, Clarisse. You're luscious in that way. You know what I mean, right? It was fast though, wow, like instant coffee, a speeding bullet, something like that." Luke laughed a little, but they both sensed his words falling flat, and a long silence ensued.

"You really don't like me, do you?" she said, slowly reaching for her clothes.

He raised his eyebrows and spoke as if that question had never occurred to him. "Uh, gee, Clarisse. Are you kidding? I mean, I like you enough. But, is this really about liking? It's an interesting question. Do you really think I could *like* you? I suppose. You and I have this strange thing. First, you slap my kid, then I pour chocolate milk on your rug, then you send me a stupid letter. I don't know. So, you really think we like each other?

"Who cares? No one. Sex is sex. Wasn't it kind of great, in a sort of you-and-me type of way? You knocked on my door, right? I mean, do you like me?"

Clarisse was crushed. She wanted to say: *No! I didn't mean to slap your son and maybe I was wrong to send the letter! It's like there's two of me. Can't you see? I'm sorry, I'm sorry! I thought . . . I thought . . ."*

But instead, she sat up, amidst the mess of her own clothes and the chaos of the sheets on Luke Spoon's bed. It was as if a dollhouse had just collapsed around her.

"It's no big deal, Clarisse, trust me." Luke said kindly. "Look, I'll wait for you downstairs."

She dressed, loathing every inch of herself, and when she came back downstairs their parting was awkward. As Luke opened the front door for her, Clarisse could not bring herself to look at him. They were strangers, passing through a hallway that was much too narrow.

"Clarisse, honey, we're both adults," said Luke. "I'm glad you came by." Though he was trying to smooth things over, it felt to Clarisse like a slap in the face. In that way she supposed he'd gotten even, but more than ruffling her pride, it hurt in a way that things used to hurt when she was five years old. She'd given him the best of her, and he didn't seem to know it, and he didn't seem to care.

EIGHTEEN

FELIX SPOON SAT alone on the school steps during the lunch recess. Across the playground, boys in their heavier autumn jackets ran back and forth kicking a ball; some gathered in circles throwing jacks, and in the far corner girls were busy with clapping games. The clouds, gray and purple, rolled far out into the sky, and at noon the air had already turned chilly. Felix twirled a stick in a small dirt pile.

Recently he thought about his mother less and less, but today, as it was nearing Halloween, and they all were told to draw pumpkins before lunch, his mind wandered to another Halloween, when his mother had dressed him up as a devil and brought him to a place called The Duchess. Though the memory floated in and out of clarity, in red footed pajamas, rubber horns, and a tail, he remembered feeling proud about his costume. It was a whiskey and beer bar with a sign on the door that said *Women Only*. Dark and smoky, and dotted with muzzy red lights, the place roared with talk, and loud music from the jukebox. He recalled that a woman had lifted him onto a stool, and his mother came toward him with a tall glass of beer in her hand and raised it to his lips. When he felt its bubbly foam under his nose, he licked it, drawing back from the bitter taste, and some of the women laughed. Some of them wore costumes, too. One chomped on vampire teeth while one sported a bright orange wig and smoked a cigar. Felix remembered how he sat on his red rubber tail and fingered its pointy tip, observing how the women's shoes made patterns in the sawdust on the floor.

Most of the time, thoughts of his mother filled him with longing, but today the memory gave him a good idea. He'd be a devil for Halloween, but this year he'd find a real pitchfork, and he'd be a fire-spitting devil, the very one who stole God's rock, and had superpowers. He'd have to ask Luke how to make the costume.

Oh, if only. The first thing he'd do was crush Mike Fitzpatrick in the jaws of a garbage truck, and Jimmy Ginty would get it between the eyes with the pitchfork, and he'd secretly feed poison to Mike's brothers, and capture Alice O'Brien from the McCarthys, and take her to the cave of God, because he knew that God and the devil were friends, in the same way that night was just the other side of day, and sometimes boys were girls, and people were dogs or cats, and living was a dream. Felix loved to travel around his brain and wind up in a place where he decided the rules, a place where he could make a jumble of his thoughts and watch them mix with each other like the way Luke had taught him to mix paint and wind up with a new color. But people interrupted him, pulled him away from this place, and he didn't like it.

Now, as he sat on the steps, he saw the one-eyed nun, making a beeline toward him.

She walked as if she wished she could run, and always seemed to have her eye on him. Maybe she even saw him with that magic, ugly, missing eye that had worked its way into his drawings, and he didn't know why. Was he in trouble again? He thought about the day so far and couldn't remember anything he'd done. He put on his worst face as she came closer.

"That's quite a mope, young man," she said, standing before him.

"I didn't do anything wrong," said Felix.

"Is that how you say good afternoon, Sister?"

"No."

"So?"

"Good afternoon, Sister," he said, poking his stick in the dirt.

"Better. Now, I have a question for you. Where's my rock?" she said.

Felix peered up at her, pretending not to know what she was talking about.

"Do you have it? Have you kept it for me like you promised?"

Felix thought about lying. He didn't like to lie, as it proved more difficult to keep track of the truth, but at the same time he didn't want her to take the rock back. "What?" he said.

"I want to know if you are trustworthy. As I recall, you promised to keep it for me. Well?" she said.

"I have it, yes," and his eyebrows furrowed to a deep V.

"You mean, yes, Sister?"

"Yes, Sister." It would be bad to have to part with the rock. It was one of his favorite things.

"So, then, where is it?"

He reached into his pocket, pulled out a wad of toilet paper, and unwrapped it to reveal the rock, holding it out for her to examine. "Are you taking it back?"

"Let me have a closer look." Felix handed her the rock and she rubbed it together in her palms and then held it up to her eye to inspect it. "Interesting," she said. "It looks pretty good. It's the only one I have, so I'm glad to see you're taking care of it. That's one incredible rock." She threw the rock in the air and caught it with her other hand. He was surprised that she would throw it around like that. She handed it back to him and he carefully wrapped it back up and put it in his pocket.

"Usually, I keep it in a velvet box that belonged to my mother, but for recess I put it in my pocket."

"I see. Interesting. Well, I suppose that's as good a place as any to keep it. Whatever you do, don't lose it," she said, and Felix was relieved that their exchange had come to an end, but the nun wasn't done. "Oh, and one other thing," she said. "Did you and Alice O'Brien go to the cafeteria together after school the other day?"

Felix thought quickly. Was there something wrong with that? The fact that he had shown the rock to Alice might have not been such a good idea. Maybe the nun would get mad. But just being in the cafeteria didn't seem like such a big deal to him.

"I guess," he said.

"What were you doing there?"

"Just . . . Nothing."

"Now that I know you're trustworthy, I suppose you wouldn't tell a lie," she said.

Why couldn't she just leave him alone? On one hand, he liked that she called him trustworthy, but she was hard to figure out. She seemed mean, but maybe underneath, she really wasn't. "If I tell you, you'll probably get mad," he said.

"Then tell me a lie," she said.

"A lie? What? But then . . . then I won't be trustworthy," he blurted out, regretting that she could see that he cared what she thought.

"Your choice," said Sister A.

The nun towered over him like a huge tree and blocked his view from the rest of the playground. For a fleeting moment he wondered what it would be like to be wrapped in her arms, with all her robes around him. "Maybe what I did was bad, but I wasn't trying to be bad," he said.

The sister frowned. She straightened the patch on her eye and took a deep breath.

"Felix, just tell me what you did."

"Okay," he said. "I . . . showed her . . . the rock of God."

Sister Annunciata said nothing for a moment, and Felix couldn't tell if she was angry or sad, because she lifted her face up to the sky, closed her eye, and shook her head.

"Oh Mother of us all," she said.

"I'm sorry, Sister," said Felix.

"There's nothing to be sorry for. Alice must be a good friend of yours."

"I don't think so. She doesn't have any friends. She told me she lost her friend."

"Oh? Who would that be?" she said.

Felix shrugged. "How do I know?"

"Perhaps you should ask Alice about her friend. Sometimes a simple question can shed light on things."

The school bell clanged, and it was time for all the children to line up and go back to their classrooms. "Sister," said Felix, as she turned to go. "My father said there's no such thing as the cave of God."

The sister smiled.

"Did he? Well then how come you have a piece of it in your pocket?" Sister Annunciata paused, and reached her hand to Felix's cheek. "Just remember, boy, I like you."

Felix pulled away, but there was something about the touch of her fingers on his face that felt okay.

Sister Annunciata took a last look at him before making her way back across the playground. "You'd better get going, your class is all lined up. And child . . . one of these days you're going to have to learn how to tie your shoes. Maybe Alice-who-has-no-friends can show you how."

As school was letting out that day, Felix waited for Alice to pass him in the hallway. He tugged on her jacket sleeve.

"What?" she whispered.

"Can you help me do something? Just for a minute, under the stairwell by the first-grade door?"

"I can't. I have to go. Mrs. McCarthy said don't dawdle."

"Just one little minute, it's not like the other day. No one will catch us."

Alice let a line of other kids pass and scooted under the stairwell. Felix did the same.

"What is it? Can't you hurry?" Today she wasn't quite as patient with him as she'd been in the cafeteria.

"It's my shoes. I don't know how to tie them. And don't laugh."

"You don't know how?" said Alice.

"It's true," said Felix, crouching down to show her his untied laces.

Out of the corner of her eye, Alice caught a glimpse of Mrs. Sepolino, who was rushing toward the front office, her shoes clunking on the floor.

"No," said Alice, still whispering. "Ask another person. I can't do it. I'm not supposed to talk to you." Alice hurried down the hall and slipped out a side door.

Felix felt bad. He wished Alice would be his friend. He wished he could learn how to tie his shoes. But wishes were a waste of time. He'd wished for his mother, and to know God's cave, he'd even wished that he could fly, all to no avail.

He waited until the school emptied, took off his shoes and left them under the stairs, with their laces stuffed inside. His stockinged feet were cold on the pavement as he made his way home to the Post Road. What did he care? He didn't care at all.

Later, when his father asked him what had happened to his shoes, Felix told him that he didn't like them anymore, so he left them underneath the stairs. He didn't say that he was lonely; that whatever untold sin his mother had committed he wished he could follow her right down through the gates of hell. He didn't say that he was mad, mad that other kids knew how to tie their shoes and he did not. He didn't say that he couldn't understand why his father was too impatient to teach him how, or that Alice, who had absolutely no friends, didn't think enough of him to at least pretend to like him.

Luke Spoon put a hand on his son's shoulder and said, "It's okay, Felix, we'll find you some other shoes to wear."

NINETEEN

SISTER ANNUNCIATA HAD been transferred to Immaculate Conception School three years earlier to replace an unpopular principal. Sister Linda Rose had had a fondness for rulers, not for the purpose of measuring feet and inches, but for slapping, prodding, and threatening. It was hard to believe the woman didn't take pleasure in making children cry.

By the time she was ousted, the children were terrified of nuns. It didn't help that the new principal had only one eye; the patch could be intimidating, even to adults.

In order to improve relations, Sister A. introduced the idea of a Halloween Masquerade Party that would culminate in a contest for best costume.

At first, Father Bruno had to be convinced. The notion of parishioners roaming around the convent was radical. But when Sister A. explained that he and Father Aloysius might enjoy being the honorable judges of the costume contest, he caved.

It turned out to be a savvy move, for although Sister A. remained a formidable figure at school, the party generated much good will, and created an excitement in Hanzloo that was hard to pinpoint.

This year Lil O'Brien received a handwritten invitation from Sister Annunciata:

Dear Lil O'Brien,

Remember me from church a while back? The crow? The shame? Please come to the costume party, Tuesday night at 7:00. I'm sure Alice will be there. You don't have to wear a costume. You're scary enough.

~Sr. A.

P.S. That was a joke.

Lil folded the note and put it in her apron pocket.

Of course, Alice would be there. Clarisse McCarthy took pride in making elaborate costumes, though neither of the twins had yet to win a prize. She often complained that the contest was rigged against her, and her thirst for first prize only grew.

To see Alice in public would be hard, but it was better than a visit in Clarisse's living room. She'd have to take it up with Jim.

For two weeks Lil had seen no one but her husband, and he'd been particularly icy to her. They'd had words about her refusal to take the pills.

"You need them," said Jim.

"I don't," she said, though she had an awful craving for them. The clearer her head became, the more she understood that they would only make things worse.

"I'm trying to get better, Jim."

"I don't see any evidence of that. Look at this place."

Having adamantly refused Clarisse McCarthy's offer to hire Mrs. Tanner to straighten things out, restoring the house to sanity was a miserable, all-consuming job, but essential in order to get Alice home. She'd have to clean it to the bone.

Wandering from the dishwasher to the sink, from the bathroom to the bedroom, she balled socks, dusted, and sorted and folded clothes. Restless in the quiet hours of the afternoon, without the drugs, she could not escape a feeling of dread. Still, she didn't take a pill. Sometimes, pausing at the kitchen window, she followed the sky to the end of the horizon, and was seized by a longing so deep and inexplicable that she'd resume her chores just to flee from the feeling.

She stacked her poetry books in the hall closet behind the bags of summer clothes. As she cleared a shelf for the books, she thought back to an encounter she'd had with Clarisse McCarthy at the post office, shortly after she'd moved to town, almost five years ago.

"Lil O'Brien, right?" Clarisse had said, her arms full of envelopes. "Pardon me if I look a wreck, I've been working like a dog on Father Bruno's birthday invites. I wonder why I do it. Sending a letter home?" asked Clarisse eyeing Lil's mail.

"No, it's a poem for a magazine," Lil said.

"A poem?" said Clarisse. "Well, that's fancy. You wrote it?" asked Clarisse.

Lil lied. "My sister wrote it."

"I don't get poetry. I don't know. It's a little too stuck up for me. Is your sister stuck up?"

Lil had waited until Clarisse left the post office before she slipped the envelope into the mail slot. A few weeks later, she received a letter from the magazine. One sentence:

Thank you for your submission. The memory alone was a good enough reason to hide her books.

LIL DECIDED she'd make a dinner for Jim. Maybe then she'd approach him about going to the Halloween party.

When she opened the freezer, it looked as if a winter snow had fallen there. Prying loose a frosty package, she discovered a steak. Behind it she found a box of green beans encased in frozen crystal flakes. And what else? *Potatoes.* Jim loved them, and he stored them in the basement, in his new abode.

She started down the creaky stairs uneasily, pausing at the bottom step to see how he'd arranged his things amid the taped-up boxes, rakes and shovels. The room was damp and chilly, and smelled like dirt.

His clothes spilled out of a laundry bag, and work shirts hung from wire hangers on a clothesline above the washer and dryer.

A comforter lay across his narrow cot. She sat down and ran her hand over it, noticing a photograph sticking out from under an ashtray littered with butts. In the picture, which was taken on Clarisse's front lawn at a Fourth of July party, Jim and Alice were smiling, wearing baseball mitts and Yankee caps, but Lil's gaze veered off to the side. The whole problem was right there in the photo: her remote ways, her wish to be elsewhere, to set herself apart.

Beside a small tube of ointment that he used to soothe the skin on his legs and back, Lil saw Jim's wedding ring. She supposed he had taken to leaving it at home.

It had come to this, and it struck her that making dinner was the least she could do.

By the time Jim came home, Lil had prepared the food for cooking, showered, laid her favorite cloth over the table in the dining room, and even put on a dress. She'd set the table and lit two slender tapers. The preparation had taken all her concentration, and with a relatively clean house, she felt a shimmer of respectability, and hoped Jim would be pleasantly surprised.

When he walked in the front door and found that the lights were off, he called out. She sensed the alarm in his voice.

"I'm here," she said. "In the dining room."

Seeing the candles and the set table he said, "What's this?"

"A surprise dinner."

"Uh, okay." His tie was already loosened underneath his overcoat, and he carried his briefcase. He looked worn out, and she could tell that he'd been drinking.

"I found a steak in the freezer," she said.

"Hey, hey!" he said, sarcastically, but that, she forgave.

"Go change your clothes. I'll start cooking."

In the kitchen, dread swept over her as she stared at the strainer full of potatoes. She put them in a pot of water and set them on the stove. Boiled potatoes were Jim's favorite, and something about that disappointed her. Could there be anything duller than a boiled potato? She turned her attention to the steak, realizing she wasn't quite sure about the timing. Was it five minutes a side, or ten?

Jim emerged from the basement, out of his work clothes. Even at thirty-seven, he still looked boyish. But Lil was struck by his weary eyes, the slight stoop of his shoulders, and, of course, the recent ballooning belly.

He came into the kitchen rubbing his hands together. "Smells good."

Lil smiled, but at that moment she couldn't remember ever loving him. He might as well have been a stranger. "I hope I still know how to cook a decent meal."

"Do you want a drink?" he asked, desperate for one himself.

"Nah," she said. "You go ahead, I'll bring the dinner in."

In the dining room he poured himself a whiskey and sat at the table. "The candles are pretty," he called in to her.

"Yeah," she said, carrying the plates of food.

"So, cheers." He raised his glass to hers. "But what's this all about?"

"I'm trying—feeling better—and I thought I'd do something. After all, you worked all day."

They cut into their steaks. The meat was tough.

"Potatoes," he said, lifting a forkful.

"Yeah."

"I could eat potatoes every day."

"I guess I should be making them every day.

Lil relaxed a bit. Tough meat or not, she had accomplished making dinner, like a normal housewife, and she knew that every step toward normal was a step closer to Alice.

"Hey, you know, they're having that costume party at the convent is this Tuesday. Maybe we could go. I'm sure Alice will be there, and I'm dying to see her. Have you spoken to Clarisse?" The mention of Clarisse's name drove an instant wedge between them.

"Lil. I don't think—yes, I have spoken to Clarisse. Alice is doing well. I don't know how much longer we can impose on her like this, but she insists she's okay. The woman is a ball of energy. She's been a real friend."

Lil let that be. "We could bring Alice home, you know. I mean, look, I seem better, right?" It was odd to be auditioning like this.

"Let's see how the week plays out."

Jim picked up his drink and swirled the ice cubes in his glass. "By the way, guess what? Big news. I'm finally getting that promotion."

"Really? Jim. Wow."

"Yeah, imagine: I actually did something right."

"Oh, come on."

Jim came alive recounting the meeting with his boss. "It was so funny. When Callahan called me in—you know how much I hate his guts—but then, boom, all of a sudden, the whole thing flipped around, and he started talking about what a great asset to the team I am. And I felt completely different. He said Cramsky has had his eye on me, just waiting for the right time to push me upstairs. I don't know if it was baloney or not. I mean, how bizarre, more money, finally. And then, you wouldn't believe, before I left the office, he hugged me. It was kind of awful, but—"

"No, it's great, Jim."

He stopped short. It had been a while since he'd really looked her in the eye. He reached his hand over and put it on top of hers. "No, actually, it's not great, Lil." He stared at her.

"What's wrong?" she said, pulling her hand away.

"It means nothing because you don't even like me anymore," he said.

"I'm here, Jim. Don't worry. Please. This is good news."

"I'm hanging by a thread, Lil." He got up and moved over to the liquor cabinet to refresh his drink. "You may be feeling better, but I feel like shit," he said.

"But why?" said Lil.

After a gulp of his drink, he stood behind her and put his hand on her shoulder. She stiffened as he buried his face in her curls and started to kiss the rim of her ear.

"Lil," he whispered. "Let me touch you."

She closed her eyes, smelling the whiskey on his breath. This was the moment she should turn to him and accept his kiss. He would want more, and that's what a wife should do for a husband. That's normal. But every muscle clenched.

Sensing her resistance, he returned to his glass of whiskey, and threw it back. "I don't know what I did to repulse you so much. What did I do?" He poured himself a refill and turned back to her. "Thanks for dinner," he said, and left the room. Lil could hear his heavy footsteps on the basement stairs.

SHE LOADED the Westinghouse and turned it on, washed the pans, sponged off the counters, and tied the garbage. The light above the sink buzzed and glowed faintly in the kitchen, where she sat until she was sure Jim had fallen asleep. Then, grabbing her coat from the hall closet, she slipped out the front door and quietly down the steps. When she reached the street, she ran; she ran down Mundy Lane, and then through the streets of Hanzloo, her coattails twirling in the wind. The moon, yellow as an egg yolk, was nearly full.

Around the corner from the school and the church, alongside the graveyard, the convent was a big old house that had seen better days. Leading up to the ornate doorway was a wide, stone staircase; several steps were chipped, and a few empty flowerpots sat on either side. Lil paused, breathless, at the bottom of the stairs. She held to the railing and looked up at the convent door. Some lights from windows on an upper floor were lit, but the front hall was dark. If the sisters were asleep, she'd cause a stir. She couldn't bring herself to ring the bell.

She had started back down the sidewalk when the convent door opened, and Sister A. ushered Luke Spoon onto the stoop. Lil ducked behind the graveyard wall to watch them. She couldn't hear what they were saying, just the soft murmur of their voices. Luke Spoon took the sister's hand and shook it gently, reaching to kiss her on the cheek. He hurried down the stairs, rushing past the wall where Lil was hiding.

When he was out of sight, Sister A. bent down to straighten a flowerpot. She peered out into the night and began to sing, with her hands clasped before her, her voice cracking with age.

Way down in the valley my lambs be ye found
Secure from the tempests that now sweep around
Tis low in the vale my blessings flow
But on the barren mountain bleak and chilly winds do blow ...

Despite her concerns, as if the earth had tipped slightly off its axis, Lil had the urge to laugh. Luke Spoon, the nun singing in the moonlight, and she, on her knees in the graveyard. It was all too much.

"Sister!"

Sister A. strained to see her.

"It's me, Lil O'Brien."

"For heaven's sake, what are you doing in the graveyard? Come here."

Lil stood at the bottom of the stairs of the convent, brushing leaves and twigs from her clothes. "I thought I might be able to speak to you."

"It's past midnight," said Sister A.

"I know, but you did suggest I come," said Lil.

"I didn't mean the middle of the night. But okay."

"I guess I've run away from home."

Sister A. squinted back at her. "One thing and another, you really are having a rough patch, aren't you? You might as well come in."

"Couldn't we just sit on the steps?"

"No, dear, I don't sit on steps," she said.

Inside the convent, Sister A. led Lil down the front hall. The house had a musty smell of incense. Sister Annunciata took Lil's hand and led her up a back staircase, down a long hall of closed doors.

She put her index finger to her lips as she opened a door at the end of the hall.

"This is what we call the Jesus room," she said. "Reserved for emergencies." It was dark, and a small single bed was lit by moonlight from the window. "I have things to tend to now, so go to sleep and we'll talk it out in the morning."

"But—" said Lil.

"Shhh," said Sister A., and she closed the door, leaving Lil alone.

Hours passed, and Lil could not relax in her strange new room. She sat upright, swinging her crossed legs and biting her thumbnail. If she had been trapped at home, now she was trapped here, in the Jesus room, no less. Frying pan to fire. When she finally lay down, it was late into the night, and mercifully, she slept until morning.

TWENTY

FELIX HAD RUN around the living room, kicking at his rocking chair, banging his fists up against the living room walls, punching at his own drawings.

"No! Please don't! Oh, Luke!" He collapsed to the floor and begged on his knees. When that didn't work, he upped the ante, stomping his feet repeatedly, and chanting defiantly, "I won't go! I won't go." He hollered until his face turned dark as a thunder cloud, and as a last resort, he employed guilt. "How could you send me to the convent?" he wailed. "That one-eyed elephant! She's always after me! And what about Halloween! You promised, Luke, you *PROMISED* to help me with my costume."

Eventually, though, Felix trailed off into a whimper, and curled up on the floor.

"If anyone finds out I'm staying with the nuns, they'll laugh me to death. Who do you think I am, Alice O'Brien? It hurts! It *hurts*. You have no idea what happens."

Luke put a hand on his shoulder. "Felix, if only you could see into the future. Those kids who laugh at you, they have no idea who you really are. But Sister A. She told me she likes you. She's a smart lady, and don't forget, she understands about being . . . different. She's a nun; but she won't hurt you. I'm sorry I have to go, but I'll be back before you know it, hopefully with some good news."

"THIS LOOKS like a monster's house," said Felix, as they approached the convent steps.

Sister Annunciata met them at the door and led them into the front room, where Felix sat on the edge of the couch, idly running his fingers across its embroidered cushion. In spite of himself, he was curious about the large fireplace, and Sister A. said that they would have a fire for the costume party, and since he'd be staying with them, he could help them throw the logs and watch them light the kindling.

After a few minutes of small talk, which none of them were good at, Sister A. brought them upstairs to her private rooms. She had opened a cot at the foot of her bed, and Luke placed Felix's suitcase beside it.

"I have to sleep in here with you?" said Felix, addressing the nun for the first time.

"Yes, you do."

Felix turned to Luke and rolled his eyes.

After he crawled into his cot, Luke bent down and passed his thumb across Felix's cheek. "I should go. And look, I think you're going to have a great time. This is what I'd call an adventure."

"I don't like it," said Felix.

BACK DOWNSTAIRS, Sister A. had walked Luke Spoon to the door, and he apologized that he hadn't had time to make a costume for Felix.

"He has his heart set on being a devil," said Luke.

"Provocative," said Sister A.

"But isn't that the point of Halloween? Look, I think he should have his way with this. Once, his mother made him a similar costume."

"Did she," she said blankly. "I see. Well, we'll do our best."

"He's taking a lot of flak from other kids."

"It's Mike Fitzpatrick and his cohorts. I'll watch out for him," she said.

Outside, on the convent steps, Luke leaned in to kiss the nun's cheek before heading home.

BY MORNING, Sister Annunciata had a lot on her mind. She left Lil O'Brien alone for the time being, managed to keep Felix out of sight until the other sisters were up and out, and then she brought a bowl of oatmeal up to her room. Felix had dressed himself and was sitting on the cot with his feet dangling, shoes untied.

"Okay," she said, placing the oatmeal on a nightstand. "Once and for all, let's solve this problem." With great effort, she got down on her knees and gently took the laces of his shoes. "First this. See? And then you loop the strings, and now tie, like this, and then pull tight. It's that simple. Now, you do the other shoe."

Felix hesitated.

"Just try it," she said. "No one is here but you and me."

He made some progress, but the looping of the laces proved too difficult and he gave up, dropping them in a huff.

"Think," she said. "Try to remember what I said."

Felix picked up the laces again, and this time he was able to make the bow. Sister A. helped him pull it tight.

"Hallelujah! It's a miracle! Look there!" She grabbed his knee and shook it right to left. "Now, breakfast."

In silence, Sister A. watched him eat his oatmeal, spoonful by spoonful, until the bowl was empty. Once finished, he handed her his bowl.

"Thank you, Sister," she said.

"Thank you, Sister," he said.

"Felix, your father has asked me to help you with a Halloween costume."

"Never mind. I was supposed to be a devil, but I doubt you'd let me.

"Well, I have to think about that."

"I never even asked you to. But please, don't make me be a nun," Felix said. "You shouldn't be scared of the devil. My mother said the devil is just the bad mood of God."

"That's a good one," said Sister A.

"My mother's smart!" said Felix.

"I'm sure she is," said Sister A. "Look, I've decided that as long as your devil is clever enough to refrain from being mean . . ."

"I'm never mean."

"I suppose we could strike a deal."

"You'd help me? But how? How would we get the important ingredients? The horns and tail? It has to be a good costume," said Felix.

"We'll take a stab at it. Maybe some of the other sisters can help. Today, after school, wait for me by the church and I'll walk you back to the convent once everyone else has left," she said. "We'll work on it tonight."

He sat on the bed with his head down.

"You're welcome, Felix," she said.

AS FELIX walked toward his classroom, he wondered if Sister Annunciata slept in pajamas or kept her robes on. Tonight, he hoped to stay awake long enough to watch her sleep. So far, she wasn't as bad as he'd thought she'd be.

All day, through the slow dreary hours of school, Felix thought about the convent, and what his costume might look like. He longed to tell Alice O'Brien that he was staying there, but he couldn't catch her eye.

Alice had gotten even stranger. She'd stopped raising her hand in class, which was surprising because she always knew the answers. He'd hoped that she would develop an interest in him, but now she was far off in her own world, and he doubted that would ever happen.

Mrs. Dickson didn't seem to care; no one seemed to care about Alice O'Brien, and Felix felt sad whenever he looked at her. Her face was like a delicate egg, something he would treasure if he owned it; like his marbles, like the rock of God.

Everyone knew she'd been sent to live with the McCarthy twins. She must have done something bad to deserve that, but it was hard for him to imagine what Alice might have done. At the end of the day, he left a blue jay's feather in her desk.

LATER, AT the convent, dinner was served in the formal dining room. When Sister Annunciata led Felix into the room, he felt small as he walked by the long wooden table where all the nuns were seated. Their eyes turned toward him. First, he saw Sister Clare Veronica, the ornery one with the big thick glasses who, just the other day, had yelled at him for running down the hall. Seated next to her was Sister Ann, almost short enough to be a child. Sister John the Baptist was next. Her long, sharp fingernails were notorious in the detention hall for poking and pinching troublemakers. Sister Loretta, who'd been Felix's teacher last year, was at the table too. She was young and kind, but she didn't smile when he passed her.

As he looked down the line of familiar faces, all of them framed by their black habits, he was surprised to see Alice O'Brien's mother at the end of the table, her hair pulled back into a bun.

Sister Annunciata led him to a seat across from Alice's mother, then took her place between them at the head of the table. She tapped on her water glass.

Prayers were said, and all but Felix bowed their heads, mouthing words that were unfamiliar to him. Afterward the sisters passed the dishes around in silence. To Felix's left sat Sister Rita Joseph, a woman so old her hands shook. She picked out a chicken leg and plopped it onto Felix's plate, along with a spoonful of rice and peas. Aside from some muffled thank yous when dishes were passed, the only sound was the tinkling of silverware on plates. At several points throughout the meal, Felix locked eyes with Alice's mother, but she quickly looked away. The food was warm and tasty, better than what Luke could make, and Felix ate it all.

After the dinner the nuns removed the dishes—each had a chore—and quickly the table was cleared; not a crumb remained. The clanking of pots and pans resounded from the kitchen, and Felix was, at last, alone in the room with Mrs. O'Brien. Like two hostages with only a moment of privacy to spare, he whispered to her, "Why are *you* here?"

She whispered back, "I could ask you the same thing."

"My father had to go to New York City," said Felix. Sensing he had little time before the nuns would come back in, he added, "How come Alice lives with the twins now?"

Before Lil had a chance to answer, Sister Annunciata was back in the dining room, carrying a pair of scissors and a sewing basket.

"So, Mrs. O'Brien, you know Felix, isn't that right?"

"Yes," said Lil.

"Felix is going to be a devil for Halloween, and it's our job get his costume together. I invite you to stay and advise us."

TWENTY-ONE

Lɪʟ ʜ ᴀ ᴅ ɴ ᴏ particular expertise in Halloween costumes, and Sister A.'s invitation seemed more like an order than a suggestion. She'd spent the whole day doing convent chores, and there'd hardly been a word between her and Sister A. The nuns were interesting, though. It was not unfamiliar to her, this life of silence, as a hard silence had now lodged itself in her own home. Had Jim even tried to find out where she was?

One by one, the nuns returned to the dining room. Sister Loretta, despite her soft voice, was the tallest, youngest, and most athletic of all the nuns. She lugged an old sewing machine into the room and hoisted it onto a side table, then helped Sister Rita Joseph—unsteady even with her cane—to sit down before it. Tiny Sister Ann entered from another door, carrying a bolt of red fabric under her arm. She pulled out a chair and asked Felix to take off his shoes and step up onto the dining room table.

Soon Felix was surrounded by nuns, all of whom had been assigned to one detail or another in the making of his costume. The sisters, as if they were trimming a Christmas tree, made adjustments here and there. Those who were not busy with a task sized up the situation with folded arms, inspecting the work of others, nodding, and praising the progress. Sister John the Baptist rifled through the sewing basket, found a tape measure, and proceeded to measure Felix around the waist, legs and arms. She instructed him to turn this way and that until her measurements were completed.

Shortly, Sister Clare Veronica, who was not known for cheerful enthusiasm, burst through the door, holding a devil's tail and two horns that she'd fashioned out of some industrial red rubber kitchen gloves.

"Look what I've done!" she said.

"Marvelous," said Sister Ann, her voice like a squeak. "I wouldn't mind some horns of my own." She laughed at her own joke as she unrolled the bolt of fabric on the other end of the dining room table. Under the blunt instruction of Sister John the Baptist, who corrected her every move with her long-nailed forefinger, Sister Ann drew pant legs onto the fabric with white chalk.

Felix watched them from on top of the table, while Lil stood off to the side without a task.

When the costume pieces were cut out, attention turned to Sister Rita Joseph as she crouched over the sewing machine, straining to make sense of the knobs and clearly unable to see well enough to thread the needle. Slapping her hands to her lap, she called out to no one in particular, "It's been too long. I don't know how the darn thing works anymore."

The operation came to a halt.

Sister Clare Veronica, all too aware of the punishments of age, put a comforting hand on Sister Rita Joseph's back. The nuns glanced around the room at each other.

"Well, don't look at me," said Sister John the Baptist. "I couldn't sew a button on."

It wasn't right to blame the old nun, but the women weren't accustomed to failure, and their spirits fell in a swoop.

Sister A., putting her fists to her waist said, "Nobody in this whole outfit knows how to sew a pair of pants?"

Lil heard herself speak. "I can sew." The nuns turned to acknowledge her presence.

It was one thing to take a child in, but there had been some grumbling about Sister Annunciata allowing Lil O'Brien to stay in the Jesus room. Aware of the grumbling, Sister A. had assembled them all in the kitchen before dinner, reminding them that any visitor in the convent was really Jesus in disguise, and they should put their petty grievances to rest.

Turning to Lil with surprise, Sister Annunciata said, "Well, good. Have a seat, then, and let's get this costume sewn."

Sister Rita Joseph was led away and seated in the corner. It was only natural to forget things, someone said.

Lil took her place at the sewing machine.

She remembered that the last time she'd sat at a sewing machine was when she'd made a dress for Alice, before her troubles had begun. They'd pinned the pattern on the fabric together, then cut it out with pinking shears. Alice had been still and somber as Lil fitted the dress and made adjustments. The most difficult parts had been attaching the collar and, of course, the dreaded buttonholes. But somehow it came together, and when Alice stood before the mirror in the simple blue dress with the perfectly accomplished collar, she'd said, "Mom, do you think I'm pretty enough to wear this dress?"

Now Lil was nervous. All the sisters' eyes were on her, and it seemed absurd to be making a devil's suit for Felix Spoon while she had no idea what her own daughter was going to be for Halloween. Felix was the one who'd been accused of hurting Alice. What was she doing?

For fear of breaking down, she didn't look up. Instead she checked that the bobbin was properly wound and that the thread was secure on the spool pin. She adjusted the stitch length and the tension, threaded the needle, and then, laying the fabric under the presser foot, she began to turn the wheel, carefully. When she felt the soft puncture of the needle into the fabric, she put her foot on the pedal and slowly pressed down. The *whir* of the old machine was a relief to everyone as the first seam was sewn under Lil's trembling fingers.

The nuns formed a semicircle behind her as she worked. Felix climbed down from the table and stood beside Sister Annunciata. When Lil finished with the pants, having pulled the elastic into the waist casing, she held them up to inspect them and the nuns approved.

"All right, hand over the pants, and I'll sew on the tail," said Sister Clare Veronica.

Lil set to work on the shirt, which proved to be trickier. Sleeves had always been difficult, and then there was the zipper down the back, which required extra concentration. But the costume took shape.

And when it was sewn, a sleepy Felix Spoon stepped out of his clothes, too tired and excited to be self-conscious about undressing in front of a bunch of nuns.

Once Felix was fully suited, complete with horns and a tail, Sister Agnes lifted him back up onto the table. True, there'd been miscalculations in some of the measurements, and adjustments had to be made, but they'd successfully made a devil's costume. Sister John the Baptist had donated her red sleeping cap, having hand sewn the horns onto either side of it, and, though it was odd, everyone agreed that, when Felix's face was properly painted, he'd look less like he was wearing a sleeping cap and more like a devil.

"Well," said Sister John the Baptist, "It's not bad."

"I've never seen anything like it," said Sister Ann.

"It's a good devil," Sister Rita Joseph piped in, having recovered from her failure at the sewing machine.

Felix examined his arms and legs, and felt for the horns and the rubber tail, but he couldn't conceal his disappointment.

Sister A. said, "What's the matter, Felix? You don't like it?"

Cupping his hands to his mouth as if he could speak privately to Lil, he said, "It's not realistic unless I have a pitchfork."

The boy had a point; a devil should have a pitchfork. It suddenly seemed obvious, and the sisters were sorry that they hadn't thought of it. Now it seemed like a major oversight. They couldn't help it; they wanted a chance at the prize, because, as Sister A. had said many times, nuns were people too.

TWENTY-TWO

AFTER THE COSTUME was made, Lil went back to her quarters and sat on the small bed, mad as hell in the Jesus room.

The fuss about Felix Spoon—getting the tail to pin on just right, the horns and cap to fit his spoiled little head—and in the end, all he could say was, "Where's the pitchfork?"

She should be home with Alice.

And yet the Jesus room was perfect, even its scary name, and it had the most delicate white lace curtains that she had ever seen. A vase of straw flowers had been placed on the dresser. She ran her palm across the smooth cotton bedspread. Everything was just right, down to a simple wooden chair that faced out from the opposite corner. Aside from the crucifix, even the walls were unspoiled, bare and blue.

And someone—who?—had carefully tended to the bed, folding the thin blanket back to expose the lip of a clean white sheet. Her pillow had been puffed and placed against the headboard and a square of chocolate had mysteriously appeared on the bedside table. It was meant to be an honor to stay in this room, but they should have put the little devil in there. Lil felt more suited to the broom closet.

There was a knock at the door.

"Yes, hello?" said Lil. The door swung open.

Sister A. stood with her arms folded into her sleeves. She looked to Lil like a large black tombstone.

"Thank you for helping with the costume," she said.

Lil buried her face in her hands.

"What?" said Sister A.

"You told me I should come to the convent. You invited me. And now I'm here, and you've ignored me all day, only to put me to work making a costume for that boy. What is it about little boys? Didn't I tell you what the women are saying about him? What about Alice? Doesn't she count?"

Sister A. paused ever so slightly, reaching into her pocket for her hankie. "I've been busy; I'm sorry, I should have told you. I spoke to Felix, as I promised I would, and the incident in the cafeteria turned out to be my fault." Sister A. blew her nose and went over to the dresser to straighten the doily under the vase of flowers. "Straw flowers," she muttered, and then turning to Lil, she said, "Here's what happened. I gave the boy a gift, something to make him feel better after he'd gotten into trouble, and he wanted to show it to Alice. It was all innocent. Remember innocence?" She smiled widely, exposing her golden tooth. "He's trying to be her friend, that's all. Rumors fly in Hanzloo; I'm sure you've noticed that by now. There was no hurt, no harm done."

"What makes you think he'd tell the truth? That boy seems to get his way. His father, too. I saw you on the convent steps last night."

The slightest ripple of worry crossed Sister A.'s brow. "Well, there's a rumor that could catch. I guess you've figured out we're having a wild affair?"

It took a moment for Lil to understand that Sister A. had told a joke. But in that moment, truth and logic fell apart. "Of course, it's not my business, Sister. I wasn't meant to see, but I just happened to be there."

"I tried to tell you in the church the other day that I'm a person, too. There are people in my life. The boy needs a place to stay. His father has business in New York."

"Of course," said Lil. The nun's directness was disarming, but there was peace in her expression, an offering; an invitation that Lil was not sure she could accept.

"Why don't you tell me why you're here," said Sister A., idly rolling her fingers over her rosary beads.

"Things have spiraled out of control. People are talking about me. If the priests find out, they may call child services. Clarisse McCarthy told me that, and I believe her. I'm afraid I'll lose my daughter if I don't straighten myself out."

"Slow down," said Sister A.

"I've done bad things, and to my husband, too. I can't seem to fix any of it."

"One doesn't get through life without screwing up."

"Please don't tell the priests. Can I confess to you? I can't confess to them."

Sister A. moved over to the window and looked out at the sky. "I don't believe in sin," said Sister A.

"You don't believe in sin?"

"It's not the way I see it." Sister A. sat in the wooden chair and faced Lil. "Let's not talk theology. I'm not an authority figure, Lil. Who cares? It can never be figured out. What are you going to do about your problems?"

"I don't know. I hope I can speak frankly. I seriously wonder if I'm meant to be a wife. It seems unnatural. My husband, sometimes I don't even like him, much less love him. He's done nothing to deserve that. And then, to be a mother, it's a blessing, I know, but now I've failed at it. It's probably hard for you to understand."

Sister A. looked down at the floor and clasped her hands in her lap. She rubbed her thumbnail with her other thumb. "Not so," she said, after a while. "This may come as a surprise. How can I say it? I'm old, and you may not be able to imagine me another way, but I am a mother, too."

"What?" said Lil.

"Yes." Sister A. looked at Lil, her one eye a smooth window of gray glass. "This is not something I speak about. It's difficult. One confides as an act of faith.

"Yes, I have a daughter. So, I do know what it's like. I won't go deeper into my story, but I will tell you that my daughter is a grown woman now, and she despises me. I'm only telling you because I want you to know that I understand what it's like to have a child, and to lose one, and believe me, you don't want to let that happen if you can help it. You have to try to get your ducks in a row, Lil. You have to try. And try again. Maybe pray? There must be something . . . something out in the world that can help you."

"You may not believe in sin, but I don't believe in God," said Lil.

"Maybe life would be easier if you did, but I understand that," said Sister A., pushing her hands on her knees to stand. "Faith comes and goes. I don't know what you should do, I don't know what anyone should do, but you're welcome to stay here as long as you want." Sister A. looked around the room. "Forgive yourself here. You don't have to be perfect, even this room has straw flowers."

As the nun turned toward the door, Lil could not stop herself. "But, were you married once, Sister?"

Sister A. turned back. Her eyes narrowed, and she shook her head. "No, Lil. And it wasn't the Immaculate Conception, either. I was forced. I was raped. And that's that. End of story. Let's not speak of it again."

The nun left the room, gently closing the door behind her.

TWENTY-THREE

As the days stretched into a week, Clarisse McCarthy was more and more amazed. Sometimes she had to laugh out loud. Had she really gone to Luke Spoon's house and *skaaaa-roooed* him? Truly it was a dream, a thick, gooey dream. A gargantuan secret, too, nothing she could ever discuss with anyone, even Steph.

She found herself letting the phone ring and ring. Steph would just have to wait until Clarisse could think up some excuse for what she'd been up to. Right now, the risk of revealing any detail of her escapade with Luke Spoon was too great. This was serious, and Clarisse worried that sex was written all over her face.

She replayed the scene with her lover—she liked that word, she really did. Over and over, she recaptured the moments of delight. Remembering how he cupped her knees or fingered her earlobe could set off a rush of pleasure so deep that she caught herself uttering audible sighs in the middle of the A&P. She got aroused just thinking about anything having to do with him. Even picturing the front door to his house could do it.

She'd managed to reinterpret his remarks. Those words—*fast fuck*—at first she thought it was an insult, but wasn't it kind of a raw, sexy thing to say? She chalked it up to the grittiness of his passion, or to his fear of her. Maybe he was overwhelmed by the experience. It was intense and so completely out of the blue, even cool Luke Spoon might have been thrown off his game. She had triumphed. She'd been ballsy, and it paid off big-time.

All day long, she was a wet sexy flower. Sometimes she'd put her finger in her mouth, twirl it around, then trace the outline of her lips, remembering his kisses. She was sexy everywhere: in the drugstore, at the schoolyard, even in church. Her body was alive with desire. Two nights ago, she'd crawled on top of Frank, hot and ready—Frank had said, "Hold on honey, I'm exhausted." He'd rolled over, and, in moments, the start and stop of his snores made her think of a farm animal. Poor Frank. It was funny how she loved him more now. Her capacity for loving everyone and everything seemed infinite. Wide awake, Clarisse lay conjuring her memories of Luke Spoon and his long, sensitive fingers, his salty, sweet breath, and his hard, steady . . . what else could you call it . . . but a *cock*. In her mind, she heard herself repeat the word. Oh, the ways she could make herself laugh.

Normal, everyday, annoying tasks became carefree. Since her visit to Luke Spoon's she'd stopped worrying so much about Alice O'Brien being in the house. Alice had settled into their routine; she didn't cause trouble and her crying jags had ceased. Clarisse wondered how long she'd be expected to keep Alice, but there wasn't any hurry. She intended to call Jim and see how things were going, but for the moment, Alice was easy enough.

Halloween and the party at the convent were sneaking up, and though she usually felt pressure to come up with sensational costumes, this year she allowed the girls to decide for themselves what they wanted to be. They'd chosen characters based on the old maid card game.

Fawn chose Fifi Fluff, who wore a mink stole and walked with a poodle, and Dawn picked Ballet Betty, which was easy enough; all Clarisse had to do was find a pink leotard, slippers, and a ballerina skirt.

The twins had jumped up and down insisting that Alice be the old maid, and Alice stood there staring at the wall, twirling a strand of hair, clearly not pleased. Clarisse patiently bent down on one knee and told her that the costume would be fun, as it required a gray wig and spectacles, and she'd fish out some old-lady shoes from Goodwill and stuff them with tissue paper. Alice wrinkled her nose and confided that she'd rather be Flirtina Fairytoe, but when the twins got wind of that they started screaming No! Not fair! And Alice eventually acquiesced.

Honestly, Clarisse couldn't care less, and instead of agonizing over the costumes as she drove down Route 16 to the Farrow's Corner five-and-dime, she found herself lost in thoughts of Luke Spoon while humming along with Patsy Cline on the radio—*Crazy*.

Once inside the store, Clarisse stopped at the makeup counter and tested some rouge to add color to her cheeks. She examined herself in the small round mirror, puckering her lips and turning her face from side to side. The woman behind the counter offered her a sample perfume. She put some on her index finger and dabbed it behind her ears. Who cares, who cares?

She'd carried the three old maid cards in her purse so she could refer to them while shopping for the costumes, and she waltzed through the aisles of the five-and-dime picking up little things here and there—a pink bow for Ballet Betty, a hat for Fifi Fluff. She tossed her items into the basket and was in such a good mood that she toyed with the idea of making a costume for herself.

While walking back to her car, off on a side street, she discovered an antique shop that she had never noticed before. In the window, on big cardboard cutouts, hanging side by side, were the most wonderful Marilyn Monroe and JFK costumes. The Marilyn costume was a replica of the famous white dress that blew up around her legs in the movie *The Seven Year Itch*. Clarisse stopped short when she saw the costumes. People had often remarked that she looked like Marilyn. She'd have to do some convincing to get Frank to wear a costume, but it would be a riot, and he always appreciated a good joke. Clarisse marched into the shop and bought both costumes without even trying hers on.

As she left the store with her hands full of shopping bags, she wondered if Luke Spoon would be at the party. She fantasized about going *with* Luke. What if? Wild, wild scenarios. Suppose she married him. What if she and the twins and that boy and Luke were a . . . *what*? What if Frank . . . What if Frank *what*? There was just no way that any of this could come to pass, but in her private musings, her longing had become an ache that would not quit, and she flip-flopped between elation and despair.

Like a ferocious animal chained to a fence, she felt herself lurching to get free. I *have* to see him, she whined to herself, as she turned the key to unlock the car door. How could something so right be wrong? Her stomach churned with nerves, she almost felt sick, and she fished around in her purse for a cigarette but couldn't find one. Draping her arms across the steering wheel, she rested her forehead on her hands and closed her eyes. She saw herself in her Marilyn dress, twirling around the convent with Luke, like Marilyn . . . like Jackie O.

TWENTY-FOUR

In Farrow's Corner or Silverton, the day after Halloween was no big deal. Children sat with their friends or siblings, bags of candy dumped on their bedroom floors, examining the contents of their stash. They traded boxes of Good & Plenty for Tootsie Rolls or pennies for Gold Rush gum.

But in Hanzloo, the festivities were far from over. November first, All Saints' Day, the Catholic Church's celebration of its holiest souls, was a bigger deal than Halloween. Kids put their costumes back on, mothers painted their faces all over again, and families headed over to the convent for the costume party, where the nuns had been on an all-day super-cleaning fest, functioning as an elite special force, organized, obedient, and precise.

Early in the day, Sister Rita Joseph, now too old and weak to knead the dough for her goblin cookies, supervised from a chair, while Sister Loretta followed the elder's instructions. She squeezed the dough with her bare hands, adding orange food coloring until Sister Rita Joseph cried, "Enough, you'll turn the cookies red!"

The convent rooms were swept, and extra chairs were brought up from the basement. Sister Ann and Sister Clare

Veronica bickered about which candles should go where, but afterward, laughing about their foolishness, they made up and agreed to light the candles just before the guests arrived.

Vodka had been added to the fruit punch, and orange slices floated on its surface. Ovens were preheated, and pigs in a blanket, stuffed mushrooms, and bite-size spinach pies were arranged on baking tins and set out on the long dining room table, ready to be warmed.

SISTER ANNUNCIATA assigned Lil O'Brien the task of dressing Felix Spoon. The boy waited on his cot in his underwear. His bare feet dangled, not quite reaching the floor, and his hands rested on his lap. When Sister A. led Lil into the room, he looked away.

Felix's devil costume had been ironed and laid out on the bed. The shirt, pants, horns, and tail were arranged with care. On the floor sat the red slippers and leaning up against the bed was a pitchfork. They'd managed to find him one, which was not quite real and dangerous, but not exactly a plastic toy, either. Really, thought Lil, and he's still pouting.

"Felix, Mrs. O'Brien will help you dress." Felix idly banged his legs against the bed. "I must have cotton candy in my ears. Did I hear you say, 'yes, Sister'?"

"Yes, Sister." Felix had learned that it was best to say the things she wanted to hear.

"Hurry. The party's about to begin," she said, and left the room with a tablecloth hanging over her arm.

ONCE ALONE, Lil and Felix fell silent. Both were bewildered and deflated by their circumstances and had little to say. Felix finally spoke.

"Is Alice coming to the party?"

"I think she is," said Lil.

"What's she going to be?"

"I don't know," said Lil, as she moved over to the bed and picked up the devil's shirt.

"Are you mad at me?" asked Felix, lifting his thumb to scratch the back of his ear.

"No," said Lil.

"It's because I'm not your own child, right?" Felix was still sitting on his cot, looking at his lap.

"Let's just get the costume on, okay?" She held up the shirt and stood before Felix. "Can you raise your arms for me?"

"Did Alice tell you about the cafeteria?" asked Felix, reaching up.

Lil stiffened. "No."

"Most kids would tell. But Alice is trustworthy," said Felix, using Sister Annunciata's word. Felix put his head and arms into the shirt as Lil pulled it down to his waist.

"My father thinks she's a special person. He said she's beautiful in a very different way. He said that you are, too. He's a painter, and he knows," said Felix.

"That's silly," said Lil as she approached him with the devil pants. "You want to put these on?" She flapped them in the air in front of her to straighten them out.

Felix stood and looked squarely at Lil, who was kneeling before him, ready to have him step his foot into the pant leg. He put his hands on her shoulders to steady himself, and their eyes met. "You want to see what I showed Alice in the cafeteria?" asked Felix.

Lil pulled away.

"Everyone is always so sour," he said.

"Okay, I'd like to see."

"Really?" Felix smiled. "Can you close your eyes?"

Lil pretended to close her eyes. From her squint she could see Felix reach under his pillow and pull out a small red velvet box. "You can open up now," he said, holding the box in the palm of his hand. He opened it for Lil to see.

Lil stared at the dull gray stone. "What is that?"

"It comes from God's cave."

"Oh yeah? God's cave?"

"Don't you believe me? The nun gave it to me," said Felix solemnly. "She has powers. People don't know about her. I have to sleep in here and I wake up every few minutes, just in case she tries something."

"Oh, please," said Lil.

"No, I mean it." Felix began to whisper. "I think she might have taken my mother. And now my father's gone. Can you help me? What if he doesn't come back, and I'm stuck living here? She told me I'm a lot like her. I don't want to be like her. If I have to live here, I'm afraid my eye will fall out."

Lil softened. "Look, I'm sure your father will come back."

"But my mother said that she'd come back, too. You're not my mother, and I'm not your child," said Felix, as a matter of fact. "Everything's wrong."

"Felix, I really don't think that Sister A. took your mother. Your imagination is running away with you. Don't you ever ask your father about your mother?"

"He doesn't like to talk about her," he said.

"What happened to her?" Lil asked gently.

"I don't know." Felix turned to Lil. "I guess you don't know."

"I don't," said Lil.

They were silent once again while she zipped up his shirt.

After she finished clasping the devil horns to his red cap, and his tail was pinned on, she helped him into the red slippers. Lil handed Felix the pitchfork and led him into the other room to stand before the mirror.

He stared at himself blankly. "Does it look good?" he asked.

"I think so," she said.

"Really?"

"Seriously, Felix, it looks better than I thought it would. You do look like a devil," she said.

"Do I look mean? I don't want to get in trouble."

"No, you don't look mean, but you look scary enough that no one will bother you," said Lil.

Felix lingered in front of the mirror examining his costume, turning at different angles to see it from all sides.

"Kids are mean to Alice," he said, still looking in the mirror. He talked on, as if looking at himself made it easier. "They're mean to me, too. But I don't mind as much as she does. How come you sent her to live with the twins? The twins are bad. It's not her fault that kids are mean to her, she's just different, that's all."

"But, Felix, that's not why she's staying there. It's not anything that Alice did. It's really about adult things," Lil said.

"Well, if I were you, I'd take her home," said Felix.

"It's time. The party's starting."

Lil sensed that Felix was losing his nerve as she ushered him to the back stairs.

"Aren't you coming?" he asked her.

"I'll wait a little while," she said.

"Do you want me to sneak Alice up here when she comes?"

"No one has to sneak," said Lil.

"I spend my whole life sneaking around," he said, feeling for the horns on his head, like an athlete adjusting his gear.

"I will come down to find Alice. You don't have to worry. But, wait," she said. "I think you could use some special eyebrows." She fished a small stick of red chalk out of her pocket and drew two downward pointing lines above his eyes that gave him a permanent scowl. "Am I ready?" said Felix.

"Yes," said Lil.

Felix took his pitchfork and turned to go.

TWENTY-FIVE

SKELETONS, PIRATES, A milkmaid, witches, and several cowboys were among the contestants who trickled into the convent on the unseasonably warm first night of November. Most of them held the hand of a parent as they filed into the front hall quietly; their footsteps could be heard shuffling across the wooden floors.

Sister Clare Veronica had put the sound effects record on, and the old house resounded with the racket of hooting owls, screaming witches, and creaking doors. The combination of dimmed lights and flickering candles caused shadows to quiver on the walls and ceiling, and some young goblins peered out from behind their masks, more than a little spooked. Entering the gigantic front room, they came face to face with their hosts.

At the bottom of the grand staircase, the nuns, shrouded in black habits, stood in a line, ready to receive their guests. Families made their way past the nuns, exchanging awkward and respectful greetings.

Sister John the Baptist, first in line, looked through coke-bottle glasses and colorless eyes. Known for pulling children by the ears, she now held a basket of M&M's and candy corn. She offered her goodies to those who passed in the welcoming line, and children warily reached in for their treat, half expecting a whack on the wrist.

Sister Rita Joseph had to sit on a chair, and beside her stood Sister Ann, who made a point of complimenting all the costumes, careful not to play favorites. But Sister Clare Veronica, crabby by nature, just kept saying, "BOO!"

Sister Annunciata was last in line. With her worn-out face and ragged eye patch, she looked more like a contestant than a host. Upon seeing her, one small, confused witch, who didn't recognize her principal, shouted out to no one in particular, "What kind of creature is that?"

Stephanie Conte and her husband, Victor, were among the first to arrive. One of their boys was Bozo the Clown and the other was Frankenstein, although his plastic mask was already up on his forehead.

"I always forget how strange this party is," Victor whispered to his wife.

Soon the children started to relax and interact with each other, while most of the adults found their way to the punch bowl.

Father Moore, looking eight months pregnant in his long brown cassock, stood nearby, rosy cheeked, with glass in hand, having already dipped his cup twice. He had a taste for the drink, and the round, bumpy nose to prove it. His assistant, Father Aloysius, was bald with a pockmarked face, but for whatever reason, people seemed to like him more because of it. The priests couldn't resist making jokes about taking bribes for the contest.

FELIX STEPPED carefully down the back staircase. With every step, he imagined becoming more and more a devil and less and less a boy. He endowed himself with special powers, like a finger that could burn a hole in someone's arm, and a foot equipped with an automatic knife, easily activated by kicking. He thought of his tail as a poisonous snake in disguise, and if need be, he could use it to squirt venom into someone's eyes. By the time he reached the bottom step he felt ready for the party. Roaming stealthily among the guests, he tried to make out who was who behind their masks. He passed a cowboy and a cop—boys from the fourth grade whose names he didn't know—and he spotted a rather lame pair of ghosts, who'd simply cut eyeholes into a sheet. Presumably a baker, Margaret Lawler, Felix's classmate, clutched a rolling pin and wore a big white hat. She was holding hands with her best friend, a nurse with a stethoscope around her neck. But there were no other devils, as far as Felix could tell. Adults towered above him, faceless, and for the most part, nameless. He looked for Alice but didn't see her.

Chubby Thomas Walsh approached him. Thomas wore a black choir robe and held a gavel in his hand. "I'm supposed to be a judge," he said with a smirk. "I like your costume. Where did you get that?"

Felix offered him a menacing stare.

"Stupid. You can't scare me," said Thomas, but he veered away.

Felix headed to the food table and took one orange goblin cookie. There he ran into Sister Annunciata, and she bent down and shouted in his ear. Her breath was heavy and hot. "Are you up to something?" she yelled above the din.

Her head was so close to his face that her eye patch brushed against his cheek. He longed to see the empty socket, as if it would be a hole into her brain. "Where have you put my mother?" he wished he could ask, but instead he just said, "No, Sister, I'm just being me."

She smiled at him and placed her hand firmly on his shoulder. "Okay, then, run along."

Felix took his cookie and snaked his way through the party until he found a spot for himself underneath an end table. He crouched there and watched.

His mood slid quickly, which led him to thoughts of his mother. And then, where was his father? Maybe his parents weren't dead but simply through with him. Even Mrs. O'Brien, who seemed nice enough, had made Alice go live with the McCarthys, and look what happened to her. Alice had gotten so strange. The problem was that if your parents left you somewhere, the real you could wind up disappearing, and even though you would look like you, you wouldn't really *be* you anymore. If he got stuck with the one-eyed nun, he'd have to run away.

A COMMOTION stirred at the entrance to the party room. The McCarthys had arrived. The guests parted to make way for them, delighted that the whole family had dressed up.

First came the twins. Dawn, a ballerina in pink leotard, wide net skirt, and white tights, had her hair pulled into a tight bun on the top of her head, and she wore a jeweled crown. Next, Fawn, in a tight red skirt, wrapped in a fake mink stole. She wore a pillbox hat adorned with a peacock plume. In her hand, she held a leash and dragged a stuffed poodle alongside her.

Behind the twins, Mrs. McCarthy was there with her husband on her arm. Her shiny white dress, which tied around her neck, drew even Felix's eye to her rather large *bazookas*—as the boys at school called them. Her hair was curly and wild in a way that it never was. Mr. McCarthy, who was a pretty fat man, was wearing a suit that hardly buttoned. He stood beside his wife, grinning.

It took Felix a moment to find Alice.

She was standing off to the side, but even as he spotted her, it was hard for him to believe that it was Alice. Instead of her long orange braids, her hair was gray and pulled into a low bun on the back of her head. Her dress was the color of charcoal, and it fell to the middle of her legs. A lumpy red sweater was buttoned over her shoulders, and a large purple purse hung on her arm. Her shoes reminded Felix of Sister Annunciata's, black mounds of clay. Even her face looked old behind a pair of wire-rimmed glasses. She looked to Felix like a tiny grandmother.

LIL O'BRIEN had slipped into the room in time to see the McCarthys' entrance. She zeroed in on Alice, who stood by the wall, her gaze fixed on the McCarthys as if she were the family dog. Clarisse and her family made their way to the food, leaving Alice behind.

Lil quickly skirted around the edges of the room. Above all, she didn't want to make a scene. Alice's eyes brightened as Lil approached her.

"Mom! *You're* here?"

"Yeah," said Lil, crouching down. She took Alice's hands with both of hers and held them to her lips.

"I'm the old maid," said Alice, blankly.

"Oh, Alice," said Lil.

Alice frowned. "Is it not a good costume?"

"No, it's a . . . wonderful costume. A very interesting one," said Lil.

"I didn't want to be the old maid. I had to," said Alice. She stared out into the party.

Lil wrapped her arms around her. "Are you okay, sweetheart?"

Alice whispered urgently into her ear. "Sneedler's gone, maybe dead." But as quickly as she said it, she pulled away, changing the subject. "Are you sure my costume is good? Please don't muss it, Mom," she said, shaking free from Lil's arms. "I think I have to go stand with them."

"No. Stay here with me," said Lil.

"I don't think so. Mrs. McCarthy said we're a team. We have to stick together."

"Alice, it's me . . . you don't have to worry about them."

"I have to do it, Mom."

"I don't understand. What do you have to do?"

Alice looked across the room where Teresa Sepolino, was forming a line for photographs. A small platform, draped in velvet, had been set up for the photographer who'd been hired to take photos of all the children in their costumes. He adjusted his camera on a stand.

Some of the children stepped up for their picture in groups of four or five, and some in pairs. Clarisse McCarthy stood in the middle of all the children supervising, a glass of punch in hand. With her other hand she frantically waved for Alice to come over.

"I have to go," said Alice, quickly hugging her mother.

Mike Fitzpatrick and his friends closed in on Alice as she crossed the room. They were laughing at her.

"Hey, Grandma!" said Mike Fitzpatrick, holding his nose.

Felix left his post under the table and met her in the middle of the room, and the boys dispersed.

"Alice," he said. "It's me, Felix."

"Yeah, I know. You're supposed to be the devil, right?" said Alice, looking him over. "Pretty good costume."

"Yeah. But yours is *so* good. I didn't recognize you at first."

Alice shrugged. "I'm the old maid."

"You should be on TV."

"I should?"

"Would you get your picture taken with me?" he said.

"I'm not really allowed. I have to do it with the twins because we're all from the same card game," she said. She started to walk on, but Felix grabbed her arm.

"Please."

"I don't know," she said, glancing around to see if anyone noticed she was talking to him.

"Come on," said Felix. "No one else will take their picture with me."

"Okay. Maybe. But first I have to do it with them."

CLARISSE MCCARTHY, having quickly downed her glass of punch, zigzagged over to Alice, swooped in, and grabbed her by the hand. "We're waiting for you!" she said, ushering her over to the photographer's station, where she arranged the girls on the black velvet platform, placing Alice in the center.

"Now, sweetie, just stand holding your pocketbook in front of you and stare straight into the camera. Don't smile!"

She directed Dawn to Alice's left, and Fawn to her right.

"They look darling," declared Ginny Rice, from a cluster of mothers who had gathered to watch the photo shoot.

"I smell first prize," she whispered to Vicki Thomas. Clarisse McCarthy had done it again. The photographer snapped the picture and the flash went off.

Felix tugged on his coat and said, "Can I go next, Mister?"

The fact that Teresa Sepolino had a line of children waiting didn't seemed to matter to the photographer.

"Come on, quick. It's our turn!" said Felix, grabbing Alice. They climbed onto the makeshift stage, and Felix held his pitchfork to one side as he took hold of Alice's hand.

"No, no, NO! What are you doing?" yelled Clarisse. The photographer stepped back from his camera, as Clarisse clunked up to the platform in her white high heels. "You've had your picture already, Alice. You don't belong in this one." She pulled Alice by her purple purse. But someone called out, "What's the problem here?"

Clarisse, recognizing Luke Spoon's voice, swung herself around so quickly that her foot slipped off the platform, and her left breast popped out of her dress.

"Darn it!" she said, embracing it with both hands as if it were a newborn puppy. The slightest smile brushed across her lips. There he was—her *lover*—standing before her, his arms akimbo.

Luke laughed. "Come on, let them be, Clarisse."

"Luke!" cried Felix, raising his pitchfork.

"Hold on, son, stay right there. I brought my camera, too.

Luke Spoon peered through his camera. "Clarisse, you're in the shot." He waved her away, slightly amused.

Frank McCarthy, who had been outside smoking, now wandered back into the party and, sensing his wife was at the center of a commotion, came to see what was up.

"Sweetie, what the hell?" he said, when he pushed to the

front of the crowd. Clarisse was breathless, on the verge of hysterics, whether it was tears or laughter, or some kind of impression of Marilyn Monroe, he couldn't determine.

"Oh, Frank, I'm fine," she said. "It's no big deal."

And everybody laughed. What better entertainment could there be than the juxtaposition of Luke Spoon and the exposed breast of Clarisse McCarthy? It really was a high-light.

Luke called out to Felix and Alice, "Stay right there you two. Let me grab a few more shots." He snapped five pictures in rapid succession.

LIL WATCHED the picture taking from across the room. It was surreal to be an onlooker, as if the town had taken possession of her daughter.

Lil couldn't help thinking that Clarisse McCarthy, with all her rules and regulations, had killed Alice's Sneedler.

She ducked up the back staircase to the Jesus room and began to gather her things. Once the party was over, she'd take Alice home. She'd have to make it right with Jim somehow, and she'd tell Alice that Sneedler wasn't dead, and in fact, he'd never die; he'd be with her forever.

Lil left the Jesus room determined to go back to the party with her head held high, but she stopped when she saw a woman sitting in a wooden chair by one of the doorways in the long hallway. The woman was wearing a satin dress, the color of orchids, and it hugged her body's every curve. Her black hair was cropped close to her head, like a boy's, and she sat with her legs crossed, one foot nervously bobbing up and down. She was smoking a cigarette and flicking the ashes on the floor. She looked up at Lil. With heavily made-up eyes and thick red lips, she looked like an actress in a French film—pretty, but not dainty—and Lil didn't get the feeling she was dressed up for Halloween. Nor did she get the feeling that she was glad to be discovered there.

Before they had a chance to speak, footsteps trampled up the back stairs, and Felix Spoon charged through the door. One of his horns had fallen to the side of his cap. The boy's father followed close behind him. Felix stopped short, as Joni snuffed her cig with her foot.

A REUNION with his mother was something that Felix had imagined many times, though on this crazy night, when everyone seemed like someone else, it took a moment for him to believe that she was really there. Silently, he looked her over.

First it was her big black eyes, then her cheeks, and then . . . her lips. He knew the way she turned her lipstick tube, how she pressed her lips together, how she checked them in the mirror. *Com'ere, Felix, let me put some color on your cheeks.* And there were the tiny lines around her eyes.

"Mother," he thought he said. But no sound came out. He tried again, and then again, until he heard the whisper of his own voice. "Mother."

"Hey there, buster," she said, reaching out her hand.

A terrible sadness crept into his face. He felt his lips pull into a frown, and his breath took him by force until tears flowed down his cheeks.

Joni knelt down in front of him and took his hands. "Felix, what's the trouble? It's okay."

Felix just shook his head no. He closed his eyes, and crawled into the cave of his mother's arms, giving way to a kind of resting that he hadn't felt since the day that he'd come home from school and Luke told him she was gone.

In time, Joni set Felix back on his feet. "You look so grown up and *beautiful*. But where did you get this crazy costume?"

With his eyes locked on hers, he whispered, "All the nuns made it. And her." He pointed at Lil.

"Her? Who's her?"

"Alice's mother."

"I heard about Alice. Luke told me about her." Joni turned to Lil. "Hello, Alice's mother, I'm Felix's mother, Joni. You must be Lil." She reached out her hand and shook Lil's.

Lil was not accustomed to feeling envious. But the sheer strength of Joni's handshake stirred her. So, this is what happens when you live in New York City. You wear shiny dresses, you paint your face with bright colors, your eyes are fierce, and you *know* you're right. Strength is beauty. You don't mince around.

"What about this contest?" said Joni to Felix. "Are you going to win? What do you think?

"I don't care about it," he said. He looked at Lil. "I don't care."

Joni put her hands firmly on his shoulders. "Come on, sport. Let's have some fun, like we used to do."

Felix wiped his eyes with two fists, but then he took his mother's hand, and his father's, too. Joni led the way, a vision in purple, and Luke Spoon, who had scrambled the wild imaginations of the women in Hanzloo, now seemed demystified, following his wife and child in benign devotion.

Lil wondered how it could be so easy. What kind of confidence was this? To leave your child for a year, and then come back one Halloween and say, "Now let's have some fun?"

Maybe it was that easy. Maybe, if you had a little nerve, anything was possible.

THE KIDS were lining up for the big moment. Huddled in the far corner of the room, Father Moore and Father Aloysius looked over their list of contestants.

"Who the hell is that?" Clarisse blurted out to no one in particular when she spotted Luke and Felix Spoon being led across the room by the raven-haired bombshell in the purple dress.

"Huh?" said Frank, and then, "Wow."

Everyone took notice. It had to be his wife. So that was Mrs. Spoon.

Clarisse glared, idly licking her bottom lip, as Luke and his family made their way through the guests. She seethed as Lil O'Brien followed close behind them. Of course Luke Spoon would pull a gorgeous, young, sophisticated wife out of his back pocket.

Clarisse could have sobbed right then and there. She could have fallen to her knees in anguish, but she had the good sense to know when a battle was lost; you don't look back, you forge ahead. It was time for the contest, and she wanted to win.

MOTHERS RUSHED to straighten their children's costumes and prepare them to parade across the room.

Frank snuck up beside Clarisse and slipped his arm around her waist. "Hello Marilyn," he whispered into her ear.

He wasn't Luke Spoon, but he was hers. "Frank," she said. "I have to get the girls ready."

"Okay, sugar. I want to see a prize this year!"

"Ha," she said, and pecked him on the cheek.

Clarisse pushed through the crowd, deciding how to arrange the girls. When she caught up with them, they were a mess. The twins were jumping up and down. First, she rearranged Dawn's ballerina bun, pulling it tightly on the top of her head until the girl cried, "Ouch!" Moistening her fingers with her tongue, she flattened a few loose wisps of hair. She reapplied their lipstick. Fawn's peacock feather had drooped and needed propping up.

"Now, Alice, darling," Clarisse said, as she yanked Alice's dress and buttoned her sweater, "I want you to walk a few steps behind the girls and stare straight ahead with a frown. Don't look around, okay? Remember, you're the crabby old maid. Do you think you can do that?"

Alice nodded yes.

To her girls, Clarisse said, "You two wave and smile, okay? And Dawn, you can do some twirls. And Fawny . . . just pretend you're Mommy and give 'em heck. Now, all three of you, listen to me carefully. When you get in front of the priests, for heaven's sake, look them in the eye. Got it?"

The girls held hands and danced in a circle.

NOW THAT masqueraders were ready, their parents lined the sides of the room, revved up on cookies and punch. Lil had wanted to speak with Alice, but when she saw her with the twins, she thought better of interrupting. Instead, she secured a spot beside the Spoons.

The parade of masqueraders began. Though many of the costumes were unremarkable and ordinary, having been conceived in a hurry, without much thought, no one minded. There were some repeats from last year, a tired Raggedy

Ann costume had worked its way down through a family of four sisters, and everyone recognized the Harris kid's scarecrow for the third year in a row. Early on, little Julie Murphy, dressed as a cat, ripped off her ears and stood pouting at the front of the line, until her father was called in to remove her.

One of the favorites was a two-headed monster: two boys from the fifth grade who'd managed to fit themselves into a ketchup-stained sheet with one neckhole. Fake fangs in their mouths, they growled as they crossed the floor, trying not to trip over each other.

Alice and the twins had been placed toward the end of the line, and when it was their turn, they rose to the occasion. Lil waved at Alice as she passed, but Alice stared ahead, walking slowly in her heavy shoes and clutching her purse. The twins, like contestants in a beauty pageant, blew kisses as they went.

The girls presented well, each taking a moment to turn in a circle so the priests could examine them closely.

A reluctant Felix Spoon was the last child in the line. His mother stood behind him, and when his time came, she gave him a push.

Sisters Ann, Clare Veronica and old Rita Joseph paused, dirty paper plates in hand, to watch the boy. It wasn't right for the sisters to be partial, but they were rooting for him.

Felix Spoon blossomed. He held his pitchfork high in his hand and marched triumphantly across the floor. When he reached the priests, he bowed deeply, causing an uneasy ripple of laughter to flow through the crowd. There was no denying he was a captivating devil.

Father Moore and Father Aloysius stood with pad and pencil in hand, scribbling their observations. Now they compared notes to decide upon the finalists, while Sister Ann stood by with a bumpy sack of prizes.

Father Aloysius stepped up and tapped a fork against a water glass to hush the crowd. "May I have your attention," he bellowed. "We'd like to see the following contestants back on the floor." The room settled.

Sister Annunciata emerged from the kitchen, dishrag in each hand, and poked through the crowd in time to hear that Felix had been called to step into the center of the room with the other finalists: the two-headed monster, the McCarthy twins, and Alice O'Brien.

The six finalists lined up before the priests, who stood with crossed arms. "Can we see the two-headed monster, please?" said Father Moore.

The two-headed monster had trouble maneuvering. After a long night of operating as one entity, the boys had grown irritated with each other. Their neckhole had loosened considerably, exposing the tops of their shoulders. But they had made their own costume, and originality certainly had to count for something.

Dawn McCarthy was called up next. She performed an impressive assemblé but lost her balance at the last minute. She made a graceful recovery, lifting her chin to finish, and the two priests nodded approvingly.

Fawn followed her sister. Dragging her stuffed poodle behind her, she posed coquettishly with her hand on her hip. When she took her final turn around, Father Moore said, "Lovely, dear. I like your feather!"

Alice O'Brien was next in line, but her nerves began to eat at her, and she froze when Father Aloysius called her name. "Earth to Alice," said Father Aloysius.

"I'll go," said Felix Spoon. "She's scared."

"But there's nothing to be scared of. This is supposed to be fun," said the father, looking around for confirmation. "Come ahead, Felix Spoon."

"What am I supposed to do?" asked Felix, as he stepped forward, holding his pitchfork, tines up.

"Well, do what the devil would do. Within reason, of course," said Father Aloysius.

Felix thought about it.

"I don't like this game," he said, laying his pitchfork before the priests. He looked back toward the crowd to find his parents. A murmur ran through the party. When Luke Spoon stepped out onto the floor and took Felix's hand, Clarisse couldn't help but whisper to her husband, "Great, you can cross him off the list."

Now the focus turned back to Alice, as Father Aloysius said, "Okay, Miss O'Brien, this is your moment. It's now or never."

Dawn pinched Alice's arm. "Don't be dumb!" she whispered.

Alice stepped up and faced her judges somberly, still clutching her purple purse with both hands as Clarisse McCarthy had instructed her to do.

"Well, dear, I understand you're the old maid from the famous card game. Show us, what would the old maid do?" said Father Moore.

Alice lifted her hand and pointed at the priests. She drew her face into a knot, and wagged her finger at them, as if they were children who were being punished.

The last thing the priests expected from Alice O'Brien was a scolding, and they burst into laughter, which quickly spread to the audience, as Alice took her place beside the twins.

The priests spent some long, tense minutes coming to their decision, while the finalists fidgeted in the center of the floor. Finally, Father Aloysius tapped on his water glass.

"We've chosen," said Father Moore. Silence fell over the crowd, but for one small child, who could be heard whining, "I want to go home!"

"And third prize goes to: Tom Harris and Joe Echy as the two-headed monster!" said Father Moore. Cheers went up, and the two boys, as if they couldn't wait a moment longer, threw off their sheet and separated with great relief.

Tiny Sister Ann came forward with the prizes: two plastic statues of St. Patrick. The boys examined the statues, and then hoisted them high into the air.

Father Aloysius tapped again on his water glass. "And second prize goes to Fawn McCarthy! AND . . . Dawn McCarthy! Let's hear it for the twins!" The girls glanced around, confused. "You both won!" said Sister Ann, rushing in with two ceramic statues of the Blessed Mother. "Look how special these are," she said, as she handed the girls their prizes. "They came all the way from Rome!" Though the McCarthy twins understood that they had not won first prize, Sister Ann's enthusiasm was infectious. They took their statues and kissed them and then held them high, just like the boys had done.

As Alice O'Brien watched them raise their statues, she longed to be included, and wished that she, too, could hold hands and hug them. But now the attention fell on her, standing alone before the judges.

"Alice O'Brien, why so glum?" said Father Moore. "You've

won first prize!" Sister Ann scurried out once more, this time with Alice's prize: a large crucifix, about a foot long. Nailed to it, a silver Jesus. She placed it in Alice's arms like a baby, and applause rose to fill the room. When the twins gathered around to examine her prize, it didn't take long for all the little girls of Hanzloo to come running out from the sidelines and circle around Alice in a frenzy of congratulations. Everybody loved the winner.

TWENTY-SIX

AFTER THE CONTEST, the party thinned out. The floor
was littered with soiled paper plates, crumpled napkins, and
discarded masks. Sister Ann pushed a wide broom across
the floor, and Sister Clare Veronica collected the melted candles. Clarisse lingered by the punch bowl, receiving congratulations from guests who were on their way home, while her
husband helped the nuns with some of the heavier chairs.

Her girls didn't win the top prize, but the fact that Alice
O'Brien had triumphed turned out to be working in her favor.
The women, who had been standoffish of late, now warmed
to her. Even Ginny Rice offered a compliment on her way
out. But out of the corner of her eye, as she shook hands and
smiled, she saw Luke Spoon, his arm around his wife.

"What you did for Alice," whispered Steph, as she collected her cookie tin and prepared to take her family home.

"Well, it's about time something good happened to
her," said Clarisse. "I really didn't do anything anyone else
wouldn't have done."

Clarisse didn't quite believe that and hoped Steph might
take a minute to point out that none of the others had been

willing to step in on Alice's behalf. But Steph said nothing more, and despite the endless stream of compliments, Clarisse felt lonely and unappreciated. Still in her Marilyn Monroe dress, she stood by the punch bowl wolfing down pumpkin cake, consumed by disappointment and humiliation. What had she thought? Luke Spoon would run away with her?

Across the room, Luke's wife idly ran her fingers through her son's hair. Soon those fingers would be all over Luke, like his had been all over Clarisse. And now Lil O'Brien was sidling up to both of them, and Luke was waving his hands in some expression of thought. Clarisse could tell they'd all made friends. Dammit. Poor Jim O'Brien. She envisioned him slouched in his chair in front of the TV, popping Cheez-Its in his mouth.

But then Lil headed across the floor, stepping among the fallen paper cups and napkins, to speak to Clarisse. "Thank you," she said. "Alice will never forget this."

Clarisse's eyes tightened slightly. "I'm sure you'd do the same for my girls." But Clarisse knew it wasn't true, and she sensed that Lil couldn't say goodnight fast enough. "Why don't you let Alice stay with us one more night. I promised them an ice cream party if they won."

The girls, as if on cue, skipped over to their mothers.

"Mom," said Alice. "I won!"

"You did!" said Lil.

"Was I good?" The bobby pins had loosened on her wig, and strands of her real hair were falling in her face.

"You were great, Alice. I laughed out loud."

"Mrs. McCarthy said we could have an ice cream party when we get home."

Lil flinched at Alice's use of the word home.

"Well, gee, an ice cream party. But . . . I thought you and I would go home and see Dad. He'll be so excited."

"No!" said Dawn. "Why? *Alice!* Why can't you come with us?" She glared at her mother. "You said!"

"*Pleeeease,*" begged Fawn. "We can have chocolate sauce, all we want!"

Alice looked to her mother. "It would be fun to have an ice cream party. Mom, can I come home tomorrow?"

Lil didn't have the heart to say no.

"Don't worry, we'll bring her home first thing in the morning. I don't know about anybody else, but I'm pooped. I've got to get these kids home and get myself out of this dress," said Clarisse.

Alice walked away in the jumble of Clarisse's family, and though Lil didn't like it, she knew it was only for one more night. Things would get better now. She sat on the stairs and watched as Clarisse and Frank gathered the children's coats. Alice turned back and waved just as they slipped out the door.

SISTER ANNUNCIATA had taken Felix upstairs to her room to pack his things. She flopped his open suitcase on her bed.

"You do the shirts and I'll take care of the pants."

They folded the clothes quietly, until Felix spoke. "Do I have to get out of my costume?"

"The party's over," she said.

"I wish you didn't have to be so grumpy all the time," he said.

"Am I being grumpy?"

Felix continued to fold the shirts. Once the clothes were

in the suitcase, Sister A. went around the room to check for anything that might have been left behind. She pulled down the covers on his cot and lifted his pillow.

"Look here," she said. "The rock." She picked up the box and set it on the dresser.

"But that's mine. Are you taking it back?" he asked.

He sat down on the cot with his head drooped, too tired to do battle with her. "You once told me you liked me.

She lifted her hand to adjust her eye patch. She was tired, too.

"Everything about me is not like other kids," he said.

"Yes," she said, sitting down on the cot next to him. She took his hand and put it in her lap. "In answer to your question about whether I like you or not . . . the truth is, yes, I like you very much."

He looked up at her, surprised. "Sister, would you let me see your eye socket?"

"For heaven's sake, Felix, why in the world you want to see it is a mystery to me. But, all right. Have a peek." With difficulty, she drew the elastic band over her head and removed the patch. Felix stared. Where the eye should have been there was only rough skin, and a scar. "Oh, no," he said, sucking air through his teeth. "I feel bad for you. May I touch it?"

"If you must."

He reached his hand up to her eye, and carefully moved his fingers over the area, as a doctor might do.

"It feels like lips that were sewn together," said Felix.

"Interesting," she said.

Sister Annunciata closed her other eye. The gentle roving of his fingers was oddly comforting.

"Does it hurt?" he asked.

"No. Not anymore," she said.

"What happened?" he asked.

"You know, Felix, I've never quite figured out how to describe what happened. But there are worse things than losing an eye."

"It's pretty bad," said Felix, taking a moment to think about that, as he continued to touch her scar gently. When he was done, he stood before her, and studied her missing eye from further away.

"You have taken care of the rock," she said. "You kept your promise. Now I'm sure you're trustworthy. Here, pack it with your things." She reached for the red velvet box and put it in his palm, closing her hand around his. "You'd better run downstairs and find your parents. You don't want them to forget you, now. Go."

Felix rushed to the door, but then stopped and turned back. "My mother said we're moving back to New York City."

"I guess so," said Sister A.

"She said you are my grandma. She said you are her mother. Is that true?"

"Did she?" Sister A. looked away for a moment. "Well, maybe it's hard to believe, but yes, I guess I am your grandma."

Felix shook his head. "Everything about me is unusual. Why?"

"Join the club, Felix. It's a mystery."

"Will you ever come and visit us?" he asked, idly turning the doorknob back and forth.

Sister A., slouching now, just looked at him, holding her eye patch in her hand.

"Should I just leave now?" he asked.

"Oh Lord. Let's think about that," she said.

Felix shrugged, embarrassed that he'd asked.

"Come," she said.

He walked slowly toward her and she put her arms around him. Soon he was cloaked in her robes, and it was warm in there, almost hot. He felt her hands move up and down his back, and she rested her chin on the top of his head. For a moment he thought it was possible that Sister A. *was* God's cave. It made sense to him in a way.

"Am I ever going to see you again?" he asked.

"I hope so, Felix, but for now goodnight," she said, releasing him.

Felix took a long look at her.

"Sister, I'm sorry you have something like that on your face. Maybe you should put your patch back on. Someone might make fun of you."

"That's good advice, Felix. Thank you."

He ran out the door and down the stairs, suddenly worried that his parents might leave him there again.

TWENTY-SEVEN

LIL CAME HOME from the costume party and found Jim asleep on the couch in his boxers and socks. It crossed her mind that they should throw the couch away; maybe even rearrange the furniture in the room. The moon, shining like a spotlight on a dark stage, lit a glass of whiskey and an ashtray full of cigarette butts that had spilled over on the table beside the couch.

Jim bolted upright, half asleep. His hair stuck out and he tried to palm it down. "Lil? Is that you? What's going on? Did something happen?" His slender arms held him up on either side, and his belly protruded over his boxers.

"Nothing's wrong. The costume party was tonight, and I decided to come home."

"Oh God, Lil, thank you."

He was a silhouette across the shadowed room.

"Come sit down," he said, patting the couch beside him.

Lil took off her scarf and coat and hung them up. The smell of her own house came at her like a bad memory. So much had happened, but nothing had changed. Keeping the lights off, she walked over and sat next to her husband. He nestled his face into her neck. "Oh, sweetie," he whispered.

"I'm sorry that I left, Jim. I needed a little time." She let him nuzzle her neck and shoulders. "Alice won first prize."

Jim pulled back in surprise. "No kidding! That's great! What was she?"

"The old maid," said Lil.

"Ouch," said Jim.

"I know, but somehow it was okay," said Lil.

"I've been thinking. Maybe this Clarisse thing isn't such a good idea."

"I tried to bring Alice home, but she wanted to stay with the twins for one more night, and I didn't want to tell her no. Clarisse had promised them ice cream. She was having a good time; it was sweet. Tomorrow she'll come home, and we can start from scratch around here."

"I love you," said Jim. "These past few days have been hell. I'm sorry I went behind your back with Clarisse. She means well."

"It's okay," said Lil. "I'm the one to blame."

"It's not your fault. You've had to put up with me," he said, with a sorry smile. Lil wondered why he said things like that.

"Things have to change," she said. "I'm not sure how, but . . ."

Jim kissed her cheek. The kisses accelerated, and soon he was down the road to his own particular brand of love-making. His breath smelled sour from sleep and whiskey, and though everything in her rebelled, she succumbed. Just minutes after arriving home, her days at the convent seemed like a hazy dream, and any yearning to return to them was futile. No matter what Sister A. had said, a nun could never understand that sex was part of the job of marriage.

Jim reached for her hand and placed it on his crotch. He panted softly. "I love you," he said again. "You have no idea."

"Jim, not here, let's go to the bedroom."

"No sweetheart, it's okay," he said, maneuvering her around. He wriggled out of his boxers and tossed them across the floor, leaving his socks on. "You are so damn beautiful." He pulled up the skirt of her dress, rubbed himself against her legs, and with his free hand kneaded her breast. She turned her face into the couch cushion, and waited for him to finish, knowing it wouldn't take long. He pushed himself at her thighs in desperate thrusts, and then, with one final heave, he shot his love all over her legs and dress. Uttering a muffled sigh, he called out her name, collapsed his head onto her chest, and began to cry real tears. "I'm sorry, I was too fast. I love you," he said again.

Underneath him, Lil felt the full burden of his weight, and his stickiness all over her legs, as she stared at the ceiling. She didn't doubt his love. But where was hers? Vaguely, she noted how an hour ago she'd been talking to Luke Spoon about New York City, as if it were perfectly possible that she might go there someday. If he could see her now, pinned underneath her gently weeping husband.

Lil patted Jim on the back.

"Oh, Lil, life is so short," he said, after a few moments. "You just never know what can happen. Sam Chinsky had a heart attack today."

"Oh no," said Lil. "Really?"

Jim lifted himself off her and climbed around to sit on the edge of the couch. He grabbed for his glass of whiskey and straightened a snuffed cigarette from the ashtray. "Yeah, the ambulance came, and I saw it from the front window, so I went out. Hedda was a mess, crying and everything. They wheeled him out of the house on a stretcher and put him in the ambulance, but they wouldn't let her ride with him, and said she'd have to follow in the car. Apparently, he stood up from the dinner table, and just fell over. I should have offered to drive her, but I . . ."

"What? But you what?" asked Lil.

Jim lit the stub of the cigarette. "I'd already had two drinks, and I didn't want to drive. I'm such a jerk. Not only was she hysterical but also, you know, she doesn't see too well. Sam does everything for her. I felt like a shit."

"Is he going to be okay?" she asked.

"I have no idea."

Lil gathered herself on the couch, leaving a space between them. She sat with her elbows on her knees and her chin in her hands. "I just spoke to him a few weeks ago. About pruning the rosebushes. He was so kind. I must have looked like a wreck. They're good people even though the kids don't like them."

"The *kids*? I think it's obvious who doesn't like them."

Jim got off the couch and put his shorts back on, relieved that Lil was home, and some semblance of closeness hung between them.

"Poor Sam," said Lil. She'd have to visit Hedda tomorrow, maybe make her some cookies. But now, all she wanted was a hot bath.

AFTER THE girls had eaten all the ice cream they could, Clarisse tucked them into their beds, not bothering to bathe them or braid their hair. Traces of Halloween makeup still smudged their faces. She kissed them goodnight, nestled their prizes under the covers beside them, and left them in the attic room with the lights out.

"Good job tonight, girls. You made me proud," she said half-heartedly. Despite sweeping the top prizes in the contest, Clarisse felt sick to her stomach. Her love affair meant nothing. It was over, and now there was only life as it had been before.

She thought about Lil, who would probably make friends with Luke's pretty wife, and they'd all have dinner parties and talk disparagingly about Clarisse. Lil only had to be her nutty little self, and everybody fell at her feet.

Clarisse paused by the mirror in the hallway to examine her image in the glass. Her made-up face stared back at her. All the prizes in the world could not make Luke Spoon love her. Forget about love, how about a little affection? He'd barely said hello to her tonight. She ran her hand across her lips and watched herself kiss her own fingers. She'd been duped. The whole thing was a big fat joke. She felt empty, yet full. Full of pumpkin bread. What an appetite she had. Insatiable, it seemed.

As soon as Clarisse was down the stairs, Dawn sat up in bed, reached for the lamp on her nightstand, and turned on the light. "Let's get up!" she whispered.

Alice was so tired, she couldn't think.

"I'm almost asleep," whined Fawn.

"Come on. Up," said Dawn, pulling down her sister's blanket. "You too, Alice. I'm too happy to sleep. Let's compare prizes." In a flash, both twins were standing over Alice's bed holding their Blessed Mother statues. Fawn rubbed her eyes with her free hand.

"Can I see the cross?" said Dawn, shaking Alice's shoulder.

Alice sat up, clutching the crucifix in her lap.

"It's *really* pretty," said Dawn. "I like the way Jesus is silver. You're so lucky."

"I like yours, too," said Alice.

"Can I touch it?" said Dawn, putting her hand around the crucifix.

Alice tightened her grip, and a slight tug-of-war ensued.

"Pretty please," said Dawn, "I just want to hold it by myself."

"It's mine," said Alice, softly.

"I *know* that. You're being selfish," said Dawn, crossing her arms. "Can't you share?"

"Do you promise you'll give it back?" asked Alice.

"If you don't share, I'm telling," said Dawn, turning to her sister. "Fawn, let Alice hold yours for a minute." She took Fawn's statue and handed it to Alice in exchange for the cross. Fawn didn't seem to mind.

"Sister Ann said ours are from Rome," said Fawn.

Alice took the Blessed Mother statue and moved her fingers over the ceramic folds. "I know," said Alice. "It's nice."

"Big deal. Everybody knows Jesus is more important than Mary," said Dawn. She turned the crucifix around, examining it from every angle. "This is so neat. You know, if I keep yours and you take Fawn's then we won't be stuck with two of the same."

"But . . . I won, and it belongs to me," said Alice, trying to be reasonable.

"It's not fair that we have to share a prize. We always

have to share, just because we're twins. My mother made your costume, and that's the only reason you won. You should be nicer to us," said Dawn.

Alice looked to Fawn to see where she stood on this, but Fawn shrugged. Dawn twirled around the room cradling the crucifix in her arms, until she made her way over to her bed, where she laid it on her pillow. "Oh, pleeeease, Alice, I love it so much! Can't you just give it to me? I promise to always be your friend."

In a rare show of nerve, Alice rushed across the room, and stood over Dawn. "No," she said. "It's mine. It's the first time I've ever won anything. You have to give it back."

Alice, taking advantage of her size, managed to pull the crucifix away from Dawn and scamper back to her own bed. She pulled the covers up to her chin and curled up around the crucifix, turning toward the wall.

Fawn stood uneasily in the middle of the room in her flowered flannels, as Dawn hopped off her bed and headed back toward Alice.

"You're mean," she said, growling in Alice's ear. "Nobody likes you. Especially my mother. She said it's like you're *retarded*. Even your own mother wants to get rid of you. There's something wrong with you, and people think you're ugly, too. Because of all your freckles. Freckles are poison spots."

With both hands, Dawn grabbed Alice's head and pulled her hair. Then she dug her fingernails into Alice's cheeks, making deep scratch marks across her face. Alice felt the sting of tears spread over the scratches.

"Give it!" said Dawn in a low whisper, and Alice handed over the crucifix. Dawn stomped back to her bed. "Everybody, go to sleep," she snapped. Fawn scurried across the room. None of them said a word, as they turned in their beds, and Dawn switched off the light.

AN HOUR later, Alice lay awake. With Dawn's scratches sore and puffy on her cheeks, she tried to suppress her tears, and the result was a kind of quiet sniffling. In the darkness, terror gripped her. Dawn had morphed into a monster, lurking at the far end of the room.

She wanted Sneedler. But he would never come into a house like this, even if he were alive.

He had been her best friend, and she never treated him the way she should, making him wait outside of school, thinking of him last, considering him a bother. No wonder he died. It must have been from sadness because she left him on his own. Alice imagined him curled up and stiff, with a trickle of blood coming out of his nose, like a dead cat that the neighborhood kids had found in the woods.

Her cheeks were hot, and she covered them with her palms. The ridges of blood had hardened. Across the room, the twins' light snoring was steady, and a reminder that they might wake up at any moment. Alice dared to open her eyes to the darkness as images of the Halloween party raced through her head. The two-headed monster, Felix Spoon in his devil's suit, and even some nuns tumbled through her brain in chaos.

She sat up, swung her feet to the floor, and saw by the light of the moon that her clothes lay folded on the end of the cot. *I'm going home.* She'd have to walk in the dark, but the streetlights would be lit.

Careful not to wake the twins, Alice stepped into her

pants and pulled her shirt on. She clutched her shoes in one hand and crossed to the stairway. By the dim glow of a night-light, she grasped the railing with her free hand, and tiptoed down the stairs, stopping short when the third stair creaked. More slowly now, she reached the bottom step.

She had to make it past Mr. and Mrs. McCarthy's room without disturbing them. Their door was ajar, and a slant of light confronted her as she turned the corner, giving her a start. She held her breath until she was safely past them, and down several steps to the living room.

Opening the front door could be a problem. If it slammed or squeaked, Mr. McCarthy might think she was a thief, and he'd come bounding down the stairs, mad enough to hit her. She gathered her nerve and turned the knob, relieved to find the door unlocked. It opened easily, and a cool gust of night air blew in against her. Her arms began to tremble as she stepped outside.

Night had no borders. The vast darkness offered little to rely on. Now she was in a wilderness. She sat down on the porch steps to put her shoes on, feeling the cold con-crete against her feet and bottom. With her ragged nerves, it was hard to tie the shoes, and she left the right one undone, impatient to get home.

All she had to do was walk down the driveway, turn left, and make it past the Chinskys' house. Her parents would be glad; they'd think she was brave. She hoped her mother would make a cup of Ovaltine and wipe her face with a warm cloth. She hoped her father would say that Dawn McCarthy was in big trouble now.

Alice made her way down the driveway, running her hand against the McCarthys' station wagon to steady herself. It was hard to see anything, even her hands. By the time she reached the end of the driveway, she had nothing to hold on to, and she stood where the driveway met the cul-de-sac, peering into the darkness. To her right were the black, silent woods. Across the street, the Contes' house was dark. As far as she could tell, not one light was lit on Mundy Lane; even the streetlamp was off. Only the moon offered its glow.

A rustling of leaves in the trees on the edge of the woods to her right startled her, and fright propelled her out into the pool of darkness toward home. She hurried down the street, clutching her arms. On her left, the outline of the Chinskys' house reassured her, but when their mailbox seemed to dance, as if it were alive, she began to run, and she tripped on her loose shoelace. Falling to her knees, she curled her face into her lap, and rocked back and forth, gasping for air.

"Alice! Turn around!"

Who's voice was that? Like a talking doll.

"It's me! Sneedler."

Alice lifted her head. Had she imagined this? She knew that Sneedler never spoke with words. Was it a trick? She dared to turn toward the voice, and there, as clear as he had ever been, Sneedler stood at the mouth of the woods, waving.

"Hi!" he called, as if it wasn't the middle of the night, as if he wasn't worried, as if everything was fine. Her heart flooded with relief at the sight of him skipping down the street. He smiled with big rubbery lips and knelt before her. But when he saw the scratches on her cheeks, his head crumpled, like a wrinkled beach ball. His face turned blue, and red sparkles floated in his eyes.

"What happened to you?" he asked, taking her hand.

Alice noticed that he had a dark bruise on his chin.

"What happened to *you*?" she said, reaching for his face, but her fingers went right through it.

"Don't worry, I fell down in the woods is all. Why so sad? We're back together again."

"How come you can talk now?" she sniffled.

"I've always been able to talk, but I never had to, because you were listening." And for a moment, Sneedler disappeared.

"Please, don't go!" she said. "I'm scared!" When she opened her eyes, he was there again.

"Easy. Easy. Relax," he said. "Tell me who scratched your face."

"Remember Dawn? Remember how I got sent away?"

Sneedler looked at one of her cheeks and then the other. "Ouch," he said. "I don't like Dawn. I know what, let's get out of here," and his head ballooned back up.

"But, I want to go home. I'm *homesick.*"

He sucked air into his balloon head. "Yeah, but you belong with me," he said, sadly. "I'm the only one who can take care of you." His lips puckered up.

Alice looked up at him. "But, you're . . ."

"What?" asked Sneedler.

"You're . . . *imaginary,*" said Alice, trying not to hurt his feelings.

Sneedler's head collapsed again. "But you could say that about anybody. What's wrong with being imaginary? It doesn't mean I'm not real."

Alice almost understood what he meant. She studied him in the darkness. Sneedler, with his plastic face, was like a toy. No doubt his clothes were painted on. Yet he was real as the moon. There'd been many days that she'd been impatient with him because he was hard to understand—he was *there,* but then he really *wasn't* there. She thought about the time she'd forced him into her bottommost dresser drawer and left him for hours, even though she knew it was mean. She told him he was dumb. And, now, all this time, it turned out he could have said something to her, but he didn't, and that was confusing, too. Certainly, he was smarter than she'd imagined, and what if he was right about being the only one in the world who could care for her? She spoke up, not sure she wanted to hear what he might say next. "But . . . I want to see my mother. Can't she take care of me?"

Sneedler's head formed a parallelogram. "Alice, you've got to listen to me. Your mother is . . ." He paused here and clasped his hands. "She's like a trampled flower; it's as if her stem got broken and the flower part of her is face down in the dirt. It's hard to take care of anyone if that happens to you. You see what I mean?"

She searched his face, trying hard to understand.

It was then that a bleary-eyed Hedda Chinsky, at her wit's end, having spent the night in intensive care holding the hand of her dying husband, came barreling up Mundy Lane in her 1955 pale yellow Oldsmobile. Hedda didn't see Alice O'Brien kneeling in the middle of the dark road.

Alice heard the car and turned in time to see the wide vehicle and its bright headlights, like a spaceship that had landed on the street.

Alice felt a terrible pain, she felt it deeply; it was everywhere, all over the world, and her heart exploded like a bomb. For a split second, she thought she saw her mother; but it was Sneedler. He took her hand, and the pain stopped, as if she, too, had turned into a rubber toy. Sneedler knew her inside and out, and he was her friend. He was the one who told her the truth, and though she didn't want to hear it, she felt it wash over her like a warm bath, and her cheeks felt better, and her breath slowed down, and she and all her tears evaporated into the cool autumn air. "Hold on," said Sneedler.

Alice watched—wide-eyed—as her street got smaller. She saw the whole town of Hanzloo shrink below her, and shortly, the entire state of Pennsylvania took its long rect-angular form. And then, the United States, like a puzzle map with different colored states, appeared in its entirety, and the earth eventually rounded into a blurry distant orb.

TWENTY-EIGHT

ALICE O'BRIEN'S DEATH changed the town of Hanzloo in ways that would only become clear in time.

The tiny cemetery, out on the county road a half mile from Ginty's Stables, had twenty-five plots, and couples crammed under umbrellas in the drizzling rain that Friday to watch in disbelief as Alice's small casket was lowered into the muddy grave.

Lil O'Brien, seeming lifeless in a pale pink raincoat, stood with Jim at her side. His arm was curled around her shoulder, and he held an umbrella above her head. It was odd the way she didn't react much, and Father Bruno droned on, reciting prayers for the dead.

Earlier, at the wake, Jim hung around the entrance to the funeral home unable to stop weeping. He chain-smoked on the steps while Lil sat in the parlor with her head down. Sister Annunciata claimed the chair next to hers, and served as a sort of guard dog, waving people away who lingered too long.

It was only when Felix Spoon arrived with his parents that Sister A. got up. The Spoons had heard about Alice and postponed their trip back to New York City. Felix was the only child there. He was dressed in a little suit and wore a red bowtie. His hair was slicked back from his face with some kind of gel. Who would bring a child to another child's wake? Mourners looked askance at the sight of the boy who was holding his father's hand as he approached Lil.

He stood before her in silence. Lil took his hand. "I'm sorry about Alice," he said. Finally, and for the first time, tears flooded her face, but she could not speak.

"May I see her?" asked Felix, turning to Sister A.

Sister Annunciata took hold of his elbow, gently leading him to the open casket.

The two of them knelt at the coffin, and Felix rested his fists on the white satin cloth that fell in ruffles over its edge.

"I'm not afraid," he said.

"Good," said Sister A.

"What happened to her cheeks?" he asked. The scratches remained visible under the waxy makeup. "Did the car do that?"

"I don't know," said Sister A.

"She looks like a doll," he whispered reverently.

"She's asleep," said Sister A.

"She's dead, Sister."

Sister A. put her hand on top of his.

"It feels like she's still here, though," said Felix. His eyes moved slowly from her orange braids, down the length of her green velvet dress, and all the way to her shiny patent leather shoes. "I tried to be her friend, but it never really worked," he said. "Don't cry anymore, Alice."

"Hmmm," said Sister A.

"Can I tell you a secret?" said Felix.

Sister A. tilted her head to hear his secret.

"I wanted to grow up and marry her," he said.

"Oh, Felix," said Sister A.

"And look," he continued, opening his palm. "I have the rock. Do you think it would it be all right if I put it in the bed with her? When I showed it to her, she kept her promise. I want to give her something that's important."

Sister A. lifted her arm and cloaked the boy with her heavy robe. "Okay," she said. "Do it now."

"Yes?" he said. He slid the rock under Alice's satin pillow. "Is that good?"

"There," said Sister A. "And now starts your new life."

THE MARKS on Alice's face were a much-discussed mystery. The police had concluded that the scratches were self-inflicted, adding to the general assumption that Alice had been troubled and perhaps couldn't handle winning first prize in the contest. No wonder, considering her mother's recent difficulties.

Lil would not allow an autopsy; even the mere mention of it sent her into hysterics.

But many questions lingered, and when asked why Alice might have wandered out into the street in the middle of the night, the twins looked confused, giving no indication that anything had been wrong when they went to sleep that night. In fact, Dawn, with a whimpering Fawn beside her, told the police officers the story of how Alice had traded prizes with her. Clarisse repeated to anyone who would listen: "I wish you could have seen how happy Alice was."

In the following weeks, the leaves fell off the trees, and winter crept in. Lil felt like a snowman, melting in the sun.

At first her feelings had been frozen, but with every passing day, the painful thaw set in, and chunks of her seemed to disappear. Jim kept his distance.

And what does one say to a mother who's buried her child? Her sisters called from faraway cities but were relieved when no one answered. Eventually the phone calls stopped, a deadly silence gripped the house, and one day the door to Alice's room, slightly ajar, beckoned, and Lil went in.

Alice's orderly room had little clutter, and the bed, with its soft white quilt, was neatly made, just the way she'd left it. Alice's legless doll lay on the pillow with its head cocked to one side. Lil picked up the doll and buried her face in its hair, smelling it frantically, like a dog might.

Lil sat rocking back and forth on the bed clutching the doll and looked around the room. On the dresser, Alice's baseball mitt lay folded like a big brown butterfly.

"By the time you grow up, girls will be able to play baseball. They will. You wait and see. When I'm an old lady, you'll be pitching at Yankee Stadium in New York City, and I'll be in the bleachers cheering for you."

"How do you move to New York City?"

"It's easy enough," Lil said. "When the time comes, we'll go there, and you can have your pick of things to do. In New York City, you can be anything you want."

"You'll come with me, right, Mom?"

Lil closed her eyes, her nose nestled in the dress of the legless doll.

JIM GAINED six pounds by Christmas. Every night, when he came home, a hot meal awaited him. Lil avoided conversation.

"This is delicious," Jim would say.

"Thank you," Lil would answer.

The only person Lil saw was Sister Annunciata. She first came two weeks after the funeral and then once a week after that. An odd ritual developed between them. The first visit had been awkward. Lil welcomed her into the living room and offered her a cup a tea, but there was little to say after that. Sister A. noticed a copy of the children's book *Charlotte's Web* on the coffee table.

"Are you reading *Charlotte's Web*?" Sister A. asked.

"Sort of," said Lil. "I don't know why."

"Well, it's such a great story, isn't it? Would you read a few pages to me?" asked Sister A. "Just to refresh my memory. It's been a while."

Lil sat down beside her on the couch and began to read. After the first chapter, Lil closed the book.

"Oh, I loved that," said Sister A.

"I read out loud sometimes," said Lil, shrugging.

The conversation wandered to other things. Sister A. told Lil that Joni had sent some postcards from New York City. "I grew fond of that boy, I really did."

"You must feel sad," said Lil.

"Sad, yes." Almost everything was too painful to discuss with Lil.

"I never really said goodbye," Lil said, vaguely.

From that day on, their visits began with a chapter from *Charlotte's Web*, as if all that passed between them lay nestled within the unlikely friendship of the pig and the spider.

ON A cold January day, when the doorbell rang at the usual time, Lil wondered why Sister Annunciata would be coming again so soon. She opened the door and saw Clarisse

McCarthy instead. She almost slammed it shut.

Clarisse, bundled in her winter coat, wore no hat, and her blonde hair flew around in the bracing wind. She cradled Alice's crucifix in her arms.

"May I come in?" she begged.

Lil reluctantly opened the door. Once inside, Clarisse stood there, lost. "Oh, it's just so cold out there," she said, blowing on her fingers.

She offered Lil the crucifix with both hands. Lil noticed that some of her nails were broken.

"It was hard for me to come," said Clarisse, nervously looking around the room. "But this belongs to Alice," said Clarisse, as if the crucifix was a simple box of crayons.

"Are you crazy? I don't want it!" said Lil.

"Well, neither do I." Clarisse raised her hand defensively. "I know you're hurting, Lil. How are you?"

The two women stood awkwardly in Lil's living room.

"My family suffers too. Fawn is afraid of everything all the time, and Dawn . . . has been off the deep end with rage."

"Dawn has been off the deep end with rage since the day she was born."

"Please don't insult my children, Lil. I realize this is terribly difficult, but I didn't come here to fight," said Clarisse, looking down at the crucifix as if it were a small sacrificial animal.

"Why did you come?" said Lil.

"Well, this . . . it's an accomplishment of Alice's," said Clarisse, meekly.

"You're scaring me."

"It's a prize," said Clarisse. "I don't know. Something to take pride in."

"Clarisse, Alice is *dead*!"

"Don't say that! I feel so bad."

Lil stared at the crucifix. "Did you come here to be forgiven? Is that it?" Her arms began to shake.

"For what, Lil? What are you saying? I took her in. *You* weren't *able*. Alice *wanted* to come to my house that night. Why is everyone picking on me, dammit, I made the costume. She wouldn't have won if it weren't for me. She was so happy, Lil. You remember that." Clarisse was pleading.

"Won?" asked Lil. "What did she win, Clarisse?"

"The prize. *This*," said Clarisse, grasping for the literal meaning of things. She set the crucifix down on the coffee table.

"Who killed Alice, Clarisse? Who gets the prize for that?"

"I didn't do it. That's so unfair!"

"But I didn't say you did."

Clarisse threw up her hands. "It's easy to blame me. I give up."

"I'm not blaming you. It must have been my fault or mean old Hedda Chinsky's. She never hurt a fly, but let's blame her. Maybe the whole town did it. Thanks a lot for the crucifix, Clarisse," Lil said sadly. "Look what happened to God's child. Nailed to the cross. How about that for first prize."

"Oh Lil," said Clarisse. "That's not it at all."

"You explain it then."

Clarisse wrapped her coat tightly around her and looked down, speechless. For that moment, they shared the weight of Alice's death. Would there be no end to the blame they would now shoulder—inseparably—forever?

"I took a big risk coming here," said Clarisse.

"Clarisse, what happened that night? I'd like to hear it from you," said Lil, quietly.

Clarisse took a breath. "Lil, I don't know. Honestly. Nothing. We had some ice cream. I tucked them into bed. The girls said they got up after I left the room and played with their prizes and . . . that Alice traded with Dawn. Maybe she regretted that. I don't know what happened. Lil, I have to tell you that Alice was troubled . . . I mean, the poor girl, those scratches . . ."

"No, no, no, Clarisse. That's way too easy. Alice was sensitive. She was very sensitive. What happened in that bedroom?"

"What? My children are the pride and joy of this town!" said Clarisse, not able to control herself, or bear the thought that her girls were in question. "Frank and I are good people."

"Good people!" repeated Lil.

"You've always thought you were better than me, I know," said Clarisse. "But take some responsibility. You reserve the right to go crazy, as if you're somehow excused from the rules. Not everyone has that kind of permission." Clarisse was getting desperate. "Why do you even live in Hanzloo? You could have run off to New York City with Luke Spoon and his wife."

"Luke Spoon? This is ridiculous," said Lil. "I think you should go, now."

"I can't!" Clarisse tightened her arms around her coat and bent over, succumbing to tears. The loud, lurching sound of her cries was shocking. Lil didn't know what to do.

"Clarisse, get a hold of yourself."

"Don't kick me out. Please. I thought we were friends."

Lil had never seen Clarisse in tears before.

"Clarisse, we *can't* make this right, don't you see that? What do you want from me?"

Finally, Clarisse calmed down enough to speak. "Lil, I'm in a terrible mess."

Lil's eyes narrowed.

"Can I sit down for a moment?"

Lil was still shaking, barely holding back a torrent of rage, but she moved aside, and allowed Clarisse to sit on the couch.

"I'm pregnant," said Clarisse quietly. "From Luke Spoon."

"You can't be serious. Are you sure?"

"Yes, I'm sure. I use . . . birth control with Frank."

"Oh jeez," said Lil, not wanting to picture any of this.

"Obviously I have to do something, and I know that you know what to do."

Lil froze.

"Look, don't fly off the handle, but I know you were pregnant. Steph overheard a conversation between you and Doctor Garufee as you were coming out of his office, and she was in the waiting room. I figured it out, when I saw you . . . well . . . fall apart."

So, they both knew. She wondered now if the whole town knew but was not about to ask. Instead she said, "Really, Clarisse! Luke Spoon?"

"Please. It's painful enough," said Clarisse, pulling out a crumpled pack of cigarettes from her coat pocket. "I made a fool of myself. Will you help me, or not?"

"I can't help."

"Please. I need the number of the doctor who did—who can do—an *abortion*," said Clarisse, barely able to say the word.

For the briefest moment, Lil felt bad for her, but she resisted the urge.

"Oh, it's a sin, Clarisse, isn't it? Any priest will tell you that," said Lil, sure that Clarisse and Steph had condemned her to hell for it already, probably over cookies and tea.

"I have to do it," Clarisse said. "You know I do. I can't go to Garufee. He plays golf with Frank. Life is impossible, it's just impossible." She fumbled with a cigarette until it snapped in half and she threw it on the table.

Lil might have thought she'd be glad to see Clarisse this way, but she wasn't, and whatever ridiculous series of mishaps had led her to Luke Spoon's bed seemed irrelevant now. She hated that they were hopelessly tied together in the mess of their lives.

Lil tried to calm down. "There's a woman in Philadelphia," she said.

"A woman?" said Clarisse, afraid. "Is it safe?"

"It's illegal. But it was clean, and she seemed to know what she was doing. But, I . . ."

"What? Wish you hadn't?"

"No. I don't regret it," said Lil, emphatically, but then she looked away. There was no reason to rail against her because Clarisse was no longer Clarisse; she was somebody else now—just like Lil wasn't Lil. She bore little resemblance to the previous version of herself; someone that she'd never really been anyway.

Clarisse, rattled, stood looking at the rug, whimpering.

Lil went over to the piano bench and lifted its seat. She was not about to comfort Clarisse. Frantically rifling through the old music books, she found a thin wallet. In the wallet was a scrap of paper with the name and address of the doctor, Agnes Morris, in Philadelphia. She handed it to Clarisse.

"I took the bus from Silverton," said Lil.

"The bus?" said Clarisse, realizing how daunting that trip would be. Absurdly, she thought for a moment about asking Lil to go with her, but knew it was out of the question. "Thank you," Clarisse said under her breath. She turned to go.

Lil picked up the crucifix from the table. "Take it, Clarisse. Get rid of it."

A hollow expression crept over Clarisse's eyes as she took the cross, yet Lil remained unmoved.

Before she went out the door, Clarisse looked back. "Lil, why can't we be friends? We could set a good example."

Lil let out a desperate laugh. She shook her head, addressing Clarisse as calmly as she could. "Our acquaintance is an *accident*, if you'll excuse the expression. We live on the same street, that's all. That street is now the street where Alice was run over by a car! I can look out my front door every morning, afternoon, and night and see the exact spot where she drew her last breath. If there's any significant connection between us, Clarisse, it's that you and I both know that the scratches on Alice's face were not self-inflicted. Now please go away, and don't come back."

They locked eyes, momentarily paralyzed. Clarisse was frightened. She inhaled, as if she had something to say, but hurried out the door, firmly shutting it behind her.

TWENTY-NINE

By April, people were tired of the cold and the wind. A punishing ice storm froze the first crocuses and left trees burdened with heavy, glistening branches.

But May brought a welcome change in the weather and in other things, too. A young couple expecting their second child bought the Chinsky home. On a mild and sunny Saturday, neighborhood children sat in a line on the Contes' lawn, hugging their knees to their chins, and watched as the huge moving van pulled up to the curb.

To many in town it was a big relief. Having that house sit dark and empty for those winter months only served as a reminder of the accident. Some hoped the O'Briens would move, too. Wouldn't they be happier somewhere else, far away from the tragedy, where they could start over?

On a life-affirming note, Clarisse McCarthy had ballooned up rather nicely, expecting her third child, surprising everyone in town.

"At least it's not twins," she'd said to Steph, rubbing her belly when she broke the news.

"Another baby. Well, you and Frank make beautiful kids,"

said Steph, but she wondered: had they never heard of birth control? No one is *that* devout.

Clarisse had spent the past few months ruminating on her last visit to Lil's house. For Lil to suggest that her girls had anything to do with Alice's death was downright mean. The twins could be feisty, but it didn't make them murderers. No one in their right mind would accuse her six-year-olds—really—after all Clarisse had done for poor Alice. Lil was crazy.

The twins were victims, too. One day, while changing the children's bedsheets, under Fawn's pillow, Clarisse had discovered a drawing; a frowning face with black and red crayon marks drawn harshly across it. Clarisse had taken Fawn aside for a private talk.

"Why draw something like that?" she asked, cutting the picture up with a scissors. "It puts bad ideas in your head."

Fawn stood there sucking her thumb, twisting a strand of hair with her finger. When pressed, she blurted out, "I'm scared. Of Dawn." Tears followed.

"Oh, honey. Take that thumb out of your mouth and listen to me. Dawn is just going through a phase." Fawn stared at her blankly. "A phase is something . . . that you go through. Oh, com'ere." Clarisse drew Fawn into her embrace and kissed her forehead. "In the meantime, drawing pictures like that can only lead to nightmares."

Clarisse would not allow herself to get pulled into gloominess. She wished she'd never made the visit to Lil's, and one day, she threw Alice's crucifix in the trunk of her car, drove to Farrow's Corner, parked behind the old abandoned movie house, climbed up onto the filthy, rusty dumpster, and tossed the prize into the jumble of garbage, snagging her nylons in the process. The crucifix landed underneath the legs of a discarded rocking chair, and Clarisse lifted a damp, mildewed rug from the rubbish and threw it across the chair.

Back in the car, she wiped the dirt from her hands and skirt with a Kleenex, then checked her face in the rearview mirror, feeling like a common criminal. But at least the crucifix was gone.

Still, the troubling behavior with the twins continued, and between Fawn's fearfulness and Dawn's tantrums, Clarisse had her hands full. One night, Dawn threw a sharp knife across the length of the kitchen. It flew through the air like a hatchet.

She'd grown weary of her children.

Of late, Dawn was refusing to wear the same outfits as Fawn, and where they used to be inseparable, now they were at each other's throats. One night at the dinner table, Clarisse shrieked, "You're getting harder to love!" The twins froze when she said it, and Clarisse ran upstairs, leaving Frank to handle the aftermath.

Sometimes, in the middle of folding the bath towels, or picking up Frank's work shirts from the cleaners, she'd be overcome by an intense longing for Luke Spoon, so powerful that she could almost smell him. Like an allergy attack, her desire would flare. And though she could not have him, she could have his child.

Once she had made her decision, she found that big-time lying was a piece of cake. Even to Frank. "I guess the rubber broke," he'd winked, hugging her tightly and grabbing her bottom. In fact, he was so thrilled to hear that she was pregnant, he had a dozen red roses delivered to the house the next day.

There was such a thing as a truth that worked for everyone. In a way, it was a sinless lie. One had to choose one's sins, and abortion was too frightening for Clarisse. Maybe it was that long solitary bus ride to Philadelphia that swayed her.

But still, there was the lie, and the deception weighed heavily. Clarisse retrieved her Bible from the basement and took to sitting with it once a day when the house was calm and quiet and the sunlight made patterns on the living room rug. She struggled to read one page at a time. It was boring. But touching the translucent gold-edged pages of the sacred book made her feel worthy.

That kind of effort had to count for something. She was sorry. For everything. She prayed herself raw until she sensed forgiveness for her affair, for lying about the baby, and she prayed for it to be true that Alice O'Brien had scratched her own face. No matter what Lil O'Brien said, the McCarthys were good people, and they would welcome the baby, their baby. Clarisse would have someone to love.

MONTHS LATER, when Clarisse ran into Lil at the pharmacy, Clarisse had ironed things out in her mind. All fixed up again—hair thoroughly blonde, nails manicured and painted pink for spring—Clarisse came barreling around the corner from the prescription desk and practically collided with Lil, whose eyes immediately fell on Clarisse's polka-dot maternity blouse. Clarisse looked around to see who might be nearby, as if she'd just stolen a tube of toothpaste.

"Lil," said Clarisse, in that way that everyone addressed Lil now, with a slightly downward tone, as though her very name was an expression of sympathy. Lil was pale from a winter of mourning, but her flawless skin was smooth as a pearl, and her reddish hair had grown full and long, curling past her shoulders.

"You look so nice, Lil," said Clarisse.

Lil said nothing.

"Beautiful day. Finally, right?" said Clarisse, witlessly glancing at a watch that wasn't even on her wrist.

"Don't talk to me," said Lil, and she hurried by to the exit.

LIL LOOKED forward to a time when she'd run into Clarisse and not be able to remember her name.

Some days were okay, even better than that, but sometimes she slipped into a darkness that scared her. She held on to household chores, because without the constant motion, blankets of grief could smother her.

She'd found a gentle soul in Sister A. Their weekly visits had continued, and Lil looked forward to them. They'd finished *Charlotte's Web* and were now a third of the way through *Stuart Little*. Once in a while, over the two jelly donuts that she always brought, Sister A. would share news of Felix. He was enrolled in a school in New York City that focused on the arts, which was mildly intriguing to Lil. And apparently Luke Spoon, upon leaving Hanzloo, had immersed himself in his paintings. As for Joni, she had softened toward her mother, perhaps because she was grateful to Sister A. for being kind to Felix, or perhaps because she was growing older. She was pursuing, well, Sister A. didn't really know. Something about a new kind of folk music. "Do you think she can sing?" said Sister A., always managing to make Lil laugh a little. Sister A. stayed clear of difficult subjects, but felt it was good for Lil to hear news from New York City.

SECRETLY, LIL started working on a poem. She couldn't be sure that she would finish it, but daily, after Jim drove off to work, she sat at her kitchen table with a yellow lined pad and a Montblanc ballpoint pen she'd found on the library floor. The sleek green pen felt smooth in the palm of her hand, and she'd slipped it into her purse instead of turning it in.

After two months, she'd filled up half the pad with her scribbles. Lines were written and crossed out or rearranged in different stanzas. While she sat there writing, time stood still, but no poem seemed forthcoming.

Inevitably, she'd scoff at what she wrote, close up her pad, and hide it under the cloth napkins and the coupons that she carefully cut out but couldn't remember to bring to the store.

ON A rainy Tuesday night Jim came home and, instead of pouring a drink, he stood in the kitchen with his hands in his pockets.

"I've been going to Alcoholics Anonymous. Do you know what that is?"

Lil was at the stove lighting a match to the burner. He stared at the floor waiting for her to turn around and say something, but she didn't.

"Do you think less of me?" he asked, his heart hammering.

There was a long pause. "No. Of course not. I love you," she said flatly, still fiddling at the stove.

Jim pulled a quart of milk out of the refrigerator, poured himself a glass, and sat down at the table, noticing that one of the bulbs had burned out in the overhead light. Maybe that was why the room looked so dim.

"Do you love me?" he asked, hunching over the table. He waited for her answer. Lil wore a faded brown shirtwaist dress, and her figure was so slight and delicate that just the sight of her made him worry. It occurred to him that he'd always been worried about Lil, ever since he'd met her. "Can't you look at me?"

Lil turned to face him and smiled blankly. "I'm here. I think it's good to stop drinking, it's wonderful, really, but I love you no matter what." She sat down, too.

What was she saying? She seemed a million miles away. "I'm a bozo," he said.

She laughed, or it was more like she pushed air through her nose. "You're funny. A bozo? That's why I love you, you make me laugh."

"You haven't laughed in forever."

"Laughed in forever, you see, that's funny too. I laugh inside," she said.

He watched the sorrow pass over her eyes, and he grabbed her wrists, urgently, as if he could somehow push it back. "Oh Lil, come on. I know that you think you've lost everything. But you haven't. People get through things. The stories I've heard at these meetings I go to, you wouldn't believe." Jim felt himself getting animated, in that way he used to do, before her illness, before the accident. "You and I have each other and there's no reason to think we couldn't—I don't know—move away from here. Have another child!"

Lil pulled her hands away from his and wiped them on her dress.

"I'll try, I really will," she said. "She's gone—that's that— right? We have to get on with it." She smacked her fist down on the table, causing Jim's glass of milk to tremble, and Jim pulled away, alarmed. "Why couldn't I be the one to die?"

A pot of water was heating on the stove. She got up and took a package of peas out of the freezer.

"Are you hungry?" she asked.

Jim was tired, and he wished he could have a whiskey; he could almost taste it in the back of his mouth. Instead he got up and took some plates out of the cupboard and set them on the table. He watched his wife, in her old brown dress, as she poured the peas into the pot, as she placed a hand on either side of the stove and leaned there, waiting for the water to boil. Everything about her seemed entirely ordinary, yet he knew that she was far out of this world.

THIRTY

"THE DOOR WAS open," yelled Sister A. "And nuts, I forgot the jellies," she added, hobbling across the room in her habit, fidgeting with her eye patch. Her rosaries swung into a small pile beside her as she thumped down on the couch.

Lil came out of the kitchen, drying her hands on her apron. "You're early," she said. "I'm just heating up the coffee."

"Never mind the coffee, Lil, come sit, and see what I've got here. Open this. Luke Spoon is having a show in New York City," said Sister A. She held the envelope out to Lil with an excited, shaky hand.

Lil took the glossy card out of the envelope. Luke Spoon's name jumped out at her; the letters appeared to be cut from magazines or newspapers, and the title *Descent to Hell* in bold type was under his name.

"Oh, is that the name of his show?" she asked, running her finger across the words.

"Who knows?" said Sister A.

Under the title was an abstract painting, and at first glance it looked like a jumble of colors and nothing more. The earthy grays and browns, purples and blues were cool and edgy. But then she saw that, no, the painting was *of* something. When she recognized the devil horns, the image snapped into clarity like an optical illusion that suddenly reveals itself.

Lil let the envelope drop to the floor and held the card closer to her face with both hands. *No, no, no.* It couldn't be, but it *was*: Alice, dressed as the old maid. Strands of orange painted into her gray wig, and she was holding hands with the devil, Felix. It was Halloween all over again. Alice and Felix. *How could he?*

Lil's eyes raced back and forth from the image of Felix to the image Alice, as if by staring at them they might disappear. There must be some mistake. How could that man have used Alice like this? And what about Felix, what must he feel? *Descent to Hell?* She flipped the card over, as if there'd be an explanation or something redeeming there. On the back of the card was a handwritten note.

Dear Mother,

> *Luke is having a new show in the city. Isn't the portrait of the children pure genius? Please come and stay over. September 10, at Boonswell Gallery on Sullivan Street. Luke insists on providing transport and putting you up in a hotel.*
> *Bring Lil O'Brien.*
> *Felix says hi. The other day his teacher compared him to Picasso. He'll be excited to see you both in July when we have a chance to come and take the last of Luke's junk out of Hanzloo.*
>
> *~Joni Spoon*

The last of Luke's junk? Lil read those words again and cringed, wondering if Clarisse's baby would fall into that category.

As she knelt to the floor to pick up the envelope, more of Joni's words came back at her. *Isn't the portrait of the children pure genius?* Genius? As if the children had simply sprung from a whim of The Great Spoon and weren't real children at all. As if they were his to paint and play around with, to make a name for himself in the art world.

She raised her eyes to Sister A., who was leaning forward with her hands on her lap, anticipating Lil's reaction to the news. She saw nothing in the nun's expression that showed that she understood. Was it possible that Sister A., with her one eye, could not really see the painting? Or did she think it was perfectly fine?

"So?" asked Sister A.

"A show. How wonderful. September," said Lil, quickly putting the card back in the sleeve. Lil was talking too fast, grasping for something to say. "Such great news."

"What's wrong?" said Sister A.

"Nothing. Nothing at all. I couldn't go. But thank you," said Lil, and she handed the envelope back to Sister A.

"No, tell me. Something's wrong. You must go. You're the one with the eyes."

"Jim wouldn't like it, and honestly, I—"

"I'll speak to your husband," said Sister A.

"No, please, don't. It's not a good idea," said Lil, a little too loudly. She looked around the room for something to do. Seeing that the curtains on the picture window were not equally drawn, she went to even them out.

"Lil, why? Why not get out of this town for a few days?

New York City!" said Sister A. "What's the harm in it?"

Lil paused, struck by Sister A.'s urgency. She took her usual seat across from the sister and stared at her hands in her lap.

"Sister, I grew fond of Felix, just like you did. And Luke Spoon, well I guess he's a real artist, or something—but I don't belong in New York City, and I don't want to go."

Lil glanced up at Sister A., the words now falling from her mouth. Lil smiled, racing through her thoughts. "I wrote some poems when I was young. I won a talent show. I can't remember now. You know, once I dragged Jim to an art fair. His reaction made me laugh. He said, 'People really spend all day long painting pictures?' How did he come up with that? Jim says funny things—the way his mind works." Lil shook her head. "The truth is, I know nothing about art, and I'm no New Yorker." Lil stopped talking.

"How do you know what you are?" said Sister A.

"Oh, what difference does it make?" said Lil.

She looked at her friend. Sister A. had helped her through the last few months with regular visits; all the reading they had done, and the talking about nothing. Now, as the nun peered at Lil with her solitary eye, holding Luke Spoon's invitation in her hand as if it were a ticket to the moon, Lil was filled with a cavernous ache. She felt herself disappearing and wished that the nun would just go away.

"Don't be silly. We'll take the bus to Philadelphia and the train to Grand Central Station. Come on." Sister A. slapped her hands on her lap. "Oh, Lil, I've often thought of you when I go in and out of this town. Have you ever noticed those signs, the ones that say:

You are now entering Hanzloo
Where dreams come true

On the other side of the side of the sign it ought to say:

You are now leaving Hanzloo
Where dreams come true

"Maybe you don't belong in Hanzloo," said Sister A.

Lil lowered her head, remembering how she and Alice used to plan their trip to New York City. All those years they could have gone. Lil never had the nerve. And what about Alice's dreams? They never really went farther than the five-and-dime in Farrow's Corner or the annual trip for Buster Brown shoes in Silverton.

"I don't want to go," said Lil.

"Give yourself a chance," said Sister A., so agitated that her breath was short. "There's a world out there."

"No. My world is here." Lil opened her arms to her living room and glanced around.

Sister A. stood up, as if to go.

"How do you think I would feel looking at that painting of Alice and Felix in a gallery in New York City?" The words flew in anger out of Lil's mouth.

"What do you mean?"

"Sister, take out the invitation, and look at it closely," Lil said.

Sister A. opened up the envelope and held the card up to her face. Lil watched the old nun's eye dart back and forth, straining to see with her one good eye. Slowly she realized the painting was not a simple mash of colors, and she fumbled with the invitation, shoving it back in its case. Her face tightened with regret. Lil wished she hadn't said anything.

Sister A. stood helplessly before her.

"Sister, I . . ."

"No need to explain. I was careless, caught up with myself. Lil, I didn't see it at first. Maybe I didn't want to see it. How cruel it must seem."

"I'm sure that no one meant to be cruel," said Lil.

Sister A. raised her hand. "Please, you don't have to say a word," she said, crossing over to stand in front of Lil. With some difficulty, she got down on one knee, and took hold of Lil's hand. It frightened Lil to see Sister A. on her knees.

"Listen to me. No one can know another's sorrow, but even from the distance between us, I've seen yours, and I guess you've seen mine. I got attached to that boy, and in my desperation to belong, to be forgiven, or something like that, I've managed to let you down. I hurt you, the last thing I wanted. *I'm sorry* will never do."

There was nothing else to say. Lil turned her head away, and Sister A. gathered her skirts and rosaries and struggled to stand up, quickly making her way out the door.

PEEKING THROUGH the curtains, Lil watched her friend turn out of the driveway and walk down Mundy Lane. The nun mumbled to herself as she walked down the empty street, and Lil thought about how strange it would be to live under those dark heavy robes. Sister A. might never come back.

Lil stood for a long time, resting her forehead on the windowpane. There was Hedda Chinsky, confused, standing in front of her car with her arms outstretched. And there were the whirring red lights of the ambulance turning in the darkness and the ring of neighbors looking on in horror, hugging their coats over their nightclothes. Every time she looked out the front window, Lil saw Alice die.

From now on, it might just be Jim; the two of them sweeping toast crumbs into their palms, washing dishes with a dirty sponge, and changing light bulbs. How long could they rattle around this empty house?

After a while Lil went into the kitchen. From the drawer beside the refrigerator, underneath the napkins and the coupons, she fished out her yellow lined pad and her smooth, green ballpoint pen, and sat down at the table. Outside, in the backyard beyond the fence, the sky was blue, wide, and empty. Fresh air came through the screen. Was it really spring?

Absentmindedly, Lil examined her hands. She allowed her thumb and forefinger to turn her wedding ring around.

A cereal box behind the cookie jar caught her eye, and she picked up her pen. *Cheerios,* she wrote. The clock ticked on the wall. Out the window, she saw two birds. They flew as one entity, squawking at each other, tumbling in the air.

The afternoon lingered, but time flew, and when she put the pen down and looked up at the clock, it was almost four thirty. Hours had passed, and not another word had reached her page. *Cheerios.*

She hadn't planned dinner. Was it pork chops or lamb chops that Jim said he wanted? She'd have to rush.

The kitchen shivered with silence; dishes rested in the drainer, her coffee pot cooled on the stove, and a stainless-steel spoon lay on the table. Lil reached out to it, as if it was a hand.

The sudden ring of the phone—out of nowhere it seemed—caused her to jump, and she rushed to answer it.

"Hello?"

"Lil, it's me."

"You scared me. Is everything okay?"

She could hear Jim's chuckle through the phone.

"I scared you? Everything's fine," he said. "It's nothing, really. I just thought—"

"What is it? Where are you?" she asked.

"I'm here, I'm here at the office. Nothing's wrong. I was just thinking that . . . you know," he said, and his voice broke the way it always did whenever the slightest emotion escaped, as if a tidal wave might follow and wash the world away. "I was thinking. Let's get out of here. Let's move. Let's get the hell out of Dodge," he said. "We could even go to New York City."

Lil was silent. "Hello?" said Jim.

"Jim. Not New York City. Let's go the other way. Some place where the sky is bigger than the town," said Lil.

"Huh? Okay, sure. Lil, I'll do whatever you want. Whatever you want."

Lil twirled her finger in the cord of the phone.

"Lil, did you hear what I just said?"

"Yes. You said, 'whatever I want.'" Closing her eyes, she touched her lips to the mouthpiece of the phone.

"Yeah! We'll talk about it tonight. Big change coming. So, what's for dinner?" said Jim, his voice breaking with hope.

"Who knows, I might cook some potatoes," Lil said absentmindedly.

"Hey!"

"Mmm?"

"You know, what you just said—*who knows, I might cook some potatoes*—it's a poem. Get it? It rhymes."

"Oh. I guess so. That's pretty good, Jimmy," she said, realizing that she hadn't called him Jimmy for a long time.

"I don't know what you see in me," said Jim.

Lil thought it was an odd thing to say. At that moment, she saw everything in him, all there was and what might ever be. Within him was her universe of dead feelings, of sorrow and of loss. He was the one who cared if she lived or died. She hung up the phone, went back to the kitchen table and laid her forehead down on her folded arms. "Oh, God, where have I been?"

THIRTY-ONE

THE SUMMER OF 1962 was cooler than the summer of
'61, but the women of Hanzloo still managed to complain
about something as they drank whiskey sours in Clarisse
McCarthy's driveway and watched their children run across
the lawn and through the sprinkler. The lazy late-afternoon
klatch had expanded to include some new neighbors.

Miranda Sellers, who had moved into Lil O'Brien's place
in the middle of June, was a force to be reckoned with. Feisty,
and a few years younger than the others. Clarisse thought
she was a lot of fun. The Sellerses had resettled from Georgia,
and they both had that charming Southern twang. Miranda
was Clarisse's new best pal, and lately they could be seen
shopping together in town, rolling their baby boys in brand
new strollers, the twins trailing behind.

"Three kids, and there goes your waistline," Ginny Rice
had made the mistake of saying to Clarisse shortly after
Frank Jr.'s birth. That was the final straw for Ginny; she was
no longer welcome at the driveway gatherings, especially
since she'd recently been getting sloshed at parties.

"No drunks allowed," Clarisse had told Miranda over drinks, to which Miranda had replied, "Ha ha, except for y'all and me." Clarisse had laughed heartily. Miranda was a riot, comic relief after a weird year. Weird was the new word.

On September 3, the women convened for the last time before the start of school. In the sky, angry clouds threatened; there'd been weather reports of a late summer thunderstorm. But the women agreed to meet anyway, because today was a memorial of sorts.

Marilyn Monroe had died in early August. What a shocker. All summer, for the sake of their new neighbors, the women had spent hours rehashing—from every angle—the saga of the famous artist Luke Spoon and the heartbreaking details of Alice O'Brien's death. But today they were ravenous for photos, articles, or any insights into the life and death of Marilyn Monroe. Each woman came with a stack of magazines to share.

"To think that people always said I resemble her," said Clarisse as Steph passed around a magazine that had a photo of Marilyn in beaded white, her arms outstretched, standing in the murky shadows of the stage singing "Happy Birthday" to the president. "I never thought she looked like me."

The women, engrossed in their magazines, didn't comment, except for Miranda, who said, "But, honey-pie, you drive all the fellas wild."

"Did you hear that?" said Clarisse, in baby talk to Frankie as she jiggled him on her lap. Frank Jr., who'd arrived with all his fingers and toes on May 30, was a jewel, and Clarisse adored his every bubble and fart. He'd emerged with a full head of black hair, which was a detail Clarisse hadn't planned for. Luckily, Frank had never said a word about the color of the baby's hair. As only Clarisse would know, Frank Jr.'s tiny lips were identical to Luke Spoon's, and every day she kissed them at least hundred times.

"Look at this one," said Vicki Walsh, turning her magazine upside down to show the others a shot of Marilyn at the age of five, smiling in a wooden chair, with one leg dangling, her foot in an anklet sock and patent leather shoe. "Isn't this the cutest, saddest thing? If someone had told her then that she would take her own life. What a tragedy."

"That is sad," said Gwen Tormey, who had moved into the Chinskys' house. "But that's showbiz."

"Hmmm," said Clarisse.

"Mamma mia!" said Stephanie, pointing to a page in her magazine. "Clarisse! Look at this!"

"What is it?"

Vicki rushed over to Stephanie to take a look. "Lil O'Brien!" She quickly downed the last sip of whiskey in her plastic cup.

"What do you mean Lil O'Brien?" asked Clarisse.

"It's *her*, she's in this magazine!" Steph flipped to the front cover. "In *Redbook*!"

"What? Why?"

"She's one of three. Look, it says right here, Lil O'Brien from—what the heck?—Ennis, Montana? So that's where they ran off to?" said Vicki.

"Ennis? Let me see," said Clarisse, as she leaned over Steph's lawn chair.

"It's poetry. Her poem is printed in the magazine. And there's a photo, too," said Steph.

All the women were clustered around Stephanie now. "Miranda, look. That's Lil, who lived in your house, the one we've been talking about all summer. Alice's mother," said Vicki.

"Here, Clarisse, here it is." Stephanie laid her index finger down under the title of Lil's poem. "It's called 'Rivulets.' What does that mean?"

No one volunteered a definition.

The women read on in silence, until Vicki looked up and said, *"The stove I boil my heart upon? The stitches on my soul?* I don't know, that's disturbing. Is that poetry?"

"Well, Lil was different," said Stephanie. "In a good way, I always thought."

"Rubbing babies from my eye," chuckled Miranda. "I'll tell y'all one thing, my baby's way too fat for that! What the heck is she talking about? I mean, jeez."

"Shhh," said Clarisse. "I'm reading it."

Steph put her hand on Miranda's arm to stop her from making any more comments about the poem. She noticed that Clarisse seemed choked up.

"I like it," said Clarisse, almost to herself. "Can I have this?"

Steph closed the magazine and handed it to Clarisse.

"What's wrong, Clarisse?" said Miranda.

Everyone got quiet, only the bickering and squealing of the children could be heard from across the yard. Miranda lifted her baby out of the playpen and laid him on her shoulder.

"Oh, well. Poor Marilyn," said Vicki.

Steph sat with her elbow on the arm of her chair and her chin in her hand, thinking about how Lil and Jim O'Brien had left Hanzloo without warning. Not even a goodbye. It was like they disappeared. "You know, I miss Lil, she added a lot to this town."

Clarisse lit a cigarette and turned to watch the children. "I think it's about marriage. It's about *us*. And Hanzloo. And other things, too," she said to no one.

"It's about us?" said Steph.

"What is?" said Miranda.

"The poem. Rivulets are meant to be tears," said Clarisse, blowing smoke into the air.

"I didn't know that *rivulets* meant tears," said Steph.

"It's poetry," snapped Clarisse. "Nobody really knows what it means."

Just then, the purple clouds broke open with a violent thunderclap and a zigzag of white lightning. Torrents of rain quickly followed, pelting the driveway and the lawn, sending the mothers scrambling. They held magazines on top of their heads and babies in their arms as they tried to corral their children, who now ran in all directions, screaming, crazily, in the rain.

Thanks to

Alexandra Shelley, Harriet Goldman,
David Bumke, and the gang

Gail Hochman

Nancy Burke, Deb Robertson, Mary Bisbee-Beek,
and Karen Sheets de Gracia

Loudon Wainwright

Stewart Lerman

&

Lucy Wainwright Roche

SUZZY ROCHE is a singer / songwriter / performer / author and founding member of the singing group The Roches. She has recorded more than fifteen albums, written music for TV and film, and toured extensively in the U.S. and Europe. In addition to *The Town Crazy*, Roche is the author of the novel *Wayward Saints* and the children's book *Want to Be in a Band?* She tours with her daughter, Lucy Wainwright Roche, and lives in New York City.

GIBSON HOUSE PRESS connects
literary fiction with curious and discerning
readers. We publish novels by musicians
and other artists who love music.

GibsonHousePress.com
GibsonHousePress
@GibsonPress
@GHPress

FOR DOWNLOADS OF READING GROUP GUIDES
for Gibson House books, visit
GibsonHousePress.com/Reading-Group-Guides